Here Comes the Sun!

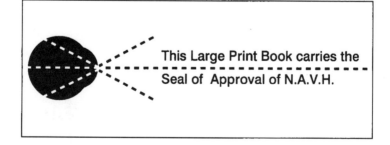

This Large Print Book carries the
Seal of Approval of N.A.V.H.

HERE COMES THE SUN!

Emilie Loring

Thorndike Press • Thorndike, Maine

Published in 2000 by arrangement with
Little Brown & Company, Inc.

Thorndike Press Large Print Candlelight Series.

The tree indicium is a trademark of Thorndike Press.

The text of this Large Print edition is unabridged.
Other aspects of the book may vary from the original edition.

Set in 16 pt. Plantin by Rick Gundberg.

Printed in the United States on permanent paper.

Library of Congress Cataloging-in-Publication Data

Loring, Emilie Baker.
  Here comes the sun! / by Emilie Loring.
    p. cm.
    ISBN 0-7862-2834-2 (lg. print : hc : alk. paper)
    1. Large type books. I. Title.
  PS3523.O645 H4   2000
  813′.52—dc21   00-056821

The sense of the world is short, —
Long and various the report, —
   To love and be beloved;
Men and gods have not outlearned it;
And, how oft soe'er they've turned it,
   'Tis not to be improved.
               — *Ralph Waldo Emerson*

Chapter I

The engine shrieked a warning. Porters shouted, "All aboard!" As the train shivered into action a black cocker spaniel jumped from the baggage car. Long ears flopping, red tongue hanging, the blue tag at his collar flapping, he dashed into a trail which zigzagged up the hillside. With an exclamation of dismay a girl on the step of the Pullman jumped to the ground and gave chase. The man on the forward platform of the car behind executed a spectacular leap and followed. The conductor of the train yelled a protest.

On sped the spaniel. When his pursuers were almost upon him he dodged into the underbrush only to emerge higher up with a broad grin, a triumphant yelp and minus the blue tag. From below came a frantic whistle, then the puff-puff of the engine as the train pulled away. With a disturbed frown darkening his fine eyes the man looked down into the valley where a haze of smoke lay lightly.

"Good Lord, they've left us!" he muttered angrily.

"Come quick! Oh, come quick! I've caught him," called a breathless voice.

With a smothered anathema on train-crews in general and this one in particular the man picked up the soft hat the girl had dropped and joined her. She was on her knees in a small clearing with the spaniel clutched tightly in her arms. The light from the slanting sun dusted the waves of her fair hair with gold, the color of her eyes fused from blue to violet with every change of expression; her cheeks, her sturdy chin were dented with dimples; the fine frills at throat and wrists were in rags, the straight lines of her smart heliotrope crêpe frock accentuated her boyish slenderness; her gray pumps were scratched irredeemably but her voice was vibrant with triumph as she held out the wriggling black creature in her arms.

"Here is your dog."

"*Mine!* Isn't he *yours?*"

"*No!* I saw him jump, feared that he might get lost and dashed after him. I adore dogs. When I heard someone behind me I concluded that his owner had joined in the chase. I couldn't endure the thought that the little thing might be gobbled up in this wilderness."

She hugged the spaniel closer and sprang to

her feet. With a quickly controlled shiver she glanced over her shoulder at the dark pines and their forest affinities which stretched up and back as far as she could see. She looked down into the valley. With a last fiery glare at the human atoms in the clearing the sun slid out of sight behind the hill. As though encouraged by the retirement of the orb of day a few clouds crawled forward. The air cooled. The mysterious sounds of unseen things hushed to a murmur.

The lovely color ebbed from the girl's face. Her eyes were deeply darkly blue as she looked up at the man looking down at her. He seemed superbly fit. There were two creases between his brows, there were stern lines about his clean mouth, the gray eyes which steadily sustained her scrutiny harbored a smile in their depths. She relaxed with a sigh of relief. There was a suspicion of unsteadiness about her lips, a slight catch in her voice as she asked:

"Has that silly train really gone?"

"It has. I'm sorry."

"I heard them shout 'All aboard!' but it didn't occur to me that they would dare go on without us. This is the worst predicament in which my impulsiveness has landed me to date and goodness knows my previous record didn't need beating. If the dog isn't yours why, *why* did you follow me?"

The charm of his smile brought a responsive gleam to the girl's eyes.

"Because when I saw you dash madly after the runaway I thought you might need help. I know these woods." For an instant he regarded her colorless face, the strained white knuckles of the hands which clutched the dog's black coat, then he went on lightly:

"I have a mother who is a twentieth century model in all ways except her dislike of being out after dark without a male escort. In that respect she is hopelessly mid-Victorian. I have contracted the habit of looking after her, so when I saw you race up the hill regardless of possible consequences I instinctively followed to look after you. I hope that you don't mind?"

"*Mind!* I should say not." A golden thread of camaraderie ran through the velvet of the girl's voice; her eyes smiled with the frank responsiveness of a boy's as she confessed:

"I'm hopelessly mid-Victorian too. I hate the dark. The dog's owner must have gone on with the train blissfully unconscious of what had happened. When he finds out will he place the blame where it belongs or will he think that you and I conspired to snitch the spaniel who is undoubtedly a thoroughbred? Will he?" There was a suspicion of tears in her voice as she protested:

"Don't stand there dumb as though I were that Gorgon female who turned people to stone!"

The man straightened as though throwing off a spell. His laugh was reassuring.

"Stone! You have quite the contrary effect. You —" He held the sentence kicking in mid-air and produced a time-table. The crease between his brows deepened as he studied it. The girl's glance followed his finger. Her eyes flashed up to his.

"Not another train north until morning! But I must get on; my aunt expects me. If I do not appear Managing Martha will wire Mother and frighten her. Can't you do *something?*"

"Where does your aunt live?"

"At Clearwater on the coast. It is fourteen miles' run by automobile from the next station. How far are we from that?" She consulted the time-table. "Is it really twenty-five miles?" she demanded in a shocked whisper.

"Yes. Is your aunt a native or —"

"No, she is at her summer home, Shorehaven; sounds like a sailors' retreat, doesn't it? Wary relatives and friends have dubbed it Match-haven. Perhaps you are going there to visit," the girl ventured in eager hope.

"I? There is no such glittering prospect before me. I stole a few days for a conference in Boston and when I get home I shall be in work up to my ears. Let's go down the trail. I saw a log house near the track. It is my best bet that it is a cabin belonging to a man I know. If it is I can get into it and if we get in we will find it liberally supplied with eats. We will have supper after which we'll organize into a Ways and Means Committee of two. Take your hat and give me the dog. If we put him down he may run away and get lost. The rascal deserves to be thrashed for getting you into this scrape."

The color stole back into the girl's face as she protested gaily:

"Thrashed! How like a man. Poor doggins fared forth on his own great adventure. *You* didn't ask us to butt in, did you, Sweetie-peach?" she crooned to the spaniel before she relinquished him. She gave an occasional backward glance at the darkening forest as she followed close at her guide's heels.

Near the bank of a tumbling, foam-flecked stream a log house snuggled between two towering pines. It was neither sinister nor forbidding; it looked to be the last word in sylvan comfort. The man groped under the wooden step in front and with a relieved, "I thought so!" produced a key. He inserted it in a padlock and opened the door.

The girl peered in cautiously. The spaniel

sniffed suspiciously. The one room was clean and dry. The built-in bunks were piled high with fresh cut balsam boughs which emitted a spicy fragrance. There was a table and three deep, roomy chairs of the type designed for the fire-worshiper. In the fireplace once-split birch logs lay ready for lighting. An open door in the rear showed a well-stocked wood-shed. The man stood aside for the girl to enter. As she hesitated he smiled down upon her.

"Welcome to our city!" Then as she stepped into the cabin he suggested, "We'll draw lots as to who shall light the fire and who shall forage for eats. For some reasons it is a pity that we weren't marooned at a station, but we shall be a lot more comfortable here."

"Why did the train stop? When it pulled up I went to the platform for a breath of this glorious air. Just as I was about to inquire what had delayed us I saw the dog, dashed after him and — here we are. I feel like Goldilocks in the House of the Three Bears. There are three bunks and three chairs. Hunt in the cupboard for the porridge, which should be steaming on the table, while I touch a match to those shavings," she suggested as she dropped to her knees by the hearth.

"The train stopped for a hot box. The place is a repair station of sorts." The man's muffled explanation oozed from the depth of the cupboard. "We are playing in luck — Goldilocks. Here is tea, condensed milk, canned corned beef, fifty-seven varieties of crackers and candles to burn. We'll take what we need and leave money to pay Father Bear." He deposited the supplies on the table and seized a shining tin pail. "I'll go for water while you prepare the collation."

He left the door ajar as he went out. When he returned the fire was casting fantastic shadows on the walls. The spaniel lay stretched on his side, his back within comfortable toasting distance of the blazing logs. He opened one eye as his rescuer entered, thumped on the floor languidly with his tail, drew a prolonged sigh and relapsed into the arms of Morpheus. The table was set with cups and dishes. A tin dipper full of ferns served as a centrepiece. Candles stuck in bottles flickered decoratively.

"Behold the festal effect," laughed the girl as the man halted on the threshold. "What happened to you? Your shoes are wet and muddy. Did you fall into the stream?"

The lines between his brows deepened at the question. "No, I did a little investigating. I told you that I thought I had been here before. I came hunting with a fri— a man but we approached the cabin through the woods back of it. You've transformed the place. The home-making fairy with the shining wings

14

must have endowed you royally."

As he filled the kettle with water and swung the crane over a heap of red coals he hummed softly:

" 'You remind me of my mother,
My mother was a lot like you,
So many little things you do,
I find . . .' "

"Go on," the girl commanded as he stopped. "I love to hear a man sing."

"Don't you sing?"

"No, I whistle."

She breathed a few soft notes, whistled a trill like the call of a bird to its mate, minors, more experimental trills, a fragment of a dance, then the notes of his song:

"You remind me of my mother —"

She broke off with a laugh and a little curtsey.

"Good Lord, I should say that you could whistle. I heard that song in a musical comedy last night and the refrain has been phonographing in my head ever since you boarded the train this morning."

"Then you had seen me before I did my spectacular dash-for-a-dog act?"

"I had. Will Mademoiselle be seated?"

15

He drew out one of the chairs with a grandiloquent French-waitery bow. As the kettle began to purr he made a cup of tea which he deposited in front of her with a flourish. He abandoned his stage-centre manner and took the chair opposite. He cut a piece of the corned beef and presented it on a tin plate.

"I am not hungry. I had rather plan what we are to do next than eat," the girl protested.

"Nothing doing. No supper, no plan. Drink the tea, eat that meat and the crackers. I refuse to discuss ways and means during this festive meal. Let's pretend that a taxi outside is gobbling our cash-on-hand while waiting to take us to the next station. Be a good little sport, forget our predicament and tell me what you meant by Managing Martha and Match-haven. Methinks the lady across the table beareth a grudge against her august aunt, what?"

The girl dimpled in delighted appreciation of his raillery. Her skin was rosy from the fire, tiny curls lay moistly against the nape of her white neck, her eyes had the velvety softness of purple pansies as she answered:

"Do you insist upon hearing the story of my young life? 'Then listen my child —' My father is a clergyman in a country town. He is a darling but he belongs between book-covers, not in this hustling world. I am the youngest

16

of his six daughters, his boy, he calls me, perhaps because I whistle. Mother's sister married a man of enormous wealth. She is a widow now and as she has no children she just naturally tries out her theories on her nieces."

"Managing Martha accounted for. Matchhaven?"

"That stands for the worst phase of her managing. Somehow, somewhere she was bitten with the matchmaking mania, only she calls it astrology. She apparently believes that if marriages are made in heaven she is a divinely appointed earthly deputy. Three years ago she bought a glorious summer home and she adds an additional pearl to her rope for every matrimonial engagement which materializes under that roof. Gunman stuff. A notch for every victim, see? As her pearls are the size of able-bodied peas she hands herself some bonus. That is why we call the place Matchhaven."

The man threw back his head and shouted with laughter. The girl regarded him with stormy eyes.

"You wouldn't think it such a huge joke if you were one of her victims."

"Are you?"

"I have been summoned for the sacrifice; the command was camouflaged by an invitation. The high priestess has taken us girls one at a time. Never before have I been invited to Shorehaven. I am the last of her Lorraine nieces unmarried. Do you wonder that I detest Clearwater and everything connected with it?"

"You don't mean that she hit the matrimonial bull's-eye five times in one family?"

"I do. She did. Her successes are spread over a period of ten years. I don't wonder that you are incredulous. Aunt Martha claims that by studying the horoscopes of her victims she has brought the right persons together. I claim that my sisters were easy marks. As children they contracted every disease to which they were exposed. What could be expected when they were plucked from a manless, small-town atmosphere and flung into a heaven of luxury which teemed with eligible males? They caught love as they would a cold. Now Aunt Martha is concentrating on me, 'little Julie, the last of the Lorraine girls,' " she quoted with a theatrical sigh.

"Then she warns you of her dark and dour design. I call that sporting of her."

"If you persist in chuckling about it —"

"I won't. I promise. Go on. Who is to be wished on you?"

"Her late lamented's nephew. I understand that he is a charmer with thirty birthdays to his credit, has innumerable female scalps dangling from his belt and that he is the re-mainder-man or ultimate consumer of the Marshall fortune. As the stars ordain that this is his year as well as mine to slip into double harness Aunt Martha has cannily decided to keep the money in the family. August and September being the open season for en-gagements here I am on my way to Shore-haven."

"Is the nephew such a poor fish that he can't select his own wife?"

"Don't growl. You are not being lured into the spider's parlor."

"Why are you walking into it?"

At his tone a tint of color crept to the girl's hair. She threw a cracker to the spaniel who, head tilted, tongue hanging, tail thumping the floor, sat up and begged. She kept her eyes on the dog as she explained:

"Partly for the thrill of defying Destiny — for Destiny see Managing Martha — even when I was a child she infuriated me. She was kind, she was generous but oh, so bossy. Now that I am older and ought to know better, if I find her on one side of a question I just natu-rally take the other. She can't forgive my sense of humor which I inherit from Mother."

"Was to defy Destiny your only reason for coming?"

"You have missed your vocation. You

should be Inquisitor-in-Chief for a detective agency."

She wrinkled her nose in laughing friendly derision and crossed her arms on the table. As she leaned toward him the candle-light made a nimbus of gold about her head. The laughter had gone from her voice; there was a tiny crease of determination on her brow as she answered his question:

"I came to get possession of myself. I suppose a man can't understand what that means. As my sisters have married, their duties at home — Aunt Martha has supplied any number of servants but they won't stay in our small town — their classes, their charities have fallen back upon me until I, the real I, have been buried as deep as poor King Tut. I have been at the beck and call of the parish. 'Julie'll do it!' has quite unconsciously become the family and village slogan. So when Mother's cousin wrote that she would be glad to live with us and help for her board, I seized her offer as a submerged person would a rope and accepted Aunt Martha's invitation."

"Only to drop into a matrimonial sea of trouble?"

"No. While I am at Shorehaven I shall think only of myself. I shall *not* sacrifice myself for anyone, I shall consider first *my* welfare, *my* pleasure, *my* happiness."

"Were you thinking only of yourself when you dashed after the dog? You've made a great start on your all-for-self program."

She colored richly as she met his quizzical eyes.

"I forgot for an instant, but it won't happen again."

"Did your mother want you to come? Does she approve of your marrying for money? Does your father?"

"For money? Haven't I told you that the man is attractive? Mother adores Dad but she has spent her life as the link between two ends of an income which couldn't be made to meet. Can you wonder if she hopes that I will fall in love with someone who can provide a checking account which will resemble the widow's cruse? I wanted to take a business course but I have been needed at home. However, Mother's hopes will be blasted. I can converse in three languages, I have been brought up on the classics, housework and the Ladies' Aid, but when it comes to talking to a man under sixty, my mind collapses like a pricked balloon."

"Good Lord, you don't think me sixty or over, do you?"

"How subtle! I have been garrulous but you see before you the new Julie Lorraine rising Phoenix-like from the ashes of the old Julie. I

21

have promised Mother that I will be as nice to Aunt Martha as is humanly possible, that I will accept whatever she wants to give me. Heretofore I have snubbed her whenever she has tried to be generous, so naturally she stopped trying. Never has she sent me a frock before this. I have worn hand-me-downs. Now I am wearing a Martharine and see what I have done to it!" She held up her hands and regarded her torn frills with laughing consternation.

"What is a Martharine? First cousin to a Worth or a Doucet?"

"Now I know where your women friends get their clothes. We girls coined the word for Aunt Martha's gifts. My frock is a Martharine, my shoes, what there is left of them, are Martharines."

"If you so hate hand-me-downs why isn't your aunt's plan a dispensation of providence?"

"Because I don't intend to marry at present. I am afraid of love. Love smashes friendship between a man and a girl. When I promised Mother that I would be nice to Aunt Martha, it was with reservations. I shall hesitate at nothing to combat her matchmaking. I refuse to be horoscoped into a pearl for her string. If I find that I am falling under her spell — don't laugh, her success is uncanny — I shall run away with Billy."

"Who is Billy?"

"William Jaffrey, the novelist."

"Billy Jaffrey?"

"Yes. He has been my pal since our Dutch-cut days. Then and ever since on his vacations I have tagged adoringly at his heels eager to show that I was of as stern stuff as he. He was a relentless taskmaster and an ardent believer in the survival of the fittest. He taught me to swim, to handle boats, to climb trees, to ride, to drive his car."

"Hasn't Jaffrey sufficient money and reputation to satisfy your aunt?"

Her eyes glimmered with mischief as she whispered dramatically:

"The planets are against our union!" She relaxed into a conversational tone. "Aunt Martha adores Billy. He spends part of each summer with her, but she has warned him that he is not to park his heart in my vicinity. Neither he nor I had thought of sentiment but now — you never can tell!" She sighed theatrically. Her lips curved with laughter.

"Are you in love with Jaffrey?"

She met his stern eyes indignantly. "Of course not. I shall not sacrifice my freedom for anyone. 'Julie won't do it!' is my present slogan. My life has been spent in a country town. Now I have fared forth to link arms

23

with those irresistible twins, Romance and Adventure."

"You said that you were afraid of romance."

"Love, man, love. I am looking for the romance of business, of politics, for the dragon-slayers, the imprisoned princesses, the sleeping beauties, the wicked dragons, the fairy-godmothers of real life, not for romance for myself. Dad has brought me up to believe that if I once succumb it is for life. He believes that marriage should be entered into solemnly, advisedly, only through a great love or a great purpose."

"A purpose?"

"Yes. He would be in full sympathy with a princess who formed an alliance to save her heritage. He is a 'Right or wrong, My Country!' American. He had so hoped for a son. When his sixth daughter came he determined to give her the training he would give a boy. I learned Lincoln's Gettysburg speech as soon as I learned my prayers and I was brought up on Webster's orations. Mother, fearing that Dad would make me into an unbearable infant prodigy, stuffed my mind and imagination with fairy-tales and saved her child."

"What is the nephew's name?"

"Are you back to him again? What persistence! Dallas Carfax Second. Sounds like a boat, doesn't it?"

"You may love Carfax. He may make you love him."

Julie rose with a suddenness which sent her chair backward with a crash.

"You are siding with Aunt Martha. It serves me right for confiding in you, a stranger. I suppose I did it because of your reference to your mother, possibly because you have a tinge of Dad's cry-it-out-on-my-shoulder manner. You seemed own-folksy, almost as though we had been friends in a previous incarnation. I deserve to be disillusioned for —"

Her voice caught Her eyes widened as she leaned toward him and warned:

"Don't move! Keep on listening and laugh! Laugh! There is a red, shiny-faced man looking in the window behind you! His eyes are bleak, his expression is dev-devilish! L-look at the dog!" she whispered hoarsely as the black spaniel ruffed his coat and gave vent to a nerve-rasping howl.

Chapter II

The man was at the door before she had finished speaking.

"Who's there?" he called sharply. There was no sound outside save the splash of the stream and a faint distant rumble.

"Come away from the door! *Please!* He's gone; he vanished like a hoodoo." The girl's eyes blazed with excitement. Her breath came as though she had been running. The man closed the door and slid the bolt. His tone was reassuring as he suggested:

"The poor chap was doubtless a native who knew the place and thought he'd get in out of the storm which is rolling up."

"A storm! Then we must get away at once. Hurry," Julie urged breathlessly as she began to clear the table. The man replaced tins and boxes without answering. They worked silently and swiftly. As the last dish was put in place a thunderous rumble bumped from hilltop to hilltop. The wind began to whisper sibilant little secrets down the stone chimney,

26

the windows rattled an eerie answer. The girl peered out into the night. There was a crimson streak in the west but overhead the sky was black.

"We must get away from here," she persisted.

"Where shall we go? There is no train north until morning. One goes south at midnight but what should we gain by taking that? I know this region and I know that there isn't a house within ten miles and that one is on the old lumber road which runs through the woods back of this cabin. I came over it once in an automobile but it would be suicide to try to walk it with this storm coming. A giant tree is likely to be struck or uprooted at any moment. I shan't consent to your trying it."

"But you don't mean — you can't mean that you expect me to spend the night here with —"

"Not necessarily. I will build up the fire, pile a lot of logs in this room for you and leave you, if you wish." A blinding flash turned the windows to molten sheets. A thunderous rumble shook the cabin.

"Leave me alone with that awful man prowling round? I wouldn't stay."

"Then we will make the best of it and remain here. Life is bigger than conventions, Goldilocks. Had we been caught in this predicament in France during the war we should have taken it as part of the day's work."

"But we are neither in France nor at war." The girl's violet eyes were black as she defied him. She pulled her soft hat low over her fair hair and picked up the dog who cowered whining at her feet. "I shall walk to the next station on the track. If you are afraid you need not come."

"Julie —"

"Don't call me Julie! Why, I don't even know your name and it is only a few minutes since we met."

He pulled out his watch. "It is just three hours, thirty minutes and twenty-seven seconds since you left the Pullman. You might have met me at social affairs for months and by your own confession not known me as well as you know me now."

"You're right. We are terribly old acquaintances; call me anything you like, but I am going on. Stop squirming, Sweetie-peach," she reproached the spaniel in her arms. As she pulled open the door a flash of lightning split the sky.

"You are an obstinate silly little girl, but of course I am going with you. Wait until I bank the fire." As she stepped outside he refilled the kettle and threw on some logs. He blew out the candles and closed the door behind him.

The streak of brilliant color in the west which had supplied a faint light faded as the man and girl reached the track. A cloud shook out a few drops of rain and scuttled on. There was a lantern in a chest under the signal box. With some difficulty the man lighted it.

"We'll keep to the track, then we shall be in no danger from blow-downs. Give me the dog. The wind is rising and you will have all you can do to walk without carrying him. I wish you had a coat."

"Mine went on in the Pullman with one perfectly good week-end case." The voice was the boyishly, friendly voice of the girl in the cabin. The man drew a quick breath of relief.

"Don't hurry. We have all the time there is. Take the lantern. This dog weighs tons. Your 'Sweetie-peach' is a snuffling, whining nuisance, but if I put him down he may get lost and we've got to stand by him now."

With a flash and a crash and a roar the wind furies snapped their leash and the storm broke. It tore its way through the tall timber on either side of the road bed, it ju-jutsued trees till they creaked in agony. It uprooted one which fell with a human groan. The rain descended in white sheets. The wet tracks glittered like gory snakes in the red light from the lantern. For perhaps ten minutes the man and girl struggled on. Then, as with a shriek nine parts demon and one part banshee the wind flung Julie against her companion, she clutched his arm. She put her mouth close to his ear as he bent his head to hear what she was saying.

"I give in. You were right. Let's go back to the cabin if — we can."

He nodded approval and shouted back: "We can make it. Hold tight to my coat. This confounded dog wriggles so it takes both arms to hold him. Swing the lantern so that it will shine on the track. That's right! Come on!"

The gale raged. The rain turned to pelting, stinging hail. After what seemed eons of time the dim outline of the cabin took shape in the darkness. The windows glowed softly.

"Oh, we can't go in! Someone is there!" Julie whispered.

The man dropped the dog and steadied the girl with an arm about her shoulders as a cold, playful mile-a-second zephyr flung her against him.

"It is the light from the fire, Goldilocks. I piled on the logs. I thought we might come back."

As he flung open the door the warm balsam-scented air rushed to meet them, the fire blazed cheerily, the kettle sang boisterously. The black spaniel dashed in and shook himself vigorously. Glistening drops sprayed from his wet coat like sparks from an acetylene welder.

"If only I could do that," Julie laughed as she looked down at her dripping frock. The rain had beaten the hair about her face into tiny tendrils. She shivered and approached the fire. After an instant's frowning concentration the man stuck his fingers between two logs in the wall and produced a key.

"I thought that I remembered where the owner kept it," he observed as he unlocked a chest under the window. He pulled out some blankets, then produced a woolly dressing-gown. "Take off that wet Martharine and put this on," he commanded in a tone which proclaimed that he was prepared to assist in carrying out his orders if necessity arose. A faint smile flashed behind the weariness in the girl's eyes.

"Sheathe your sword. I surrender. Of course I will get out of these wet things. I am not quite without common sense even if my previous actions so indicate."

"Good girl. While you change Sweetie-peach and I will dry our wet coats at the oil-stove in the wood-shed, at the same time we investigate the fuel supply. When you want us, knock."

As he closed the door the girl pulled off her

dripping frock and spread it over a chair within the heat's radius. She stuffed her shoes with bark which she peeled from logs in the big wood-box. In her heliotrope slip she crouched near the fire. She let down her hair and fluffed it in the heat. In an unbelievably short time she was warm to the marrow. She slipped into the bath-robe which she swathed about her and belted with the cord. She doubled and redoubled the long sleeves until her hands were free. Her hair hung in two braids which curled at the ends. Her cheeks were deeply flushed, her eyes brilliant with excitement. She tested her shoes. They were still wet. She crossed the room in her silk-stockinged feet and knocked on the wood shed door.

The man who opened it seemed to loom above her. He had substituted a leather hunting jacket for his wet coat. The spaniel bristled and growled at the girl, then jumped on her in apologetic frenzy. As she dropped into a big chair near the hearth the dog snuggled into her lap. Her companion seated himself opposite and began to fill his pipe.

"You look like an ammunition ad," Julie laughed.

"I wish that I had a cigarette. I don't smoke them but I suppose that you —"

"Didn't I tell you that I was mid-Victorian?

I neither smoke, drink nor — nor pet."

"What have I done that you should feel it necessary to add that last?"

"Nothing! Not one littlest thing! You have been an angel when it is my fault that we landed in this mix-up. And it is a mix-up. Aunt Martha will be horrified and Mother — well, Mother won't like it much."

"You have forgotten to mention Jaffrey's reactions."

"Billy will think it a joke, just a huge joke. I can hear him chuckle as he inquires solicitously, 'You never had any use for that look-before-you-leap stuff, had you, Marble-heart?' "

"Marble-heart?"

"That is Billy's foolish name for me. As I told you men and boys bore me stiff when they wax sentimental —"

"Oh, then there are men in that small town from which you came? I got the impression that Jaffrey was the only man you knew."

She flushed pinkly, thoroughly.

"I have met a few at family weddings." She expertly switched the conversation. "After this summer I intend to train for a secretaryship, then when I have learned a great deal I may go into politics.

"Politics in the best sense of the word, of course. I was too young to do much but knit and serve coffee during the war but the flags and the music and the marching men set a flame of patriotism in my heart and mind that mounts higher and higher as time goes on. I want to do something to help my country."

"Then keep out of politics yourself and make a home for some embryo politician which will keep his ideas and ideals up to the mark. You've got the biggest chance in the world right there. Blessed are the home-makers for they shall inherit the earth," he paraphrased gravely.

Julie regarded him with eyes of tormenting amethyst. "That remark smacks of the vintage of '76. Poor old Rip Van Winkle! Has he been asleep for the last twenty years?" She abandoned her tone of mischievous commiseration as she clasped her hands on the dog's black back and stared into the red coals. Her voice was grave as she admitted:

"Billy may think this predicament a joke but it isn't. Do you ever get into a mix-up that makes you say 'Darn!' every time you think of it?"

"I'll say I do, but I employ a more torrid exclamation."

A crash shook the cabin. The dog whined and burrowed his nose under the girl's arm. Her face whitened but she smiled valiantly at her companion as she admitted:

"I don't like being in a cabin between two high pines in a storm like this. Please talk, talk fast so that I will forget it. Don't you mind, Sweetie-peach, Julie'll take care of you," she quieted the spaniel as she stroked his silky ears.

Pipe in hand, knees comfortably crossed, the man leaned back in his chair and smiled at her.

"What shall I talk about?"

"Anything, everything. Tell me the story of your life. I have told you mine."

"It is hardly interesting enough to make you forget the storm, but I'll do my best. I am James Trafford, a hard-working mill-owner, the descendant of that First Trafford who landed in Plymouth with a shilling in his pocket, sapphires in his belt and a lady under his arm."

"A lady!"

"To be more exact the portrait of a lady. A regal creature with sapphires in her fair hair, sapphires at her ears, a great sapphire on her finger, sapphires fastening her blue and gold bodice and a King Charles spaniel under one arm."

"Go on! Who was she?"

"A Duchess evidently, but who she was or what she was to the First Trafford — we have acquired the habit of capitalizing him — or why he had her jewels no one knows. After he landed he married a girl who came over in the same ship. They drifted to Maine, only it wasn't Maine then — and he started a mill and after a while lived in a sort of feudal state. His son enlarged the mill and his grandson abandoned the first building with its big wheel and started a woolen mill. It was during the middle-age of the next generation that the first part of the portrait prophecy came true."

"Prophecy! Go on! You've missed your vocation. You should be a writer of mystery stories. Your technique is superb. When I am not holding my breath in suspense my teeth are chattering in apprehension. You are not inventing a fairy-tale, are you, to help me forget this horrid storm and that awful man?" She covered her ears with her hands as the lightning cracked like a pistol shot and the thunder seemed bent on ripping up the ridge-pole. Trafford's smile was like a steadying grip of the hand as he affirmed:

"It is the cross-my-heart-an'-hope-to-die truth I'm telling you."

"What was the prophecy?"

He leaned his head against the back of the comfortable chair and frowned up at the roof.

"It is printed in curious old script on the back of the portrait and goes something like this:

" 'Deep into the dark, damp earth
Bury the sapphires of the Duchess faire,
And after many days they will blaze forth
Attended by three shining knights,
Wealth, Love and Fame,
Full panoplied.' "

"And were the jewels buried?"

"Figuratively. They were sold by a black sheep who is known as the Mad Trafford in the family annals. The proceeds were used to finance a copper-mine. His interpretation of the prophecy being, evidently, that invested in the earth the jewels would insure the success of the venture."

"Did they?"

"No. When the investor's aged father discovered what had been done with the family jewels he cursed his son and dramatically invoked the spirit of the Duchess to haunt the steps of the Mad Trafford until the jewels were returned. The story of the curse spread like fire in dry grass. After a while men refused to work in the mine — there had been but a few pockets of copper there, anyway — and to this day there is considerable superstition in the county in regard to the roaming Duchess."

"Don't stop! I'm shivering with excitement. Then the sapphires never have been found?"

"No. No information could be secured as to where they were sold. They were exquisitely set. I am having them duplicated. Mother and I decided that the restoration of the sapphires would go a long way toward downing the silly stories which keep cropping up about the royal lady. Except for the Mad Trafford my ancestors have been decent, high-principled, hard-working mill-owners. Despotic, perhaps, but honest and just. It is curious what an influence background has upon one. I've seen men plunge into glittering dissipation, I've been caught in what seemed blind-alleys of temptation but something has strengthened my power of resistance. Perhaps it was the hand of some God-fearing, ideal-worshiping Trafford on my shoulder."

"Your voice gives the impression that you regret the fact that you have not followed the lure."

"Then it lies. Perhaps the tinge of regret was, because I realize that I am confoundedly conservative. I should like once to do something unusual in an unusual way. But I shan't. As I grow older I shall follow in the footsteps of my grandfather. What is there about New England that breeds repression into one?"

"I can't answer that question because my limited experiences with New Englanders has been the reverse. Mother was an F. F. from

Massachusetts, Dad an F. F. from California — that makes me Middle West, doesn't it — curiously enough the two have exchanged coastal characteristics. Mother has an irrepressible sense of humor; the world and its problems gnaw unceasingly at the domine's heart. I am forever bubbling with enthusiasm. I'm the original obey-that-impulse! Dad would approve of you. He claims that when a man resists temptation he is building character for future generations. Tell me more about yourself. Of course you were in the service?"

"I am sound and thirty; that answers that question. My father was an only son. He died when I was a boy of wounds received in the Spanish-American War. I spent my summers with Grandfather. Before I went overseas he told me that he hoped that I would carry on the mill, that I would live part of the year, at least, in Brick House, the Trafford homestead, that I would help to make the town my ancestor had founded a factor in good government. But, whatever I decided, everything he had was to be mine when he got through."

He leaned forward to rap his pipe on the hearth. The firelight shone on his fine head, gilded the faint touch of white in his black hair at the temples. He frowningly regarded the blazing logs as he continued:

"Grandfather lived till I came back from

the war, then his heart stopped. Good Lord, how I hated to take on that mill! I had other plans, other ambitions, but I was the last of the name. I had to carry on or the plant would have gone to the scrap-heap. That would have meant hundreds out of employment."

"Will you have to keep it always?"

"Your sympathetic tone is undeserved. I like it now. I like my work. I am proud of the people of my county, a people who have been trained to overcome difficulties. The war struck a spark in my heart which the disillusionment of the last few years can't snuff out. I am deep in politics. I am a nominee to defeat Cheever, our present state senator. I believe that he is a tragic example of a brainy college man of good family gone wrong."

"Do his constituents think that and *vote* for him?"

"Of course not. Most of them think him a wonder. The voters are tremendously excited by our contest. I think that they are trying to be absolutely fair."

"Are you friends?"

"We were when I spent my summers here. Cheever is eight years older than I. He was nominated on one ticket, I on the other at the state primaries in June. He is a good mixer. I suspect conditions — oh, well, I'm not talking about that. I shall win this fight on my own merit, not on the other man's demerits."

"That is an excellent policy if your opponent plays fair too. Does he?"

"No. I am convinced that if he could find a thread of evidence against me he would weave it into a cloak of iniquity. He has it in for me for another reason than this senatorial fight."

"Is the other reason a girl?"

Trafford rose and leaned his arm on the slab of granite which served as a mantel.

"Yes — in a way. Cheever pretends to be in love with my mother's ward who has money and an inordinate ambition which I am sure does not stop this side of the White House. Neither Mother nor I believe in his sincerity. He knows that but he haunts Brick House just the same."

"Is she in love with you?"

"Good Lord, no. What put such an idea into your head?"

"Does he think that she is?"

"How do I know what he thinks?"

"You're wriggling. He does. In that case you had better prepare to fight him with his own weapons."

"Not until I am back against the wall, and not even then. The newspapers are full of smudged political reputations. There is not much incentive for the boys growing up to serve their country. The men and women in my employ are behind me. It's a heart-thumping sensation to realize that hundreds of persons are looking to one for leadership; it makes one feel like an old-time patriarch. I shall beat Cheever with bare hands. I shall use no brass knuckles or stuffed clubs or defamation though I don't trust him. I can't prove it, I don't want to — yet, but I believe him to be tricky, irresponsible."

Julie laughed up at him with friendly eyes. She applauded softly:

"Here! Here! All you need, Mr. Senator, is a hand thrust into your shirt-front and you'd be Webster replying to Hayne to the life, only you are younger and infinitely better-looking than the oratorical Dan," she teased. "Is this scurvy politician — Oh-o-o!"

She sprang to her feet as a crash shook the cabin till its rafters chattered. Its Siamese twin sent a tree outside crashing to earth and sent her straight to Trafford. As his arms closed about her she buried her head against his shoulder. He rested his face against her fair hair as he encouraged:

"It will be over in a minute, Goldilocks. You are safe —"

The cabin door was flung open and banged shut. "Good God! I thought that pine would get me!" panted the man who leaned against the door as though exhausted.

Julie twisted herself free from the arms which had unconsciously tightened about her. She tried to silence the spaniel who added to the din without by barking shrilly at the intruder. She stared at the drenched figure with hat pulled low before she confided in a laughing whisper which caught in her throat:

"Enter Father B-Bear!"

But her companion was neither looking at her nor listening to her. He was staring at the intruder. The tense silence sponged the color from the girl's face. Her eyes widened in dawning comprehension as she looked from the man beside her to the man who had pushed back his dripping hat and stood as though carved in bas-relief against the door. A slow smile stretched his thin mouth. Trafford reddened darkly as he explained lightly:

"Cheever, as you see, we have taken refuge in your cabin from the storm."

The man took a step forward. His glance flicked from the frock drying before the fire, to the pile of blankets on the floor by the open chest, to the girl.

"I'm glad you made yourselves comfortable, Jim. Sorry that I butted in at an inopportune moment. Had I suspected a rendezvous —"

He bowed with exaggerated formality to Julie. Even her lips went white. The spaniel kept up a rumbling growl. The significance in the smirking tone thickened the veins on Trafford's forehead. He clenched his hands behind him but his voice was in control as he protested:

"Don't be a darned fool and turn accident into melodrama, Cheever. We jumped from the train to rescue this dog who escaped from the baggage-car and the infernal thing went on without us."

"Your dog?" Then as neither answered he laughed. "It's a bully story. I wonder if your constituents in the clean, anti-mud-slinging campaign will believe it — I wonder?"

"Believe it! Why should they care anything about it, except as a humorous incident — unless you — you —"

"Better save your ammunition for the campaign, Jim. You'll need it, believe you me. I've got you where I want you. I've got you there." He drew up the fingers of one hand like vicious claws. "You've started to beat me at the polls, you think I'm not a proper person to represent — oh, I know you've made no charges. I have no such scruples. I'll give the public to understand that never in my most riotous days did I indulge in this sort of thing." His words were muddy with inuendo

44

as he looked from the man to the girl.

Trafford's face was livid with fury. "You know that my explanation is true, Cheever, and by God before you leave this cabin you are going to admit it."

Cheever shrugged and lighted a cigarette. "Am I? I wonder. I'll trade. Promise to step out of the senatorial fight, make your mother withdraw her opposition to me, and —"

"Is that all? And if I don't?" Trafford took a menacing step forward, his fists clenched.

"I'll spread a version of this cabin episode that will take the rest of your life and the girl's to contradict. You've got to choose and choose quick."

With a rasping sob which she juggled into a laugh Julie Lorraine caught one of Trafford's clenched hands in hers. She leaned her head against his arm and defiantly regarded Cheever before she smiled up into the blazing eyes above her and inquired:

"What is all this riot about, Jim? Doesn't the silly person at the door know that we are married?"

Chapter III

The quiet which followed the girl's breathless questions was like the still instant which precedes the bursting of a shell. Even the spaniel held his breath. A burned log in the fireplace crumbled and fell. The sound broke the spell.

"Julie!"

At Trafford's hoarse protest the blank surprise on the face of the man at the door shifted to skeptical insolence. He glanced at the ringless left hand which clutched Trafford's arm. With a seventeenth century flourish he swept off his hat. The thin spot on top his head shone bravely in the firelight as he bent to the waist.

"Congratulations, *Miss — Mrs.* Trafford."

With theatrical grace the girl gave an adorable imitation of his greeting.

"Merci beaucoup, Monsieur D'Artagnan, I beg pardon, Mr. Cheever I should have said, but you are so like the irresistible musketeer in your manner that —"

"That will do, Julie," snapped Trafford.

"Now he will be sure that we are married, Jim. If we weren't you never would growl at me like that. Do come nearer your own fire in your own cabin, Mr. Cheever. We won't bite. Your clothes are dripping. You didn't walk here, did you?"

Her solicitous tone narrowed the man's lids. His glance flashed from her to her companion and back again before he answered:

"No. I came through the old lumber-road in my car. Your — your *husband* knows it. I had planned to meet a man here to-morrow. Thought that he had arrived first when I saw the place lighted. I found Willy Small huddled up in the shed. He came over to get the cabin ready. I shall have someone to back me up when I spread the news that I met you two on your honeymoon."

At Trafford's quick step forward he seized the latch of the door behind him.

"Everyone in the village knows that The Trafford went to Boston, but I'll say you kept your intentions mighty quiet. I wonder if even your mother knew it? The girl has turned a clever trick. You may find that there are disadvantages in being the richest man in the county, Jim. You'd better get her to manage your campaign. I'm off to spread the joyful news. My business here can go to the devil."

As he jerked open the door a flash of fire split the sky. Trafford sprang for him. The black spaniel, mistaking his spring for a new move in the game he had been watching, jumped for his sleeve, caught it and hung kicking and tugging. In that instant Cheever slammed the door. Trafford made a rush for it but the girl slid the bolt and backed up against it. The man seized her by the shoulders and swung her away. As he jerked open the door three derisive blasts of a motor-horn sounded weirdly in a lull of the storm. For an instant he stared into the blackness then as a jagged streak of lightning shredded the heavens he slammed the door and bolted it. His eyes were flames in his white face as he demanded:

"What demon prompted you to say that we were married? I could have handled Cheever. He is no fighter. He's a consummate bluffer. But now — why, why didn't you stop to think of the consequences?" He hurled the question. The girl's eyes were as turbulent as his as she protested passionately:

"I did, for once in my life I did. I thought of the bleak-eyed man who had stared in at the window, Willy Small, I suppose; I thought of the consequences if by accident you killed Cheever here in this lonely cabin — your face was terrible — I thought of the consequences to you if he spread a story about you and me.

If only I hadn't rushed to you when that crash came. I didn't realize that I was doing it, really I didn't. He accused you of an unspeakable thing. You had told me of his enmity, of what you were trying to accomplish. I couldn't endure to think that all you had built with consecrated purpose would topple if he attacked your reputation."

"I can take care of my reputation."

"How about mine?"

"Good God, do you think I have been raving on my own account? I have hoped against hope that you would not realize what this might mean for you."

A ghost of a smile flitted across Julie's sensitive lips.

"I am not so mid-Victorian as that. But we are wasting time while Cheever is speeding —" She clapped her hands over her ears as there came a blinding flash followed by the sound as of a Big Bertha being fired over the roof. As the reverberation rattled away over the tree-tops she opened her eyes with a shiver.

"I hope that crash shook up Cheever and his witness. We must do something to checkmate them. I still think I did the only thing possible but if I blundered — I'm sorry. Couldn't we pretend that we were married till after election?" Her lips quivered into a smile.

The creases between Trafford's brows were black streaks.

"We could but we won't. That is part of Cheever's game, confound him. If I am married I am out of his way. We'll defy him. My people ought to know me well enough to take my word against his lies."

"But they will be such insidious lies. He will capitalize this episode and ruin you."

"Let him, so long as he does not touch you. I'll make that the condition of dropping out of the campaign. He does not know your name —"

"It won't take him long to find out; he heard you call me Julie. It is too late to bargain with him; he is on his way now to start his propaganda. Don't let him ruin your career, don't. Aren't you the dragon-slayer who has fared forth to rescue the imprisoned princess whose name is Clean Politics? And it isn't you alone he will ruin. Think of the boys who have been looking up to you, believing in you. What effect will a scandal have upon them?"

The veins in Trafford's temples stood out like cords. "I shall lose them for a time but I will win them back. I shall not have you drawn into this fight, little girl."

"I am not a little girl. I am twenty-three years old."

A smile softened the sternness of the man's

eyes. "Are you really? Even so you are not old enough to take my burdens on your slim shoulders. I want you to go home. Take the train that goes through here at midnight. Wire Mrs. Marshall from Portland that you have been called back. I'll withdraw from the fight, but next year — good Lord, *next year* —"

"I won't go home. I won't be saved at your expense. Some of the most earnest men in the country have visited my father. They have deplored the corruptness of politics. They have predicted that, unless our native Americans in whose veins should flow the instinct of patriotism jump into the ring soon, we shall have imported leaders, possibly alien leaders. Wouldn't that be an immeasurable disgrace? You can't pull out! You must go on! I realize now that I effectually tied your hands with my impulsive declaration. If you denied it you accuse me of lying; what could you do but let it go? What did Cheever mean when he said that I had turned a clever trick?"

Trafford caught her by the shoulders.

"Will you marry me, Julie?"

The color scorched to the girl's hair but her eyes met his steadily.

"Is that the only way out?"

"That or for you to go home."

"Going home wouldn't kill the story.

Cheever would keep it up his sleeve for use next year. If we can save the situation by a ceremony which can be annulled and explained after election I'll do it."

"How can we manage it? What shall we do next?" she asked eagerly.

Trafford turned from her abruptly and pulled out his watch. "We can flag the southbound at midnight, go to Portland where I have some influence, be married there and take the next train back. From the first station possible we'll wire your aunt that you were delayed just twenty-four hours." The storm which was moving east flashed and rumbled an accompaniment to his words.

As though suddenly exhausted the girl dropped into the armchair by the fire. The spaniel jumped into her lap, licked her face with his red tongue, circled and settled down. There were tears lurking behind her smile as she met the gray eyes looking down at her.

"You'll have your heart's desire. You are about to do something unusual in an unusual way. Was anyone of your ancestors married as you are to marry? What explanation shall we give our friends? We can't tell them the real reason but Dad and Mother and your mother must know the truth."

She watched his strong, steady fingers force tobacco into his pipe. Now that he had made his decision he seemed as unshakable as his New England granite. Her heart shook her with its beating. She had a sudden desire to rest her head against one of his hands and cry. She gripped the arms of her chair and sat stiff and erect as she awaited his answer to her question.

"We will tell them that we met during the war — that is not necessarily an untruth, perhaps I went through your home town with troops, perhaps you gave me coffee — and that knowing your aunt's plans and fearing her sorcery decided that we would marry before you reached Shorehaven and the jurisdiction of the planets."

"That story may convince some but it won't Billy. However, it will have to serve until after election."

"When we reach home — Clearwater —"

"Clearwater! Is your mill *there?*"

"Yes."

"When I told you about Aunt Martha why didn't you say that you knew her? You do, don't you?"

"Yes, and I have met two of your sisters and their husbands. Didn't you passionately proclaim the fact that you detested Clearwater and everything connected with it? I wanted to win your friendship. Mrs. Marshall never has cared for me, apparently. She will like me less now that I have upset her project for you and Carfax."

"I had forgotten Dallas the Second. Aunt Martha will be furious. She will think I smashed her plans on purpose — perhaps — perhaps with that reckless statement to Cheever I smashed your plans too. Perhaps you are in love with someone?" Her tone begged for contradiction. Far down in the eyes which met hers steadily lurked a smile.

"I am."

"Heavens, what a mess I've made of things. I practically forced you to ask me to marry you, didn't I?" Indignation surged in the voice which had been near to tears. "Why didn't you tell me? All I thought of was that poor imprisoned princess. But it isn't too late. You'd probably rather have the girl you love than the senatorship. I will go home and —"

Trafford caught her by the shoulders as she turned away. "We'll see this thing through now, Goldilocks. My love affair has not progressed so far that it can't wait until after election."

Julie smiled radiantly back at him. "Thank heaven! The lady ought to forgive you, for ours won't be a real marriage. It will be nothing but an empty contract stuffed down our throats by that odious Cheever. After election you may tell her the true story of your married life and I'll corroborate the data." She was boyishly friendly as she teased.

"Thank you. I may need your help to convince her that I loved her even when I married. Meanwhile you and I will be the best of friends, won't we?"

"We will. I feel as though I had known you years and years. Next to Billy you are the most companionable man I ever met. When I reach Shorehaven —"

"Shorehaven! When we reach Clearwater we'll drive directly to Brick House. Mrs. James Trafford will naturally go home with her husband."

Julie indulged in an irrepressible ripple of laughter.

"Of course. There is considerably more to this marriage bluff than I had sensed. Billy is right; never will I learn to look before I leap."

"Are you sorry, Julie?"

She met his eyes squarely. Twin flames of eagerness burned in hers.

"No, a thousand times no! Cheever shan't succeed in wiping you off the political slate if I can help. We'll proceed with this emergency measure and —" Something in his eyes caught at her breath. She gave his arm a little shake. There was a trace of panic in the voice in which she demanded: "You understand that that is all it is, don't you? *Don't* you?"

"Steady, Goldilocks, steady! Of course I understand. We are partners for the purpose of beating Cheever." He looked down at the fingers clutching his arm and added lightly, "We shall need a ring. Have you one that I can borrow for size?"

The color still burned in Julie's cheeks but the smile returned to her lips as she shook her head.

"A ring! Would you expect the sixth daughter of a country clergyman to possess a ring? I have never owned one."

"Then I'll make one. Stand still a moment." He pulled a knife from his pocket and severed a strand of her fair hair. "Hold out your left hand." He wound the golden thread around her third finger. He removed the slender circlet and laid it in his pocketbook. Julie watched him incuriously.

"Will it be necessary to have a ring for such a short time?"

"Possibly not, but we won't leave any holes for suspicion to peek through." He looked at his watch. "You had better put on your gown. The south-bound train goes by in an hour. You'll find a mirror and wash-basin in the wood-shed. I'll bring my clothes in here."

Fifteen minutes later when Julie returned her fair hair was as carefully arranged as though she had dressed in her own room; her heliotrope frock was minus frills and much the worse from its exposure to the storm. She looked from her crumpled gown to the wrinkles in Trafford's coat. There was a slight unevenness in the voice she tried to keep gay as she observed:

"We look more like hoboes than a bridal couple."

"We are not a bridal couple —" Trafford contradicted gruffly.

She colored pinkly and pleaded breathlessly, "Don't notice my flippancy, *please*. I'm merely whistling to keep up my courage. I refuse to make a tragedy of the situation. I've whisked it inside out and have found the humorous lining."

"Good little sport. Remember that we are partners determined to beat a mud-slinging opponent. Are you ready?"

She caught up the spaniel.

"Yes. Of course we take Sweetie-peach?"

"We'll keep him until his owner claims him." He opened the door. "The storm has cleared. The air is glorious."

Julie hesitated for a moment on the threshold to look out upon a world silvered with moonlight and dappled with purple shadows. The sky was powdered with stars. The brook tinkled and splashed through the midnight stillness. A young breeze frisking by after a heady carousal among the ballsams stirred the soft hair at the girl's temples. The "Aolee-e" of a wood-thrush which had been deceived into a thought of dawn by the sudden emergence of the moon, splintered the silence. The singer's prelude was followed by a melody of song rich with the vibratory notes of a bell, which rose and fell and swelled into a paean. As the last jewel of sound was flung recklessly into the treasure-chest of space James Trafford smiled down into the eyes looking up at him.

"We'll take the thrush's song as a good omen, Julie. Come."

Chapter IV

The engine shrieked a warning. Porters shouted "All aboard!" As the Pullman shivered into action Julie looked from the car window. Was it only twenty-four hours since a train had stopped at this same signal-station and a girl and man had raced up the hillside in pursuit of a black spaniel? It seemed years.

She closed her eyes and in retrospect lived over the hours since she and Trafford had boarded the south-bound train at midnight. Only an enraged conductor and a fussy porter had seen them enter; the passengers were in their berths. From the first station a wire had been sent to Martha Marshall. When they had reached Portland they had left the spaniel with the baggageman and the girl had gone to an hotel. While she had breakfasted in her room the maid had pressed her frock and had sent out for fresh frills and a hat for her inspection. When Trafford had telephoned that he was waiting downstairs her heart had pounded unbearably. Had he suspected it, she wondered. As she had stepped from the elevator he had drawn her to one side and suggested in a low voice:

"You may change your mind even now, Julie." She had shaken her head vigorously in lieu of speech but when their taxi had stopped in front of a church and parsonage she had drawn back and protested:

"No, no, not by a clergyman! I thought it would be a justice of the peace!"

Asking for no explanation of her protest, Trafford had held out his hand with an imperious, "Come!" and she had followed him to the door. How could she make him understand that to her a marriage performed by a man of God seemed indissoluble? In spite of the fact that she had served as witness innumerable times in her home rectory she couldn't remember a word of what had been said. The ceremony seemed an unconnected dream. A dream! Julie's heart jumped. Perhaps the whole thing was a dream, a nightmare! She opened her eyes cautiously and from under the fringe of her dark lashes looked down at her left hand. Hope folded its wings and dozed again. The glistening narrow circlet on her third finger was not of the stuff of which dreams are made, it was real.

Julie opened her eyes wide and stared unseeingly out upon the woods and fields which flashed by. Now that the bubbles had evaporated from the champagne of excitement her sacrifice for her ideals for clean politics seemed absurdly flat. "Don't be a shortsport, Julie," she admonished herself. After all, was what she had done so preposterous? She had married a man on whose honor and kindness she would be willing to stake her life. She had done nothing in comparison to what hundreds of girls had done during the war. They had given their lives for a great cause and she had given a few months of hers, given them because she passionately believed that if a leader broke laws either human or divine his example would be followed by hundreds who would make his weakness their excuse for deviltry. Jim Trafford had not transgressed a law but his enemy would have broadcast his sordid misrepresentation of last night's happy-go-lucky accident and there would be hundreds who would not hear the retraction. Truth has never a neck-and-neck chance to overtake a lie like that.

What would her parents say? She had begged Trafford to do his best to keep the announcement of the marriage out of the newspapers until she had written them. He had succeeded. To-night she would write her mother and father a full explanation of what had happened. Suddenly, clearly she heard her father's sonorous tones: "Solemnly, advisedly, in the sight of God." Would he think that she had violated that admonition or would he understand? She looked up in relief as Trafford took the seat beside her. Her voice was tinged with panic as she asked:

"Are we almost there? Is Sweetie-peach quite all right?" she added, as though the welfare of the spaniel were of superlative importance. The gray eyes met hers with reassuring steadiness.

"He has made slaves of everyone in the baggage-car. That and running away seem to be his specialities. We'll go forward and get him."

Five minutes later as Trafford and the girl stepped to the station platform a man hurried up. His face might have been assembled from a rummage sale of all-American features. His beard, of the slap-stick variety which reared and dropped with every excited word, hid the toothless state which articulation betrayed. His assorted eyes were alight with triumph as he caught Trafford by the arm.

"Gorry-me, Jim, we begun to think you was lost when you didn't show up yesterday afternoon an' yer grip did. Pamela drove over for you; she's here agin to-day. Hev you heard the news? Ain't yer? I guess you'll git to the leg'slater all right. Cheever's as near dead as he can be an' be kep' above ground."

"What!"

Unconsciously Julie clutched the coat of the man beside her. She felt the color drain from her lips and bit them furiously. Trafford had his voice well in hand when he demanded:

"What has happened to Cheever, Captain Phin?"

"Cheever was comin' from that camp of his last night in the storm. He must have ben drivin' like the devil fer not far from the cabin a big oak crashed down on the auto. Ben was pinned under what the high school teacher called the dee-bree. He can't live through the night, they say."

"How did you hear about it?"

"Willy Small found him about midnight an' skulked into town at about nine o'clock this morn-in'. He sneaked that pink-eyed white bulldog of his out of the pound an' lit out. Mark-my-words, he'll never be seen round here again. Scared to death fer fear he'll be held a witness, but the coroner won't trouble him. There ain't no doubt in anyone's mind as to what got Cheever; it was the storm. I'm comin'! I'm comin'!" he shouted in response to a hail. "This fresh new station agent's got some express fer Brick House. It beats all how

63

some folks won't wait a minute —" As his protest died away in the distance Julie released her hold on Trafford's coat. Her face was white as she whispered:

"With Cheever almost dead and Small gone we won't have to announce that marriage, will we?" she pleaded breathlessly.

"You are to decide that, Julie."

"Then we'll forget yesterday. Take the ring, quick!" She pulled the circlet from her finger and dropped it into his pocket. "I didn't realize what a nightmare it had all been until this minute. I ought to be sorry for that man, but I'm not. I can think only of our unbelievable good-fortune. I'll take Sweetie-peach with me. There's Billy, the dear!" With a sob of excitement she darted toward the man who was racing down the platform.

William Jaffrey caught the girl by the shoulders. His fairly plump body seemed to deflate with relief. His nose had a protrusive round tip, his full lips curved up, his green eyes had the keenness of a sharp-shooter's. He was somewhat breathless.

"Had a darned blow-out on the way over," he puffed. "Thank the Lord you've materialized, Marble-heart. I was off fishing yesterday and didn't know until this morning that you hadn't arrived when expected. You'd have thought Aunt Martha would have been fit to tie at your nonappearance, but she wasn't. She took it philosophically as Sol was in parallel aspect with Jupiter which rot translated means that yesterday was a lucky day for you. Where the dickens did you get the pup?"

"The pup?" Julie looked down at the black dog in her arms who growled tentatively and ran out a pink tongue at Jaffrey. "I — oh, I found him."

"I'll bet you picked him up on the streets of Portland. Aha, I thought so; you have guilt smudged all over your speaking and fairly good-looking countenance. You never stepped out yet, Marble-heart, without bringing home some forlorn canine. Where did you meet up with The Trafford?"

"The Trafford? Who is he?"

"I thought I saw you talking with him as I raced up. My mistake. It is just as well you weren't. He is a mill-owner here, a sort of lord-of-the-manor. Aunt Martha has him black-listed. I brought your coat. Better put it on. It will be cold after we start. The sun went down behind the hill half an hour ago." He followed her into the roadster and bent to the gears. "How does it happen that you are a day behind your schedule?"

"I was on the train yesterday when I dashed out to get something and —"

"And got left. Your suitcase and coat arrived on time anyway."

Julie's voice was slightly uneven as she attempted to ask casually:

"Why has Aunt Martha black-listed — did you say his name was Trafford?"

"Yes, Jim Trafford. The morning whistle of his mill disturbed her. She asked him to have it stopped. Wasn't that characteristic of her? Of course he refused. I think that her determination never to vote was shaken to its foundations. She would have liked to help beat him at the next election. I'll arrange for you to meet Jim; you'll like him. In my no-account judgment he'll be Governor some day. You'll like your prospective bridegroom also," he added with a chuckle.

"Has Dallas Carfax Second really arrived, Billy?"

"He has. He is not at all a bad sort, Marbleheart. He is big and blond and has that my-heart-is-in-your-little-hand manner which mows down the female of the species in swathes."

Julie was silent as the car sped on. When she caught a glimpse of the ocean she drew a long breath. Far off a line of purple hills tore ragged jags in the horizon. Against the rocks — burnt umber at the base, pale umber at the top — which lined the shore a blue-green sea ruffled whitely dragging countless silvery pebbles in its wake as it receded. Pines, balsams and cedars swept up and back from shore to sky-line. The clear air was lightly seasoned with the tang of salt. From far off in the woods came a plaintive, "Whip-po'-will! Whip-po'-will!"

The mournful call created panic in the girl's usually sound, safe and nerve-proof heart. She set her teeth hard in her lower lip to steady it. She caught Jaffrey's arm and pleaded:

"Billy, don't let Aunt Martha fling me at Dallas Carfax, will you? I can't — I shan't marry him. If worst came to worst I'd rather marry you."

Jaffrey glared at her. "Me! Not on your life! You're all right as a pal but for a girl of my own I want —"

"Her mushy," supplied Julie with a ripple of laughter. "You're not fair. Can I help it if when it comes to sentiment I can't make the grade?"

"Don't cry about it. You have sentiment enough when it comes to a dog, Marble-heart. You're mushy over the mangiest specimen the street produces. I want my girl to be mushy over me and I don't care if the world knows it. Besides, you know you wouldn't have me if I roped and tied you. Just wait till you see Dallas the Conqueror. You won't have time to play round with me. He reeks of filthy lucre but he's decent and unspoiled considering the fact that since he cut his first teeth he has been trailed by hopeful mothers —"

"And aunts. Just the same, I am prepared to hate him. Do you think that Managing Martha has told him her plan for — for us?"

"Holy smoke, no. Credit her with some sense. She told me as a sort of keep-off-the-grass warning." Jaffrey's infectious grin sobered to a thoughtful frown. "I don't see why she told you. She might have known that it would set you against him. She's fallen down on her technique; usually she handles situations more diplomatically." He stopped the car.

"Look! To borrow a phrase from your Dad's Book of Books, I sometimes think that this must have been 'The exceeding high mountain from which He saw all the kingdoms of the world and the glory of them.' Doesn't that view do queer things to your breath?"

Julie nodded without speaking as she gazed down into the valley divided by a pond which looked like a molten mirror. Before it reached the bay the water churned into white falls and tumbled under a low bridge across which the road lazed. On its bank a group of mills, conjured by the afterglow into golden palaces of mystery and charm, loomed against the horizon. Nearer the shore nestled a village with two this-way-to-heaven sign-posts, the white spires of the churches. The valley was checkered with stone walls, dotted with ample farm houses, patched with green fields, fringed with tall timber. Costly summer homes, more or less architecturally fit for their surroundings, adorned or disfigured every point and curve of the inner bay which was partially separated from the outer by a disjointed peninsula of rocks and sand and glittering tide-pools. In the inner harbor boats of all types and sizes swung at their moorings. At the town wharf a schooner — picturesquely colorful in the distance — was being loaded with lumber. Toward the north the outer bay spotted with islands and reefs rippled and surged on to the open sea. Julie drew a long breath.

"So this is Maine!" she paraphrased softly. "It is wonderful, Billy. Can we see Shorehaven from here?"

"Yes. See the mills? Now look across Glass Pond. Do you see that spot of warm velvety color? That is Brick House where Traffords have lived for generations. Straight on from that are the roofs of Shorehaven. Get them?"

"Yes. How near together the two places seem."

"The houses are two miles apart in distance

but hundreds of years apart in tradition. Shorehaven is an electrified, plumbed, refrigerated, steam-heated adaptation of Tudor architecture. Brick House is mellowed with the atmosphere of the family which conceived and built it. See those falls under the bridge? I have a new stunt for you. At certain tides the favorite outdoor sport here is to shoot the rapids."

Julie observed the foaming water without enthusiasm. "It looks ticklish."

"It isn't. No girl has ever tried it but I'll have you eating it up within a week. Nothing can happen if you keep your head and I have never known you to lose yours, Marble-heart."

She colored faintly. "There is always a first time, Billy. What is that curious green house on the slope this side of the river? It looks like a mammoth dragon. Those disjointed, straggling ells make the tail, those curving steps in front form the jaws, and those two funny little windows under the eaves that the sun has set afire look like the monster's flaming eyes. Who owns that masterpiece of architecture?"

Jaffrey chuckled. "You're some little word-painter, Marble-heart. That is a bungalow, what sins are committed in thy name, oh bungalow! It belongs to Cheever, the representative from this county to the state legislature, who keeps bachelor hall there. He is up again for election but Jim Trafford is giving him a run for his money this trip. There has been a breath of rumor that Ben has not been quite straight, but such an intangible breath that it has made no impression. There has been a lot of excitement in the village over the contest but it looks now as though the fun were over. I heard at the station that Cheever was smashed up last night in the storm. They thought he was going to die but —"

"*Thought!* Isn't he?" cut in the girl sharply.

Jaffrey regarded her in astonishment. "You bloodthirsty creature! Just because there has been a rumor that a man has been crooked in politics do you want him snuffed out? Hmp! Votes for women!"

"Of course I don't, Billy. It was just interest."

"Interest! It sounded mighty like despair to me. Cheer up, he probably won't pull through, though these State of Maine men are the dickens and all for endurance. Seen enough? Let's go!"

As the roadster shot forward Julie glanced covertly at the bungalow on the hill. In one of the windows under the caves the sun's reflection slowly paled and went out. To the girl's excited imagination it was as though the green dragon had winked one contemplative, derisive eye.

Chapter V

Julie opened the door to what in Tudor times would have been known as the minstrel gallery at Shorehaven. In Martha Marshall's practical regime it housed the console of an organ. From the shadowy retreat the girl looked out into the great hall with its oak half-timber ceiling, its leaded glass windows set in stone mullions. It was lighted by a myriad electric bulbs in branching candelabra, for the lady of the manor disliked dusky corners. Two balconies extended round three sides from which doors opened into luxurious apartments. Costly rugs which in tone and coloring harmonized with those on the dark floor below were flung over the railings. Bowls of glowing flowers in the hall made splashes of color against a dark background. Behind the ornate brass doors of the fireplace logs blazed cheerily.

The fragrant warmth, the color, the stillness gently untangled the girl's knotted emotions. She dropped to the organ seat and sat for a moment with her eyes closed, her hands linked loosely in her lap. Since Cheever had entered the cabin the night before her mind had been in a tumult. For the first time she had a chance to index and pigeonhole the events of the last twenty-four hours, to take account of stock. If Managing Martha had blacklisted James Trafford there would be no danger of meeting him at Shorehaven, so that liability could be checked off. Her aunt had swallowed her explanation as to her delayed arrival without the least attempt at mastication. She had accompanied her to her rooms and left her with the serene announcement:

"I have provided a wardrobe for you, Julie, as I did for your sisters. Make yourself lovely. You are the prettiest of the Lorraine girls. I was wise not to invite you here until I had the others married."

The memory of her self-congratulatory tone brought a flush to the girl's cheeks. She had felt like a prize colt about to be knocked down to the highest bidder. She was tempted to refuse to wear a gown from the wardrobe, but she remembered her promise to her mother and with apparent enthusiasm had selected a frosted violet evening frock from among those which Carlotta, the Spanish maid, produced for her inspection.

At the sound of voices in the hall below

73

Julie tiptoed to the railing of the minstrel-gallery and looked down. Martha Marshall was standing on the hearth-rug. The girl regarded her aunt with wrinkled-brow absorption. She had the stiff manner of a general directing a campaign. She was tall. Her slightly full figure in its stately gown of black crêpe was guilty of a waist-line the fashion of which went out with Tipperary and long skirts. Her beautiful white hair was perfectly dressed, her blue eyes were large and keen, her clear skin was faintly tinged with rose. Her short upper lip and piquant nose which were so out of character with the rest of her were balanced by the challenging chin and imperiously poised head of the born executive. Her aunt's viewpoint had not shifted as much as an inch in all these last kaleidoscopic years, her niece reflected as she looked down upon her. She was kind-hearted as long as one agreed with her, just until a cause clashed with a cherished conviction, and bitterly intolerant of the modern woman with her mélange of activities.

Billy Jaffrey stood near her. The sunburn of his face topped by his red hair was intensified by the black and white of his dinner clothes; his hostess was a stickler for form even in the country. Was the man opposite him Dallas Carfax, Julie wondered. He was broad-shouldered, his small mustache was as blond as his hair; she couldn't see his eyes. He was tall, but not as tall as Jim Trafford —

The comparison brought memories of the last twenty-four hours trooping back. In an attempt to outrace her thoughts Julie hurried from the gallery and ran down the narrow winding stairs. As she entered the hall Jaffrey looked up.

"Talk about an angel —"

"Were you talking about me, Billy?"

"My word, the conceit of her! That one so young and guileless should be allowed to travel alone in this wicked world —"

Martha Marshall interrupted his theatrical soliloquy. She slipped her arm around Julie's waist and drew her forward.

"Dallas, this is my youngest niece, Julie Lorraine. I know that you and she will be friends."

The girl's lips stiffened with resentment as she looked up into the brown eyes smiling down at her with happy-go-lucky assurance. Then to her amazement she felt her aversion to the man oozing away. She liked him! She was too surprised at her own change of viewpoint to speak. Suddenly over his shoulder she caught a glimpse of Jaffrey as hands clasped on his breast, eyes crossed, lips sagging open he gazed dumbly upward. The girl

75

strangled a laugh as she dragged her fascinated eyes back to the man before her. Had Billy meant that she had been looking at Carfax like that? Her lips twitched, her dimples deepened, her voice was unsteady as she declared warmly:

"I am so glad to meet you."

Carfax's puzzled eyes met hers which were riotous with laughter. His color mounted but there was a humorous twist to the lips beneath his slight mustache as he responded:

"You seem to be. In fact you appear almost hysterical with pleasure."

Julie cast an imploring, indignant glance at Jaffrey. He jumped into the breach.

"Guests expected at dinner, Aunt Martha? Not many, I hope. A crowd cramps my style."

"Then there will be no excuse for your not glittering like the Kohinoor to-night, William," Mrs. Marshall replied dryly. "There will be three besides ourselves. Mrs. Trafford and her son —"

"But I thought you were at swords' points with the last of the mill-magnates."

His hostess regarded him with indulgent disdain. "As a senatorial candidate I am, as a dinner guest he is most desirable. He can talk on any subject and he — he has such a wonderful nose." Her tone was wistful as just for an instant she quite unconsciously touched her own insignificant pug. Julie hastily avoided Jaffrey's incredulous eyes. Could it be possible that her aunt was envious of a nose, was that the weak joint in her armor of self-satisfaction, she had time to wonder before Mrs. Marshall went on:

"His mother is charming, thoroughbred. Not at all the modern woman. She has none of the twentieth century urge for hot-box oratory."

"Soap-box oratory, you mean, Aunt Martha. Don't speak of the lovely lady as though she were a trolley-car," teased Jaffrey. "Who will make the third in your galaxy of stars?"

"William, I wish that occasionally you would take things seriously. My third guest is Mrs. Trafford's ward, Pamela Parkman, who arrived at Brick House a few days ago. She makes her home with the Traffords. I understand that the son is engaged to her."

"Wha—at!"

Julie juggled the startled exclamation into a paroxysm of affected coughing. Her aunt regarded her anxiously. Carfax approached her solicitously; she turned her back quickly on Jaffrey's contemplative eyes. She flung a stumbling explanation into the silence. She had caught her breath, she often did it — it was not really a cough, she mumbled. Jaffrey interrupted with exaggerated concern:

"You should cure yourself of that rube habit of drawing impressions in through your open mouth, Marble-heart. It isn't done in polite society."

"Mrs. Trafford, Miss Parkman, Mr. Trafford," announced the butler.

Julie retreated behind the great couch at right angles with the fireplace as the guests advanced. Her heart thumped out a measure to which her pulses quick-stepped. Was it true that Jim Trafford had been engaged to his mother's ward? Probably that fact, even more than the political rivalry, accounted for Cheever's furious enmity. What had the man meant by his gibe, "The girl has turned a clever trick!"? The sentence recurred to Julie with annoying persistency. In spite of his engagement, perhaps because of it, Trafford had recognized the importance of the marriage as an emergency measure. Fortunately the emergency had passed — but had it — had it? If Cheever were to recover — but he couldn't — how —

She thrust the man from her mind and forced Mrs. Trafford into the foreground. The charming woman justified Martha Marshall's enthusiasm. Anne Trafford gave the impression of having met life valiantly. Her head with its shining waves of slightly silvered bronze hair came about to her son's heart, just where a mother's head ought to come, Julie approved in her thoughts. Her eyes were a sunny brown, her mouth seemed fashioned for tenderness, her white lace gown was undoubtedly an advance model.

The girl who entered the hall with her was in striking contrast. Her personality was pitched in a more blatant key. Her slenderness bordered on attenuation. The sleeveless, backless bodice of her pailletted yellow frock displayed a gleaming expanse of super-white skin. The lacquered effect of her shaved eyebrows gave an oriental look to her dark eyes. The red of her lips, the flush of her cheeks, the shadows under her eyes were the work of an expert. Her black hair, guiltless of wave or ripple, was swathed in gold gauze. Her voice was keyed up to her personality. There was a strident note in it as she handed a vanity-case to the man beside her with an imperious:

"Put this in your pocket, Jim!"

Julie's eyes lingered on his fine lean face as with chivalrous deference he responded to the qualified welcome of his hostess.

"Don't look upon me as a political convert, Mr. Trafford. I've called a truce because I so admire your mother. Julie," she waited for the girl's slow approach. "Mrs. Trafford, I want you to know my youngest niece, Julie Lorraine. Miss Parkman, Julie, and Mr. Trafford."

If she had not thought it to be quite out of character Julie would have sworn that there was a slight *timbre* of excitement in her aunt's carefully trained voice. The girl met the man's steady gaze with impersonal eyes. He was evidently awaiting his cue. She smiled radiantly at his mother.

"You are entitled to hold your head high if you have won Aunt Martha's admiration, Mrs. Trafford. It is a pleasure to meet you, Miss Parkman. Mr. Senator-Apparent, it has been the ambition of my life to cross swords with an honest-to-goodness political candidate. Aren't you thrilled to the marrow by your opportunity?"

The group shifted into another pattern leaving Julie and Trafford together. The smile left the girl's lips, her brows met in a slight frown as she whispered:

"Not a soul suspects! You said that you were in love but why, why didn't you tell me that you were engaged? That's different."

The charm of his smile struck down the slim rapier of her resentment. His voice was as low as hers but rich with amused indulgence as he answered:

"Engaged! I am not engaged. I'm an old married man."

"Thank heaven he sees the humor of the situation," the girl thought as she took her place at table. He need lose no time in getting the marriage annulled or broken or whatever one did to a contract that really was not a contract. How could a man of his force of character care for a girl like Pamela Parkman? Apparently he could, for hadn't he admitted last night that he was in love? He would be eager for his freedom. Julie's spirits soared. She would get a firmer grip on that all-for-self cult she had adopted and pack this visit with pleasure. She had made a flying-start when she had accepted that marvelous aggregation of hats, frocks and accessories from her aunt.

Carfax was seated at her right. Julie found him surprisingly easy to talk to. Was the fact due to his tact and experience or had the events of the last twenty-four hours swept away the barriers of reserve which she was wont to erect between herself and young men, she wondered. He was devoted to outdoor sports, so was she. In a lull in the general conversation he spoke to Jaffrey at the girl's left.

"The law will be off shore birds in a few days, Billy. Miss Lorraine has promised to come shooting with us. Perhaps we can persuade you to join the party, Miss Parkman."

Pamela shook a dissenting head. "No shooting for me, thank you. I hate a gun."

"Julie is one good little shot if I did train her," effervesced Jaffrey vaingloriously. "But

81

we can't do much without a dog."

Pamela Parkman forgot her pose of indifference as she contributed eagerly:

"That reminds me! There was a riot at the station yesterday. Somewhere *en route* a black dog had escaped from a baggage-car and a man and girl had chased him. They disappeared in a flash and no one knew who they were. The train went on and left them. The passengers were furious as there was not another north-bound train until morning. The conductor in charge who was making his first Maine trip — as were most of the porters, defended his action on the ground that he had to meet the Bar Harbor boat and 'How'd I know but what they hadn't planned it anyway!' What do you suppose happened to the three?"

The six pink candles in the six massive silver sticks seemed to Julie to be doing a one-step about the bowl of sweet-peas and stevia in the middle of the table. What was Jim Trafford thinking? She didn't dare look at him. Would no one ever speak? She stole a glance at Jaffrey. His green eyes were fixed on the girl opposite as he exclaimed:

"What a corking situation for a story! What breed of dog was it, Miss Parkman?"

"A black cocker spaniel, someone said."

"You would want something larger than that for hunting, Mrs. Marshall," Trafford cut in easily. As his hostess protested that she did not want any kind of dog, Billy Jaffrey murmured in Julie's ear:

"Well, I'll be darned, Marble-heart!"

Chapter VI

Julie in a dripping black bathing-suit, a green silk kerchief bound about her head, perched on the bow of Captain Phineas Snow's dory anchored off shore. Her sunbrowned hands clasped one silken knee in an affectionate embrace as she gave ear to the fisherman's monologue as he tinkered with the engine. The spaniel, head tilted, gravely superintended the repairs.

"It beats all how Ben Cheever hangs on, don't it? It's jest two weeks to-morrer since he was struck down an' they say he don't git no better'n no worse. The doc says he's clingin' to life like a bulldog. They can't find no bones broken, jest had a concussion, that's all. This human frame of ours is a queer machine. One minute 'twill stand more'n 'twould take to wreck a ship an' the next 'twill go to kingdom come at a touch as light as a thistledown," toothlessly philosophized Captain Snow as he filled a grease-cup.

Julie nodded affirmatively, her eyes on the

bungalow across the pond. It was three miles away but in the clear air it seemed within touching distance. She never passed it nor looked at it without a curious shiver. Never had she lost her first impression that the house was a crouching green dragon diabolically conscious of something sinister.

"Of course this accident will settle the senatorial fight, Captain Phin. Mr. Trafford will win hands down, won't he?"

The man straightened his bent back and looked thoughtfully toward the rustic bathhouse which was set up from the rocky, kelp-strewn shore. On the horizon line back of it loomed the red roofs of Shorehaven. The air was seasoned with salt, seaweed and a slight dash of fish. With a shake of his head the man shifted his glance to the girl and regarded her with marble-like eyes. They reminded her of the two prize glassies over which she and Billy had waged eternal warfare in the days of their youth.

"I dunno, gorry-me, I dunno. You see, Cheever had his own way in the county for years an' then along comes Jim. He's always been with his grandfather more or less, but he's been all over the world an' we none of us thought he'd be content to settle here. Folks don't want to elect him an' then have him get tired of it here an' leave an' that's what Ben's

85

tellin' everybody he'll do."

"I should trust Mr. Trafford before I would Cheever," championed the girl hotly. She colored under her sunburn at the fisherman's quick retort.

"How do you know? Cheever's ben smashed up ever since you've ben here."

"One can — can judge something from what one hears, can't one?" fenced Julie.

"Sure, sure. Jim an' Ben were great friends at first, used to go huntin'. Then all of a sudden they weren't seen together an' Jim announced thet he was to run fer the leg's-lature."

"Why not? Competition is as desirable in politics as it is in business, isn't it?"

"Sure it is, but Ben got ugly. He's tried to rake up something in Jim's past to smirch his campaign but he couldn't find so much as a cobwebby corner. Jim's ben straight all his life. He's ben full of fun an' mischief but he's ben straight. He can count eight generations back up there in the old cemetery on the bluff. Sometime you git him to show you the grave of the First Trafford. It's marked by a common field stone with name and date on it. Folks come miles to see that. The family, all except the Mad Trafford, an' gorry-me, he wouldn't be thought so wild these days, have ben fine God-fearin' citizens; it would be a mean skunk who would break that record. When I heard thet Jim was goin' into politics I shouted right out in caucus:

" 'Here comes the sun!' "

Snow wiped his greasy hands with a greasy wad of waste and reached into his pocket for his pipe. When he had the richly colored abomination drawing to his satisfaction he clutched his knee in two gnarled hands and regarded the girl whose slim figure swayed with every motion of the bow.

"The papers are full of stories of bribery an' corruption in politics. If you could git the young men growin' up to think it more manly to be straight than to be law breakers an' to set to an' take hold of things, mark-my-words, 'twould be the dawn of a new day; 'twouldn't be long before the sun of righteousness an' square dealin' would be shinin' overhead."

"You're a philosopher, Captain Phin."

The old fisherman regarded the girl quizzically. "Don't call me fancy names. I'm an American citizen, that's all. I ain't got the education to talk right but you don't have to know no grammar rules to think right an' I say what we need in this country is young people who'll think more of what they owe to the nation an' less of what the nation owes them. Jim Trafford's one of the first."

"But you seem doubtful about his winning the election."

"Gorry-me, I am. I dunno why, either. I ain't heard nothin', I don't know nothin', but I feel something in the air. You never can tell at sunup what you'll bump into before sundown, Julie." It was the Captain's royal custom to dispense with prefixes. He "never could see no use in misterin' and missin' people," he contended.

"Does Mr. Trafford sense something too?"

"I dunno. You never kin tell what's goin' on behind them gray eyes of his. When he gets a certain smile in them I know he's runnin' up a 'Take warnin'!' signal. They tell me at the mill that he's campaignin' most of the day an' workin' nights at the office. That kinder looks as though he wa'n't none too sure, don't it? Kinder tough fer him to have to be away so much when thet pretty ward of his mother's is stayin' at Brick House. Perhaps though he's pleased. He must get all-fired tired hearin' women talk. His mother ain't a talker, she's a doer, but there's Sarah Beddle besides the Parkman girl."

"Who is Sarah Beddle?"

"She's housekeeper at the Traffords an' the sourest old maid in the State of Maine. She's nutty on the subject of cats. She's got one at the house now that M's. Trafford says I've got to chloroform if Sarah don't. You see, I've been sort of a handy man fer Brick House since I was twenty. I taught Jim to fish, to shoot, to sail a boat. He'd listen to what I said 'es though 'twas gospel. That kept me steerin' pretty straight myself. That Beddle woman's tongue is hung in the middle."

The venom of the Captain's tone suggested many and losing encounters with the lady of the rotary tongue.

"Cheerio, Captain Phin. You don't suffer from the companionship of women. You live alone, don't you?"

"There's only me an' the phonograph. When I want to hear talk I turn the crank; when I've heard all I want I shut the thing off, which is something you can't do with a person."

"And I have been sitting here for the last half hour talking to you and doubtless you have been wishing you could shut me off. I'm sorry. Perhaps sometime I'll find *somebody* who appreciates me." The laughter in the girl's brilliant eyes gave the lie to her lugubrious voice. Snow's glassies warmed with approval.

"You know all-fired well I don't git tired hearin' you talk, Julie. But I guess your aunt wouldn't like it if she knew how friendly we was. M's. Marshall's a fine woman but she ain't no mixer. Here comes yer beau," he observed as a man in sports coat and knickerbockers appeared among the low pines that edged the shore. "That Carfax is a nice friendly feller but don't you marry him, Julie, unless he gits to work. Don't take a man that's likely to hang around the house all day."

The girl stood on the bow preparatory to a dive. From the seat the black spaniel watched her. Straight and slim, hands clasped behind her green turbaned head, she swayed with every motion of the boat as she laughed down upon the fisherman.

"I can't picture Dallas Carfax hanging round the house. His days must be fairly full when he is in New York."

"Full! Full of what? Is he runnin' a mill? Is he goin' to the leg'slater for the good of his country?" Snow demanded jealously.

"Why don't you talk to him, Captain Phin? You might succeed in making him realize his responsibilities."

"Course I know you're foolin', but gorry-me, I will talk to him the first chance — what you sayin'?" bellowed the Captain in response to a hail from shore.

"Mrs. Trafford wants you to bring the launch to her fl-o-a-t," shouted Carfax. "Come in — Juli-e. Pic-nic!"

90

The girl waved her hand and dove. The black spaniel scrambled over the gunwale and splashed into the water. He followed at a respectful distance from her gleaming arms. As the two waded to shore Carfax joined them with Julie's cape which he placed over her shoulders with practised care.

"Captain Phin thinks that you should go to work, Dal," she teased as she looked up into his lazy brown eyes. It was surprising, she thought, how fond she had become of Carfax in these last two weeks, the more surprising that it was the result so evidently desired by Managing Martha.

"Work! We're ordered to Blue Heron Cove for a picnic and if that doesn't mean work for an unresisting male, what does? Billy is to bring Aunt Martha's boat round to the Brick House float from which we will all embark. Mrs. Trafford has succeeded in corralling her son for a few hours. Hustle into your clothes, Julie. I'll wait here."

"I won't be — a min —" the girl's voice floated back as she raced for the bath-house, the black spaniel playfully nipping at her heels. It was several minutes before she returned in her white-knitted frock and violet sweater, a soft hat pulled low to shade her eyes. She drew a long breath.

"What a day for a picnic! It's glorious!

Don't you love this, 'the-world-is-mine,' feeling, Dal?"

He smiled at her indolently. "I'm afraid I never had it. We'd better toddle along. Why take the dog?" he asked jealously as in answer to her whistle the spaniel left a tide-pool in which he had been making life miserable for a crab and dashed up to her.

"I just haven't the courage to hurt his feelings by leaving him behind."

"It's a pity about your soft heart, Julie. You remind me of one of those chocolate-coated bits of granite one encounters in the average mixture."

"Are you intimating that I am stony-hearted or as delectable as chocolate?"

"Laugh if you like, I'm in earnest. You're both."

"Then enjoy the surface chocolate. I don't like that word granite, I much prefer Billy's Marble-heart. The name suggests something nice and white and undented," she tormented.

"Your heart is undented, all right. I —"

With boyish friendliness Julie slipped her arm within his as they turned into the wood trail that led to the road.

"Please don't spoil —"

At a sound ahead she looked up. Trafford faced her with a basket in each hand. Julie dropped the arm she held as though it had flamed red-hot. Then furiously angry with herself she turned her indignation into the first available channel.

"How you startled me! You go through the woods like an Indian, Mr. Trafford. I didn't suspect that there was anyone within two miles of us."

"So I imagined. Carfax, Mrs. Marshall wants you at Shorehaven. You and she and Billy are to pick up Pamela who is playing auction at the Club. Miss Lorraine is coming in our boat when we go ahead to get the fire started."

"Why the dickens didn't Aunt Martha send you for your own guest?"

"You may search me. I'm merely obeying orders. It is Mother's birthday and I couldn't refuse to help her celebrate. When I left the office the Shorehaven chauffeur was waiting to take me to Mrs. Marshall. This is the result." He moved his basket-laden hands. With a muttered protest Carfax started on the run.

"We'll go directly to the float, Goldilocks. Captain Phin —"

"Don't call me that! Someone might hear you."

"So they might. I'm sorry."

They swung into the hard white road. The

spaniel darted from side to side to poke his nose into suggestive holes in the shrub-crowded banks. Julie had met Trafford every day but it was the first moment she had been alone with him since they had parted at the train two weeks before. She racked her mind for something to say, something which should be sophisticatedly impersonal. She had the sense of groping in a great empty room, beautifully clean, swept clear of even a shred of an idea. In despair she sank to a boulder by the side of the road.

"There is a pebble in my shoe. You had better go on and tell them that I am coming," she suggested as she struggled with a button. Trafford dropped the baskets at the imminent risk of transfusing forever their contents and went down on one knee in front of her.

"Can't I help?"

"No. Darn!" she murmured under her breath as she broke a finger-nail. Trafford took possession of her foot and unbuttoned the shoe.

"Steady, Goldilocks. Why should you get panicky because we are alone together? You are not afraid of me, are you?"

"Afraid!"

Two indignant amethysts blazed up and met his smiling eyes.

"That is better. I prefer to have a person

94

look at me when I talk to them. There was no pebble in your shoe. Put it on again and I'll button it." He hesitated and then went on gravely, "Julie, I want your permission to announce our marriage if necessary."

"If necessary! Is there a chance that Cheever will live? Oh, I didn't mean that as it sounded. Of course I want him to live . . . I — I have had the feeling all the time that he might and I've wondered what I ought to do." Her troubled eyes met his.

"Put it out of your mind. Trust me to make the next move, will you?"

His hold on her shoe tightened. She looked down at his fingers, then up into his eyes. She wriggled her foot free and sprang to her feet.

"Of course I will trust you. I have from the first moment we met. I can't stay panicky when I am with you, you are so cool and steady and friendly. Our escapade would have proved a nightmare had you been like some men I know. I am sorry that your romance had to be held up but as far as I am concerned our partnership in the interest of good government may last until you think it safe to dissolve it. It doesn't trouble me in the least."

"So I can see."

Julie looked up at him quickly. Was there a trace of irony in his tone, in the gray eyes which met hers?

"Evidently the partnership isn't interfering with your aunt's plans in regard to Carfax. He seems completely under your spell."

"He isn't really. It is his habit to devote himself to someone and as I am in the house he is following the course of least resistance. I have a feeling of guilt about Aunt Martha, though. I am accepting her hospitality and all the lovely frocks when I haven't the least intention of —"

"Don't you wear any color but shades of violet?"

"Observing man. Hooverizing on colors was a measure of economy with us Lorraines so I dyed all the girls' white hand-me-downs violet to match my eyes when they are not blue. However, why should that fact interest you? Mrs. James Trafford won't have to economize," Julie teased gaily.

"Oh, but she does, or she thinks that she must."

The girl caught her breath as she met his eyes.

"Don't say that — that way. For an instant I felt trapped. As though I were really Mrs. J — J —" she stumbled irretrievably.

"Mrs. James Trafford? Not so bad," he mused judicially. "Your signature would be Julie Lorraine Trafford. Decidedly rhythmic, isn't it?"

"Don't! *Please!* If you keep on I shall begin to think that I am married."

"Then we'll forget it. I have news for you. No, *no*, nothing unpleasant. Don't be so apprehensive. I have finally succeeded in getting in touch with the owner of the spaniel; he wasn't on the train that day, and the dog is yours."

The girl's eyes were like stars. "Really? Did you buy him for me? You shouldn't have done it. I have been brought up not to accept presents from men friends," she protested with tormenting gravity.

"But you don't consider me —" he forced his voice to coolness. "This is certainly some day! See that fish-hawk! Over your head! Quick!"

Julie looked up with an unconscious sigh of relief. For an instant she had had the sense of being drawn gently, irresistibly into smothering depths. Above her a mammoth bird circled against the blue of the sky. For a second it hung and fanned, then rose until it disappeared into the snowy depths of a floating cloud-cave. Out it came. It sank, it swooped, with outspread wings it pounced on something beneath the meringue-tipped ripples of the bay. The girl controlled a shiver as she whispered:

"That bird reminds me of Cheever. But

how can he pounce —"

"All aboard!" shouted a voice from the water.

"Coming, Captain!" Julie answered and raced ahead of her companion to the float.

Anne Trafford was seated in the stern of a trim motor-launch. She looked like a girl in her green sports coat and hat. Julie's heart went out to her as she met the smiling tenderness of her eyes.

"Your aunt arranged for you to come with us, Miss Lorraine. Are you and I equal to keeping these three men in order? I forgot, you haven't met Major Buell. Tom!" In response to her call a man who had been bent over a locker stood up. Would he ever stop looming, the girl wondered. He had gray hair, quizzical eyes behind glasses and an iron jaw.

"Oooch, I should hate to be what you wanted if I didn't want you," Julie thought as she took the hand he extended to help her into the boat. Trafford followed her and Snow pushed off. She turned to the woman in the stern.

"Dal told me that this was your birthday. Felicitations!"

"Now what have I said?" she wondered indignantly as she felt Trafford's intent eyes on hers. She turned away from them but his voice followed her.

"Won't you take the wheel, Miss Lorraine? Didn't you tell me that you were used to a motorboat?"

"Oh, may I? Would it make you nervous, Mrs. Trafford? I am really an experienced skipper."

"Take it, if it would be a pleasure. Nothing frightens me with Jim aboard."

"Anne, don't leave me out!"

The intonation of the Major's voice sent prickly thrills over Julie. He seated himself in the stern and she went forward. Captain Phin relinquished the wheel to her.

"Do you see thet bleached oak on the island? Keep her headed straight fer thet. Jim, you'd better stay kinder near."

Trafford nodded and took his place directly behind the girl. There was a laugh in his voice as he commented:

"I wish that you could have seen the color of your face when the Major protested to Mother, Goldilocks. You mustn't mind him. He has been in love with her for the last fifteen years."

"And doesn't she care for him?"

"For a young person who abhors sentiment your voice indicates considerable concern for the Major's unrequited affection."

She shook her head in laughing denial, her eyes on the bleached oak.

"But I am not the subject. The moment a man shows the slightest interest in me I feel like a porcupine, all quills. And if he attempted to touch me, I should *hate* him."

"Look out for that reef!"

Trafford thrust an arm forward on either side of her and gave the wheel a quick turn. For an instant she leaned back against him with her hands over her heart. Her boyishly cool eyes met his.

"After this, Mr. Trafford, no talking with the motorman. I —"

"Gorry-me, Jim! What do you mean by sayin' there was a reef?" Captain Phin was peering over the side of the boat. He met Trafford's eyes and subsided into a mutter. Julie had been too intent on her task to hear.

"Please give me the wheel again. I promise to keep my eyes and my mind on that tree. You look white. Did I frighten you? Do you think that I was fibbing when I boasted that I was an experienced skipper?"

"Not when you said that, but on some subjects your statements are not absolutely reliable — Miss Lorraine."

The launch with the Stars and Stripes floating at the stern entered the outer bay. The spaniel settled himself on the bow with his paws drooping over the edge, his head tiptilted as he watched for the seals whose dripping, satiny heads kept bobbing above the water on the ledges. The sea was rough. Trafford dragged some oilskins from the locker. He tossed two to Buell and held one for the girl as he directed:

"Take the wheel while Miss Lorraine gets into this slicker, Captain Phin."

"Do I need it? I think I do," Julie gasped as a wave broke at the bow and drenched the inside of the boat. Trafford tucked her hat into his pocket and drew a sou'wester over her fair hair. He dried her dripping face with his handkerchief.

"Thanks lots. Lake sailing and sea sailing are not quite alike," she admitted with a laugh.

As Snow dropped anchor in a cove from which a cliff reared almost perpendicularly Julie whispered:

"Look!"

A crane standing knee-deep in water, one leg under him, long neck arched as he poked experimentally among the seaweed, shrilled an alarm and soared. With legs trailing behind him like ram-rods he winged into the west.

"What *was* it?"

"A blue heron. They are the original first settlers. There has been a pair somewhere near that cliff since the beginning of its history."

The girl's eyes glowed with eagerness.

"You mustn't mind if I lose my breath over this wonderful coast. I have never been at the sea before," she explained with her eyes on the stretch of pebbly beach and the ferns and bushes which tufted the ledges above the cove.

"Jim, take Miss Lorraine —" Julie dragged her eyes away from the shore and faced the stern.

"Please call me Julie, Mrs. Trafford. Remember that I am a country clergyman's daughter and quite unused to formality in the parish."

"Jim, take *Julie* first and some of the baskets. Then come back for the Major and me. Captain Phin has something to do to the engine."

The girl seated herself in the stern of the tender as Snow steadied it against the gunwale of the launch. As Trafford took the oars he frowned at her thoughtfully. "I don't care for the idea of leaving you alone on the shore while I go back for the others. Captain Phin is eternally fussing with that engine."

"Silly! What could happen to me? If a great big bear came along I could swim to the launch. I'll collect driftwood for the fire while I'm waiting for the others."

She stood on the beach surrounded by baskets and watched him pull away. No wonder that his mother felt safe when he was in the boat, she thought. He was so companionable, not at all like Dal Carfax who had been showing slight symptoms of sentiment of late. Why, oh, why couldn't men stay friendly? But why, oh, why was she spoiling this glorious minute thinking of unpleasant things, she demanded of herself.

The sea and the air and rocky coast set her imagination to galloping. She picked up a basket and went slowly toward the cliff. She whistled the air of "God's in His heaven, all's right with the world!" from start to finish. As she reached the last exultant note she stopped in startled surprise. A figure struggled up from a heap of seaweed at her feet. The man got as far as his knees and stopped and stared. His glance sent a million frosty shivers stealing down the girl's spine. Then the million shivers congealed in one icy lump in her heart. The bleak eyes regarding her with mounting recognition in their depths were the eyes that had peered into the cabin window, the eyes of the man whom Cheever had found curled up in the shed, the eyes of Willy Small.

Chapter VII

"Come back to earth, Marble-heart! You're burning the bacon!" sniffed William Jaffrey. "You can't cook and indulge in day-dreams and get away with it," he protested from the other side of the circle of rocks within which glowed the red coals of driftwood.

With an exclamation of dismay the girl examined the cinder, once a fat, juicy strip, which dangled from the fork of the long stick in her hand.

"I'm sorry, Billy. I am so thrilled with this experience that I can't keep my mind on what I am doing. My eyes will roam about this wonderful country. Look at Aunt Martha! Isn't she funny? I'll wager that she would stop to put on her veil and gloves if the last trump sounded."

Jaffrey's eyes followed the girl's. Seated on a fair sized boulder in the middle of the beach was the *chatelaine* of Shorehaven. She wore a thin black gown, a mourning hat with a white lined brim, a crape banded veil drawn tightly beneath her chin and black gloves. The formality of her costume was accentuated by the white and green sports perfection of Anne Trafford who was stirring the contents of a kettle which steamed over a small upright camp stove. Major Buell, coatless and with his white sleeves rolled above his elbows, was feeding the fire under it. Pamela Parkman generously displayed her chiffon textured hosiery as knees crossed, cigarette between her lips, she perched on a rock and directed Carfax and Trafford in the laying and provisioning of the cloth. The rough familiarity of the sea-breeze seemed not to have ruffled a hair of her satin-smooth head; her hands in loose white gloves were thrust into the pockets of her yellow sports coat. She had the manner of a queen permitting her vassals the privilege of serving her. The spaniel roamed from group to group sniffing wistfully. Overhead the sky spread cloudlessly blue. Offshore a cabin-cruiser was anchored. One tender was drawn up on the beach, the other swung at the stern of the launch in which Captain Phin was busy at the engine. A few heavily wooded islands broke the illimitable expanse of sea. The clear air was rich with the spicy breath of balsams and appetizing with the aroma of coffee, broiling bacon, and cooking clams.

Julie's glance stole to the sloping cliff. She

had not explained to Billy that while the bacon burned her thoughts had been with the man who had surprised her on the beach. How had he come there? She had seen no boat. Had he recognized her as the girl he had seen in the cabin by the stream? He had stared at her a dazed instant before he had scrambled up the cliff with the sidewise motion of a crab. Half-way to the top he had disappeared as suddenly as though a magician had prestidigitated him out of sight. But in the instant he had hesitated she had recognized the bleak blue eyes which had stared at her through the window. Should she tell Trafford? Her glance flew to the group by the improvised table. No, he seemed absorbed in Pamela Parkman. Why spoil the first day of vacation he had in two weeks? Of course he must know soon that Willy Small had not left the county as Captain Phin had stated. She would tell him tomorrow, not to-day. It seemed as though she had been speculating for hours when Jaffrey's voice answered her comment.

"Patience on a monument, smiling at Grief, that's Aunt Martha to the life. I doubt if a cloudburst of emotion would stir her marcelle or flutter a ribbon. Pam Parkman will be a small edition of her when she is older. Look at her! She sits there as unruffled as though she had been recently removed from a wardrobe trunk or one of those things warranted not to crumple one's belongings."

"*Bien soignée* is the term for which you're struggling," Julie prompted.

"Righto! Now as for you —" his green eyes alight with amusement and affection appraised the girl.

"You can't do things with the tips of your fingers, can you, Marble-heart? Where is your hat? Your hair has deserted the straight and narrow and is running wild, the wind has whipped it into little curls. There is a smudge the shape of the map of Ireland on your chin and one eye looks as though it had been set in your head by a sooty finger. Don't touch it, you'll make it worse. Come along with me while I wash your face."

He caught her hand and the two raced to the water's edge in laughing comradeship. After a rough but thorough application of his wet handkerchief Jaffrey held the girl off for inspection.

"That's better! You don't look so piebald. We're coming!" he shouted in response to a hail.

By the time the cloth was cleared and the dishes washed and packed in baskets the sun had begun to slant. A few creamy clots of cloud had appeared in the sky. Martha Marshall reëntombed in veil and gloves sat erect

107

on her boulder. Anne Trafford leaned comfortably against a tree-trunk while she knitted a soft pink and white thing. Buell near her was paying out wool from a ball in his hands. Carfax was stretched flat on his back beside Julie, quoting poetry between cigarettes. Trafford and the spaniel had rowed out to the launch with Captain Phin. Jaffrey beside Pamela Parkman was immersed in a newspaper. No one had spoken for quite five minutes when he exploded:

"Holy smoke, I'll get out of the writing game tomorrow and start raising dogs. Listen to this:

" 'Owner of a blue-ribbon cocker spaniel sells prize-winner for one thousand dollars. Purchaser bought the dog for a present for his wife. His name has been withheld.' "

"I should think that a man who would pay one thousand dollars for a dog would want his name withheld," commented Martha Marshall dryly. "Julie, you had better turn that black spaniel of yours into money."

The girl looked up and met Jaffrey's green eyes observing her intently over the edge of his paper. Her heart had given a sudden jump when he had read the item but of course it couldn't be — she sprang to her feet.

"I would rather have Sweetie-peach than a thousand dollars, Aunt Martha. I am going for a row. This air drugs my mind to say nothing of my muscles. Will anyone come with me?" Six pairs of eyes regarded her lazily. "One at a time, don't crowd, please!"

"You are too darned energetic, Marble-heart," groaned Jaffrey.

"Energetic! I have done nothing but play around with you and Dal since I reached this wonderland two weeks ago. I'm used to being a working woman, not a lady of leisure. A hard row will do me good."

"Go with her, Dal," commanded Martha Marshall.

"I don't want him."

Carfax colored angrily but before he could utter the retort so evidently on his lips Jaffrey suggested blandly:

"Perhaps Miss Parkman would like to take the other pair of oars?" He carefully avoided Julie's indignant eyes. Pamela daintily ringed the smoke from her cigarette before she answered:

"Thank you, no. I am not athletic. I never venture into a boat without a man, neither do I waste time upon a girl," she added with the blunt discourtesy she affected. She produced her vanity case and dexterously powdered her nose and chin. Mrs. Trafford's lips compressed as she wrinkled her brow over a dropped stitch. Julie denatured the crisp retort on the tip of her tongue to an amused:

"My proposition appears to be as unpopular as the sixty-seventh Congress. However, I'm going. I'll row around the headland. Who knows but that I may discover a tourmaline mine and make my fortune?"

"If it's prospecting you want, scramble up that cliff and you'll tumble into the entrance to the Mad Trafford's copper-mine. Ah, well, if you persist in rowing, I suppose I can go with you, Marble-heart. That is, if no one else will." Jaffrey grinned at Carfax who with heightened color and stubborn lines about his lips stolidly contemplated his cigarette.

"I haven't the heart to take advantage of your self-sacrificing offer, Billy," Julie replied crisply. She looked at the watch on her wrist. "May I have twenty minutes, Mrs. Trafford? I'll peek at what is on the other side of the cliff and come back. I have a passion for adventuring round corners."

"Go on, child, we shan't start for at least a half hour," Anne Trafford encouraged. "Adventure to your heart's content. Nothing can happen to you with Jim and Captain Phin out there in our boat."

With practised ease Julie stepped into the

tender and pushed off with an oar. She waved her hand to the colorful group on shore and took her seat. As she passed the launch Jim Trafford looked up and shouted, "Where are you going?"

"I'm going a-rowing, kind sir, she said," she flung back over her shoulder and sent the tender forward with a long, strong pull. The sea had quieted and rolled in lazy undulating waves. A kingfisher flashed bluely by. The sun was warm on her back. She put her hand to her nose which felt like a brand snatched from the burning.

"Every day in every way you're getting redder and redder," she laughed as she squinted at the shapely member.

The tide was running strong when she reached the headland. It swept the tender round the cliff which on that side was bare and dented with cave-like hollows. It was devoid of vegetation except for one ancient oak which twisted out from the rock in the most approved Japanese-print fashion, and for a fringe of bushes at the top which gave to the promontory a pompadoured effect. As she rowed nearer the girl could see that they held blueberries. Such bouncers! Could she get them?

The sunny cove at the base of the cliff encouraged her, the step-like crevices in the rock invited her, the berries lured her, the dazzling black and white No Trespassing sign at the top dared her. With an appraising glance at the sun she sent the boat forward. A wave carried the bow up on the beach. She made the painter fast to a low branch of the oak, pulled a tin pail from the locker and jumped out. With a rueful glance at her wet shoes she began to climb.

The ascent was absurdly easy. At the top she stopped to look about her. She could see the village and the brooks that emptied into Glass Pond. They spread in all directions like the silver reins of a gigantic four-in-hand. Between the mills and the water she could just discern the green bungalow. It looked more like a sinister dragon than ever at this distance, the girl thought. What had Jim Trafford heard about Cheever? Whatever it was she could trust him to take the right step. He had told her to put the thing out of her mind. She would — if she could.

She looked at the smooth green plateau which the berry-bushes fringed. Who would believe that the rocky ledge was crowned with such velvety richness? Julie wrinkled her brows over its posted condition.

"It looks as though there had been an explosion of Danger signs," she confided to herself. What was the owner's idea? He couldn't be trying to conserve the fruit on those few bushes; that would be absurd. Whistling softly she stripped the berries into her pail. As she reached for an elusive spray her eyes wandered to the green field. With a startled sound in her throat she dropped to her knees. Cautiously she parted the bushes. Breathlessly she peered through. Was she dreaming? had a patch of earth risen slowly from the ground? It wasn't a dream! It wasn't! A head emerged slowly from the opening. Two bleak eyes shifted from end to end of the field with the wariness of those of a prairie-dog in front of his hole. The head ducked. The sod fell noiselessly into place. Julie sank back on her heels.

Willy Small! What did his presence here mean? What sort of a retreat did that trapdoor indicate? Was he hiding from the authorities on account of Cheever's accident? Had the subterranean cave any connection with Jim Trafford's suspicions about the state senator and his methods?

"Hallo-o-o!"

The hail from below sent Julie's heart into her mouth. Someone had come for her. Would Small be watching? If he saw her he might suspect that she had recognized him. With the handle of the pail between her teeth she crawled on hands and knees to the spot where she had entered the bushes. She slid part way down the cliff. When she stood up she saw Trafford leaping from ledge to ledge toward her. Below Captain Phin was steering the motor-launch in slowly widening circles. The black spaniel was stretched on a locker. Pamela Parkman sat in the stern as immaculate as when she left her room that morning. Julie was indignantly conscious of her own tousled appearance.

"Now why did he have to bring her?" she protested under her breath.

"How the dickens did you get here?" Trafford demanded as they met half-way down the cliff.

"How the dickens did you get here?"

He laughed at her careful imitation of his tone. "Captain Phin landed me on the rocks. We saw the tender in the cove. Billy has taken the rest of the party in your aunt's boat. Didn't you see that NO TRESPASSING sign? The old copper-mine honeycombs this cliff and you ran nine chances out of ten of going down a hole."

"So this is your land too. Don't scold. I kept in among the berry-bushes. I didn't go into the field. Your mother thought it quite all right for me to adventure alone. Billy didn't want to come and I didn't want Dal."

"Why? Has he been making love to you?"

The explosive quality of the question startled Julie. She slipped. Trafford steadied her by an arm about her shoulders. Her eyes and voice laughed as she shook her head.

"You force me to the humiliating confession that I really don't know what 'making love' is like."

"Shall I show you?"

The roughness of his voice sent the girl's puzzled eyes to his. His quick, cool laugh reassured in her. Was it accident or design, she wondered, that his glance dropped to the figure in the stern of the launch as he suggested:

"Perhaps I need experience too."

"Don't experiment with me. I refuse to have our friendship spoiled. I feel so secure with you and Billy. Perhaps it is because I saw my five sisters through malignant love-affairs that I have such an aversion to sentiment. I hope that I am not one of those athletic creatures who are temperamentally incapable of loving." At the unqualified dismay in her tone Trafford threw back his head and shouted with laughter. "I don't see anything particularly funny in that. It isn't a joke to feel iced the moment a man shows that he likes you," she defended indignantly as she stepped into the tender. Trafford untied the painter, pushed off the boat and jumped in.

"Don't worry about your unresponsiveness. Keep on feeling secure with Billy and me. We'll stand guard over the Sleeping Beauty till her Prince Charming arrives."

"In spite of the fact that you won't take me seriously you have a steam-roller way of smoothing out my problems." She smiled at him radiantly but the lines between the man's eyes deepened.

"I didn't smooth out that cabin situation."

"Only because I mixed it so hopelessly, Mr. Trafford." Ought she to tell him that she had seen Small, Julie considered. No, she would wait until to-morrow. He should have his holiday.

"You called me 'Jim' when you told Cheever that we were —"

"Don't whisper it! That was an emergency measure. Of course I will dispense with formality if you care to have me. I think of you as 'Jim.' "

"Thank you. I confess that I was horribly jealous when you called Carfax by his first name. You met him after you met me."

"But I have been living in the same house with Dal for two weeks. A house-party is a quick worker. It splits friendships or welds them with amazing speed."

"Then it is a pity that I cannot accept your aunt's invitation to spend the time between now and election at Shorehaven. I should like our friendship to be welded indissolubly —

Mother, Pamela and Major Buell are going over this afternoon for a visit. Your aunt proposed the plan after you left in the tender. I am glad for Mother to have the change. She keeps so everlastingly busy with her classes for the girls at the mill, visiting the sick and coddling the old ladies in the village. Then while Sarah Beddle is invaluable I'll admit that she is wearing when she dons the martyr's crown."

"It will be delightful to have your mother with us. Why can't you come?"

"I — I — oh, until after election Brick House is the best place for me. Your aunt, Jaffrey and Carfax have gone there for tea while Mother and Pam pack up. You are to join them."

"For tea! I can't go like this! Look at me! Drop me at our float. I'll dash up to Shore-haven, leave Sweetie-peach, make myself presentable and drive over in the roadster. They will need the extra car for the luggage."

As they reached the launch Trafford shipped his oars and Captain Phin seized the tender. The spaniel's tail thumped a languid greeting. Pamela Parkman's dark brows arched as she complained:

"I thought you would never come, Jim. Miss Lorraine, you have broken up the party."

"I'm sorry," Julie apologized as she stepped to the seat of the launch. The tin pail dangled from her arm. She joined Snow at the wheel. He waited until Jim Trafford had made the tender fast, then put on full speed. As the launch cut through the waves Julie confided:

"See what I found at the top of the cliff, Captain Phin! I'll come to your cottage to-morrow and make a berry-pie to pay for keeping you waiting here."

"I'd like the pie first-rate but gorry-me, what'd you go up among them bushes for? Jim was fit to tie when he see you. Didn't you read that sign?"

"Yes, but I didn't go far. Doesn't anyone ever go up on that land?"

"Why should they want to go fer? It's a wild spot an' it's dangerous. The Trafford who was buncoed into openin' up thet mine didn't quit until he'd run shafts in all directions. There used to be a lot of buildin's but Jim had them taken down an' the openin's protected as far's he could. He's kept the inside jest's it was even to some of the wheelbarrers an' tools."

"Isn't it a temptation to someone to steal?"

Captain Phin's gums showed in a grin. "I guess by the time a thief got them things out they'd cost him more'n he could buy new for. The townspeople don't trouble Blue Heron Cove much. You see, when the Mad Trafford put them sapphires in —"

"Did he bury the stones there?"

"Gorry-me, no. Not the jewels themselves; he sold 'em an' —"

"He wasn't the first man who has sunk family jewels in speculation."

"You said somethin' then. I expect this speculation business is the same bug under another name that bit them old buccaneers when they started out to pick up what they could on the high seas. Ben Cheever's jest like that. He's always dabblin' in somethin' new to make a cent instead of stickin' to his mills."

"Poor man, nothing matters to him now, does it?"

Snow scowled at a sailboat which was tacking in his direction. "I dunno, I dunno. Since I talked with you this mornin' one of the villagers who come alongside this boat to borrow a tool told me that Cheever was — Gorry-me, Julie, you look kinder white. Better go sit in the stern where there ain't so much pitchin'."

"I'm all right, Captain Phin. What were you saying about Cheever?"

"I guess perhaps I'd better tell Jim too." He turned his head and shouted over his shoulder:

"Hi, Jim! They say Cheever's up an' round again, talkin' loud about beatin' you hands down."

Chapter VIII

In a linen frock which matched her eyes when they were bluest Julie stopped for an instant in the drive to look up at Brick House. Twenty-four paned windows gazed benignly back at her from its velvety red surface. The old wrought iron door latch with its curved lift proclaimed it as belonging to that period when men occupied themselves more with making homes and building character and background than with making money. To the girl the mellow old house had a look of brooding tenderness as though in its warm embrace it had soothed heartaches, had laughed and sympathized with youth, had welcomed the coming, sped the parting guest, had celebrated births and bridals and had cared lovingly for the aged until it lingeringly released them to more tender care.

It was not surprising, Julie thought as she went on, that Jim Trafford loved the place and was eager to uphold its traditions. She paused under an arbor in the hedge. Before her stretched lawns like green velour. Beyond them was a high brick wall from the top of which tumbled cascades of white clematis. In the middle of the wall the two sides of a massive wooden door were thrown back to give a glimpse of stepping-stones which led into the cathedral-like solemnity of a forest. On either side of the door giant spikes of monk's-hood, the flame of gladioli, a fringe of pink cosmos, opaline mists of stevia, hollyhocks in pink and carmine made a riot of color, sighed a perfumed breath at every touch of the light breeze. Against the eastern wall a row of beehives hummed with industry; on one of the lawns an iridescent peacock strutted before a mirror set in the ground.

Anne Trafford, in a fan-back wicker chair of the inspired type designed as a background for lovely woman, was dispensing tea from the tray in front of her. Martha Marshall with veil thrown back and gloves removed was chatting with Major Buell whose ardent eyes were on his hostess. Julie judged from the motion of her aunt's white hands with their flashing rings that she had mounted her favorite hobby, astrology. Pamela Parkman had commandeered both Jaffrey and Carfax who were busy supplying her innumerable wants.

Where was Jim Trafford, the girl wondered. Had he sensed the full significance of the news Captain Phin had flung at him? What would happen now? Had Cheever's journey to the borderland of eternity ennobled him or was he an exemplification of that old saw:

"When the devil was ill the devil a saint would be; when the devil was well, devil a saint was he"?

"Julie, you were a quitter when you wriggled out of acknowledging that marriage," she condemned herself. If Jim Trafford lost the election would it be her fault? Suppose he were beaten by that horrid, untrue story of Cheever's? For the first time in her twenty-three years the girl's sense of expediency failed her. She felt like a caged squirrel running round and round to find a way out. She gripped her imagination. Nothing had happened yet, she reminded herself. Why was she worrying? Wasn't Jim quite equal to the situation? She had boasted that she loved to approach corners. She was afraid to peer round this one, starkly afraid. She tried to respond to Anne Trafford's smile as she looked up and greeted her.

"Here is the laggard. Come and have your tea, Julie. Jim had to call up the mill as soon as he reached the house so I haven't heard how your rowing adventure turned out."

Julie's heart warmed to the affection in the woman's voice. She matched the gaiety of her tone as she deplored:

"Could you have seen me when I emerged from the blueberry jungle you would wonder that I have appeared as soon and as presentably as I have. Am I not presentable, Dal?" she challenged as she met Carfax's reproachful eyes. She seated herself on a low wicker divan. "I should love a piece of that chocolate cake if you don't want it all."

Carfax presented the laden stand and seated himself beside her.

"Why didn't you want me to come in the boat with you?"

"Martyr! You know that you were bored to extinction when I suggested a row. A stick of dynamite out adventuring for something to blow up would have passed you by as immovable, you looked so lazy. Lucky you didn't come. You would have hated the tangle of bushes I landed in. Look at that!" She extended a scratched palm. "It feels as though it had been harrowed with a vegetable grater and seeded down with thorns. I didn't stop at Shorehaven to pull the horrid things out; I was afraid that I would be late for tea. They are mighty uncomfortable."

With an exclamation of concern Carfax caught the slender hand in his. "I can get those out, Julie." He drew a knife from his pocket and opened out a slim pair of tweezers.

His blond hair touched the girl's head as he bent over her hand. "See that — and that? Just a minute. There is one more."

"Is this a first-aid station, Carfax?"

Julie jerked her hand free and looked up at Trafford at her elbow. There was a warning rigidity about his jaws, the creases between his brows were deep, his gray eyes were black. The girl's heart stopped for a moment, then pounded on. Had he heard something more about Cheever? She must have a talk with him before she left. He ought to know that Willy Small was hibernating in the cliff. What excuse could she make to get him away? She had an inspiration:

"Mr. Trafford, won't you present me to the Duchess? I so want to see those famous sapphires."

"Billy, take Miss Lorraine to the living-room and show her the portrait. Mother, have you some tea for me?"

Julie had the sensation of having been suddenly and expertly ducked into icy water. What had she said that she should not have said, she wondered as she followed Jaffrey through the garden. Indignation tilted her chin. Why should she worry about The Trafford's election, if he didn't, she asked herself scornfully.

Her annoyance oozed as she entered the

124

living-room. The restful atmosphere soothed her perturbed spirit. The walls were a deep tan. The satin polish of old mahogany reflected the light of the fire in the Franklin grate. On the hearth-rug, like a sentinel, a yellow coon-cat sat motionless on its haunches, observing the intruders through dark slits in topaz eyes. Across the room double doors opened into a book-lined study which had French windows that faced the sea. There was a large couch at right angles with the fireplace. Over the mantel hung the only picture in the room. It was the portrait of a fair-haired woman in stiff blue and gold brocade, with eyes the color of the satin of her gown. Under one plump bare arm was a King Charles spaniel. In the fingers of the other hand, on one of which was a great sapphire, she held a round cracker. There were sapphire buttons on her bodice, sapphire clusters at her ears, a bow of sapphires against her fair hair which was bound about her head in braids. She was beautiful, stately, slightly cynical as she looked down into the vivid face upturned to hers.

"Isn't she g-grand, Billy?"

"She is. You have heard the story of the First Trafford, of course, but that isn't a patch on the thrills which came later."

Julie perched on the arm of the couch and

gazed up at the portrait.

"Tell me about it, Billy."

"Once upon a time an enterprising Trafford, perhaps of the fourth dynasty, sold the sapphires to finance a copper-mine. Thereupon his aged sire cursed him richly and racily. Whereupon the royal dame began to roam. None of the villagers will admit it but even in this age and generation you couldn't induce one of them to play round Blue Heron Cove after the R Z T hours."

"R T Z hour? What is that, Billy?"

"Radio. At exactly eight P.M. everyone commences to listen-in. You won't meet a person on the street. The Duchess has the evening quite to herself in which to search for the missing jewels."

"We picnicked near that same copper-mine today, did we not?"

"We did. It runs through the cliff you were so eager to investigate. They *say*, that on foggy nights a c-curious l-luminous m-mist floats about the entrance. Some superstitious dumb-bell started the story that it was the D-Duchess h-hunting for the l-lost sapphires." There was a shiver in Jaffrey's every syllable. In spite of her amused appreciation of his artistry his tone sent a responsive tingle along Julie's nerves.

"Nonsense, Billy! How can intelligent persons give credence to that absurd yarn? It's your bestseller imagination."

"If it is what do you make of this *fact?* When Mrs. Trafford appeared at a fancy-dress ball last summer in the costume of the Duchess — reproduced to a thread except for the sapphires — the chairman of the village committee politely but firmly requested her to go home and take it off. It had tumbled the temperature of the festivity to below zero."

"Did she go?"

"She did, like the thoroughbred she is. Hung it up and went back in the costume of the sixties she had found in the attic." He stifled a prodigious yawn behind his plump hand. "My word, but these high-noon chowder fests make me sleepy. Let's make our getaway and have a few sets of tennis before dinner."

"Just as you say, Billy. I strive to please. I love this room. I felt as though I had been caught in tender arms as I entered it. If I lived here I should fall victim to a virulent attack of ancestor-worship. Isn't Mrs. Trafford a dear?"

"Too dear for her own good. Imagine a woman like that having a girl like Pam flung at her to guard."

"They seem decades apart in manners and ideas."

"They are. Pamela's father died when she

was eighteen. He was a one-time adorer of Mrs. Trafford's. If the girl marries a man of whom her guardian disapproves, her property will be tied up in a trust. She was furious when she found that she had been left under guardianship. I'll say that Mrs. Trafford was not any more pleased."

"Why did she accept the trust?"

"Because she is like you, Julie; her duty complex is abnormally developed. She shouldered the responsibility and has Pam with her when the girl isn't traveling. The logical outcome of the situation would be for Jim to marry her and add her fortune to his own. Perhaps her father thought of that."

"Has he so much money, Billy?"

"Boy, I should say he had! So much that with his chivalrous make-up it's a wonder to me that he has escaped the innumerable snares set by fair-sex trappers. You got a nice burn to-day, Marble-heart; an Inness sunset has nothing on your face."

"It's — it's partly the fire, Billy. We had better start if you want tennis. Here comes Aunt Martha. Tell her that we are going," Julie suggested as Mrs. Marshall followed by Major Buell entered the room. The woman was triumphantly concluding an argument.

"Laugh if you like, Major, but I can prove that astrology is a science to be regarded with respect. Take to-day, for instance; the dominating influence is martial impelling to turbulent and aggressive acts, making the actions and temperament generally ill-governed. It would be well for us all to keep our affairs under firm and cool control if the fortunate aspect between certain luminaries is to govern. While you are at Shorehaven I will explain my charts, Major. Julie, Mrs. Trafford wants you in the garden. There is a rare blossom she thinks you will appreciate. She is to drive to Shorehaven later with her son, who will dine with us. She suggested that you wait and go with them. The rest of us are going now. Pamela has gone for her coat. Billy, will you and Dal —"

Julie did not wait for the rest of the sentence. As she stepped into the garden she saw Trafford and his mother standing by the teatable. The peacock on the wall above them had his tail widespread as though with its iridescent beauty to challenge the cloud-tinting sun to competition.

What did Mrs. Trafford want of her, the girl wondered. Of course she had not been summoned to see a blossom. Was the mother in her son's confidence? Was —

Julie's mind spun for an instant and steadied. Was that Cheever standing in the garden doorway or had she thought of him so much that her imagination had projected his counterpart?

"The dominating influence to-day is martial. It would be well for us all to keep our affairs under firm and cool control," Julie reminded herself under her breath. There was no doubt but that the man she saw was flesh and blood. The last time she had seen him he had been enveloped in a dripping rain coat, his thin dark hair had been plastered to his head by the storm. Now in his immaculate sports clothes he might have served for the advertisement of the well-dressed man. The long strip of plaster on his cheek gave him a malevolent look; his pallor accentuated the burning intentness of his dark eyes as he approached Mrs. Trafford who greeted him with outstretched hand.

What should she do, Julie wondered. She would not complicate the situation by impulsiveness this time. There was nothing for her to do. Hadn't Jim said that he would take the responsibility of the next move? If he would only look at her. As though he sensed her thought he turned. He held out his hand and looked straight into her eyes.

"Come here, Julie. You have met Cheever before. Ben, of course you remember my wife?"

Chapter IX

"My wife!"

The words jangled through Julie's mind like a sharply pulled bell till they tinkled into stillness. In the silence which followed Jim Trafford's announcement the hiveward humming of a honey-laden bee rumbled like an express train against the girl's ear-drum. Slow color tinted the pallor of her startled face as she forced herself to meet Cheever's eyes. To her amazement they showed not a trace of mockery. His expression was puzzled, dazed as he looked from the girl to the woman and on to Trafford. The master of Brick House was colorless. He gave the impression that his spirit was crouched to spring. Cheever's laugh was embarrassed. He brushed an unsteady hand across his eyes.

"Remember her! I didn't know that you were married, Jim. I had thought that you and Pamela — that isn't a tactful thing to say, is it? Forgive me. I am as good as new except that I can remember nothing that happened from a week before my accident until I opened my eyes a week ago. Perhaps your engagement was announced during that time. The lapse of memory is most unfortunate just now. I mean to do some of my campaigning over again, but this time I also will cut out the mud-slinging. One doesn't just escape the boatman on the river Styx without learning something. My congratulations to you and The Trafford, Mrs. Jim. Is Miss Parkman at home?"

"She is in the house unless she has already started for Shorehaven, Ben. Shall we try to find her?" Anne Trafford's voice was uneven. Anticipating his consent she led the way along the garden path.

The two left behind might have been modishly appareled garden statues they stood so still. Swaying shrubs dappled them with shadows. The peacock stared down with bead-like eyes as he cautiously furled his tail-feathers. As the house door closed Trafford turned to the girl. Julie's heart winged to her throat. She put up her hand to still its throbbing. "Keep our affairs under firm and cool control," she parroted to herself. The man's voice was rough as he apologized:

"I'm sorry that it had to come — this way, Julie." His sincerity quieted the wild beating of the girl's heart. Her protest was eager:

"Don't be sorry, *don't!* I am glad to have the

truth out. I have been living a lie and all the while I have felt as though I were dishonoring Dad and his profession. The sword of Damocles was a tin toy to what I have sensed hanging over my head these last two weeks. Even if Cheever does not remember — but do you believe that he doesn't?"

"I don't know what to believe, Julie. If I had not announced the marriage and he had made no reference to it, I should have thought that he was running true to form and attempting to lull us into security by pretending ignorance. However, he has nothing to gain by that bluff now."

"Will he refrain from mud-slinging?"

Trafford laughed. "As he can find no mud to sling he may have been sincere in that statement. I should have more faith in his change of heart had — oh, well, what is the use speculating? You and I will have to walk straight on now with our heads high. There will be the usual nine days' riot of speculation and gossip before state politics, which are hectic this year, will submerge us."

"Thank heaven for that. We will go straight on. If you can do it I can, for you must hate the situation as much as I," Julie sympathized with unflattering honesty. "Where do we go from here?" He smiled at her apt adaptation of a current phrase.

"To Shorehaven. We will make a dramatic announcement of our marriage. Then you will come back to Brick House with me."

"*Alone!*"

Trafford's spontaneous laugh showed his white, even teeth.

"Of course we could bring Mother and Pam with us, but —"

Julie's color heightened. Her eyes flashed with indignation.

"Don't laugh. Do you realize what a mix-up we are in?" She put her hand suddenly to her throat to detain a sob which was tearing it way up. Trafford's face was white as he caught her wrist.

"Julie!"

She twisted herself free. "Don't! What shall we say? How shall we explain? Who will tell them — Aunt Martha? I suppose that Julie'll —"

"Julie *won't,* this time. I will," Trafford cut in quietly. "From now on you are to drop the burden of this situation to my shoulders. I'll carry it. Here is Mother. Cry it out in her arms, Goldilocks, while I get ready to take you to Shorehaven." He started for the house as Anne Trafford entered the garden. The woman's eyes were warm with tenderness as she caught the girl's hands.

"I hope that you are not angry, Julie, but it

seemed the only thing to do. Jim heard to-day that Cheever was up and out again. He wanted a chance to talk with you so I sent for you to come to the garden. When Ben appeared so unexpectedly Jim cut the Gordian knot."

"And you knew all the time?"

"When we reached home after dinner at Shorehaven the night of your arrival there, Jim told me of the cabin episode and its results. I told him then, and I still think the same, that you should have acknowledged your marriage at once."

"Don't blame him. It was my fault. I welshed. I thought that if only he and I knew we could slip out of the contract more easily. The whole miserable business came from my impulsive lie to Cheever. It was a blunder, I suppose, but even now I don't see how I could have done differently. Don't hate me!"

"Hate you! Honey-girl, I love you for trying to help my boy. Whenever I have had qualms over the situation I have visualized your face and back has swept my confidence that the matter would straighten out. You will never know until you have a son of your own, Julie, a mother's anxiety that her boy may find the right girl. A wife can so effectually make or mar a man."

The girl's voice was hoarse with protest.

"But this isn't a real marriage. It — it is an emergency measure."

"I understand, child. I don't know what started me to moralizing; it's a pernicious habit of mine. It was an outrageous situation for you to be forced into a ceremony with a man you had seen but a few hours."

"There are occasions when a few hours are as good as a lifetime in which to become friends, and that was one of them. I liked your son the moment I looked up and saw him on the hill. By the time we had finished supper I should not have been afraid to follow him anywhere. He is more like Billy than any man I have met. They are both cool and unsentimentally friendly."

"So-o, you prefer men of the wood and stone variety. I wonder — There is a tinge of caveman in the make-up of the Traffords, and I had thought that Jim — however, you never can tell." She checked a young, delicious ripple of laughter. Her eyes shone with repressed mirth as she went on, "Have you and Jim decided upon the next move, honey-girl?" She slipped her arm about Julie's waist and moved toward the house.

"He thinks that I should come here."

Anne Trafford's voice was brisk with practicality.

"Of course. This afternoon's dénouement

136

has been heaven-sent-for me. I disliked to leave Jim alone. Now that he will have you for company I shall luxuriate in my vacation. Sarah Beddle — the divine Sarah Jim calls her — is the eighth wonder of the world when it comes to efficiency, but she gets on my nerves after a while. She is one of those from-the-cradle-to-the-grave monologists when once she gets started. We'll go up and plan your rooms while Jim is dressing, then I will break the news to Sarah. She has the second maid Charity trained to perfection so there will be nothing for you to do."

Nothing to do! The words echoed through Julie's mind as she followed Anne Trafford into the house. Was it only two weeks ago that she had proclaimed her intention of thinking only of herself? And now she had her chance. Nothing to do! It was the last maddening crooked nail driven into the wobbly matrimonial structure she and Trafford had erected.

Chapter X

The tall clock at Brick House boomed eleven. Julie released her chin from her cupped hands and looked about her. A lamp in a distant corner radiated a soft glow; the only other light in the living-room came from the red coals of the fire. Six hours before she and Billy had been chatting under the portrait, now she was back again to stay — for a time.

She sprang to her feet and moved restlessly about, the crystals on her violet dinner frock flashing into infinitesimal rainbows at every step. Her position at the present moment was grotesquely absurd, but no more absurd than that initial situation at the cabin. Julie sneakingly wondered if perhaps there were such a thing as a conjunction of planets which set extraordinary events in motion.

With a sigh of futility she curled up on a corner of the couch and stared back at the fluffy yellow cat who sat on its haunches regarding her with inscrutable topaz eyes. She had been in that same spot in the afternoon. Was she watching before the pictured remains of the Duchess as the statue of a cat had watched before the tomb of King Tutankhamen for three thousand years, the girl wondered fancifully.

Her thoughts flashed back to the evening just passed at Shorehaven. While she in her room had written to her parents a true account of her marriage, Trafford had announced it down-stairs. He had first had a private interview with Mrs. Marshall when he had told her the facts under an oath of secrecy. To the others he had made the explanation upon which he and Julie had agreed. Julie had begged her father and mother to coöperate in keeping the true inwardness of the affair quiet until after election.

When she had made her lagging appearance in the great hall she had been amazed at her aunt's triumphant tenderness; she had expected icy disapproval. Billy had been noncommittal, Carfax gloomily aggrieved, Pamela Parkman's eyes had burned with anger, fury had seethed beneath the surface conventionality of her congratulations. Major Buell had been unaffectedly radiant. Did he think that her son's marriage would give him Anne Trafford, the girl wondered.

It had been a horrible evening, a nightmarish evening, Julie thought, as she gazed into the fire. Awkward silences had been charged with electric questions which no one had had the courage to snap on. She had been honestly relieved when the time had come for her to drive back to Brick House with Jim Trafford. They were co-victims of a misadventure for which she alone was responsible; she could not blink that fact, even if he was too chivalrous to admit it, — and it would be a relief to talk things over with him.

Mrs. Marshall and her guests had waved them good luck from the veranda, but in spite of Billy's old shoe and a shower of rice the departure had taken on more the air of a funeral than a honeymoon. As they had started down the drive in Jim's roadster with the black spaniel on the seat between them, Julie had looked up at him with a laugh in her eyes but he had been intent on the wheel. They had driven in silence through cool, fragrant air under a star-stippled sky. When they had arrived at Brick House Carlotta, the maid, was taking her fluttering departure after having unpacked the trunks which Mrs. Marshall had sent over from Shorehaven. Trafford had left Julie in the hall and had driven to the village to post her letter to her parents.

Thank heaven that the suspense was over, the girl thought. She would play her part her sporting best until election. The day after she would start for home and free Jim to untangle the situation.

Would she? Her life had suddenly surged out of its worn channel to tumble and leap through new country, to change in color and speed, to confuse, to excite, to stimulate. It had swept her along in breathless expectancy but always she felt the standards and inhibitions which had been bred into her clutching at the skirts of her conscience. Emergency measure that it was, would she ever feel honest again if she broke that marriage contract?

"Silly, of course you would," she encouraged herself. "If it comes to a question of your conscience or your freedom, remember your all-for-self program. Besides, Jim Trafford's life can't be governed by your upbringing."

She glanced at the clock. Had it stopped? No. Could it be but five minutes since it had struck the hour? Jim had asked her to wait down-stairs until his return. He had been so unlike himself driving over that she dreaded his coming. What should she say to break the ice of the awkward situation?

How quiet the house was! She looked up at the portrait. The cynical eyes of the Duchess had watched many generations come and go. Did the departed spirits keep vigil over their old haunts? With her dreamy eyes on the pic-

141

tured face, her ringless hands clasped behind her head, the girl repeated Longfellow's lines softly:

" 'All houses wherein men have lived and
        died
Are haunted houses. Through the open
        doors
The harmless phantoms on their errands
        glide,
With feet that make no sound upon the
        floors.' "

The musing rhythm of the words lured the yellow cat. Fluffy tail rampant she brushed back and forth against Julie's skirts, then with a soft sound sprang into her lap and snuggled. A friendly hand stroked her silky fur as the velvety voice went on:

" 'We meet them at the doorway, on the
        stairs,
Along the passages they come and go,
Impalpable impressions on the air,
A sense of something moving to and fro.'

" 'A sense of something moving to and fro,' " the girl repeated in a whisper as though afraid of disturbing the harmless phantoms of the old house as they glided about on their

ghostly errands. The line sounded delight-
fully busy, she thought wistfully. Her mind
flashed back to Anne Trafford's, "There will
be nothing to do." Could any condition be
more boring? Since her eighteenth year her
days had been packed with duties. She had
helped her father in the parish and because of
the impossibility of securing a resident physi-
cian in so small a town, she had been requisi-
tioned in many capacities. She had assisted at
births and deaths, she had done housework
and churchwork, she had read and studied.
Her two weeks at Shorehaven had resembled
nothing so much as a lazy dream. She was
glad that the lotus-eating epoch was over. She
would find something to do.

Footsteps in the hall, a rush through the
room shattered her revery. There was a series
of explosive "Ststs! Ststs! Ststs!" from the
yellow cat as she leaped from Julie's lap at the
impact of the black spaniel. He sat back on his
haunches grinning like a dervish as he contemplated the bunch of bristling yellow fur
with lashing tail which bared spiked teeth at
him from the top of a chair back. Julie caught
the reprobate in her arms and shook him.

"Sweetie-peach, you're a nuisance. I'll hold
him while you put her out," she suggested as
Trafford entered. He seized the spitting cat.
When he returned from dropping the claw-

ing, tawny bunch outside the front door she released the dog. The spaniel with a deep sigh of relief as of a difficult undertaking satisfactorily accomplished flopped to the hearth-rug and closed his eyes. Julie crossed her arms on the back of the wing-chair and smiled at the man who was standing under the portrait.

"I have been burning up gray matter trying to think of something casual and informal to say upon your return, quite as though I had been living here for the last thousand years, when in dashes Sweetie-peach and solves the problem for me. You and I must have been born under Sirius, the dog-star. Tell me everything! What did they say when you told them?" she demanded eagerly. In the firelight her eyes were a deep hyacinth; the red glow from the coals threw a rose light on her rounded throat and bare arms. "As I descended the grand staircase at Shorehaven and looked down upon Aunt Martha and her guests looking up at me my mind blew out like a tire. I couldn't think. I hope that I said the right thing?"

Trafford's eyes smiled encouragement.

"You did. I was too intent upon getting my story across to get the full effect of their reactions. Your aunt is jubilant —"

"*What?*"

"Your aunt is jubilant," he repeated as

144

though the girl had not heard him. "She confessed to me that she had used Carfax as a blind. Knowing your combative nature — don't flare, that is her term, not mine — she made you think that the stars declared him your affinity when in reality I am."

Julie flushed furiously as she met his laughing eyes. She opened her lips impetuously to start a sentence which she abandoned and tried another.

"I — I — just can't talk about it. It — it must be because she admires your nose. It — is — rather nice," she teased, her head critically tilted. "What did Billy say?"

"Nothing."

"He didn't speak to me when I left. Perhaps it was just as well. I don't like to be cross-examined by him unless I am prepared to tell the truth. The whole truth and nothing but the truth, so help me God! What did Pamela —" she hesitated as Trafford turned abruptly to the fire and poked it. She nodded her golden head understandingly at his back and went on, "I won't ask any more questions. Where ignorance is bliss, etc., etc. That episode is behind us. Don't you like the firelight?" she asked in surprise as Trafford pulled the chain of a floor lamp and flooded the room with light.

"So much that I am afraid of it. Sit down

while I talk to you. When you stand I feel as though you were preparing to depart."

Julie's eyes laughed as she sank into the capacious chair.

"No such luck for you. I am to be a fixture here until after election."

"Do you mind?"

"Not if my being here will help. Having started to assist the best man to win the senatorship I shall carry on. It certainly complicates matters for you with Pamela, and I am sorry. I had a creepy premonition this morning that something would happen and when you held out your hand to me in the garden I knew what was coming. It took an hundred pounds' weight from my conscience when I realized that your mother knew. Why did you tell her?"

"Because she is my best friend and my wisest."

"Did she say that you had ruined your life?"

"On the contrary her apprehension was for you. She was quite sure that you would find Carfax irresistible after you had been at Shorehaven a few days."

"He is, in a way. There is something tremendously lovable about Dal."

Trafford thrust his hands into the pockets of his dinner jacket and met her eyes steadily as he cautioned:

"Watch out for shell-holes, Goldilocks. Carfax is in love with you. I knew it when I saw him bending over your hand in the garden."

"Silly! I know that he is not. You have mistaken his technique for the real thing. Any girl, even if she does not know what love-making is, knows when a man is in love with her," Julie refuted paradoxically.

"Does she? Then you must know that I love you."

The words were so quietly, so smilingly spoken that the girl doubted her ears. Through the silence in the room the old clock seemed to tick a monotonous repetition, "Love you! Love you!" Julie sprang to her feet and barricaded herself with the wing-chair before she protested incredulously:

"No, oh no, *no!*"

Trafford's face was white but the girl took courage from the spark of a smile in the gray eyes which met and held hers as he countered:

"Yes, oh yes, *yes*. Don't look so stricken, Julie. I want you to know the truth, that is all. I'll not take the chance of a stupid misunderstanding between us. I sat near you on the train the day you rushed to the rescue of the spaniel. You attracted me more than any girl I had ever seen. By the time we had finished supper I was in love with you. I have loved you more and more each day since."

"But you didn't want to marry me. I — I almost forced you into seeing the thing through."

"Of course I didn't want to marry you — that way."

"Then why — why did you do it?"

"Because loving you as I did it seemed the best way out of a treacherous situation. I took the chance that some day you would love me."

"You took some chance. I sha'n't love you — ever," the girl denied furiously. The color flooded to her hair. Eyes and voice were frankly horrified as she demanded: "You don't think for an instant that that empty ceremony will give you the right to kiss me, do you?"

Trafford's eyes shone with laughter; the smile which widened his generous mouth showed his white, even teeth, but there was a husky strain in the voice in which he answered:

"No, not at present."

"Not *ever*. You know that I hate sentiment."

"Then I am playing in luck, Goldilocks. I may be sure that you won't care for anyone else. Now I want to talk with you about my campaign. Pamela to-night declared her intention of electioneering for Cheever —"

"Not really!"

"Yes. Perhaps you remember that I told you that he wanted to marry her and that Mother and I opposed his suit. Pam has been tractable but now — of course she can marry him, and have her property tied up until she is thirty, but she won't do it unless she is certain that he will go on politically."

"Why don't you tell her what you know about him?"

"What I suspect, you mean. By the way, Julie, you and Captain Phin are the only persons who know that, so please keep my secret. Election comes the second Monday in September. If I win I shall represent two important mill towns. Can't you help me strengthen my campaign in the next two weeks?"

His voice was businesslike, matter-of-fact. Julie wondered dazedly if his protest of love had been but an imagination-storm induced in her mind by an overdose of excitement. Her voice was buoyant with relief as she answered eagerly:

"I will do anything I can, Jim. Your bride —" She crimsoned to the ears. Her tone was frankly, boyishly horrified as she apologized:

"I'm sorry! I forgot. Oh, say that it isn't

true. I can't believe it. I — I *won't*."

"Stick your head in the sand, Julie, if you please, but you can't alter the fact that I love you."

In spite of the cool friendliness of his tone the girl felt again that curious sense of being drawn irresistibly into smothering depths. The contrition in her eyes flashed to defiance.

"Why, why did you have to spoil the fun we might have had together with your old love-making?"

There was a slight unsteadiness about the long firm fingers which drew the pipe from Trafford's pocket and slipped it back again.

"Love-making! You don't call what I have said love-making, do you? You are an unsophisticated young person. I could give you a demonstration —" the laughter in his voice quieted the pounding of the girl's heart. After all, she assured herself, he was the most wonderful friend she ever had had, with the exception of Billy. She could trust him. She matched his light tone as she replied from the doorway:

"Your demonstration would be thrown away on me. Reserve it for your *friend* Pamela. She would appreciate it; there is nothing unsophisticated about her. Good-night!"

"What possessed you to drag in the Park-man girl?" Julie demanded of her reflection as she sank to the chair before the old-fashioned mirror in her bedroom, propped her chin in her two hands and frowned at the troubled violet eyes frowning back at her. "As ex-president of the Ladies' Aid you should have met the situation with more dignity. But when he told me that — that — he roused my horrid old demon of opposition. I realized that I was in the clutch of a steel-hand-in-the-velvet glove sort of person. Oh, if I just hadn't dashed after Sweetie-peach."

Urged by her turbulent thoughts she walked about the rooms in which Mrs. Trafford had installed her. The furniture was rosewood. The four-poster bed would have wrung agonized tears of envy from the eyes of a col-lector. The passage between bedroom and boudoir was paneled with wardrobes. The mahogany and brass in the sitting-room was rare and beautiful. A secretary with innumer-able pigeonholes invited correspondence; the bookcase was filled with rare editions. The one modern note in the room was the violet negligee which Carlotta, with a nice sense of artistic values, had thrown across an end of the wide couch. A smile lightened the shad-ows in the girl's eyes as she caught it up and pressed her cheek against it.

"How I adore frillies! You lovely —" the word trailed into a whisper. She stood motionless. Could that be Jim Trafford's footstep on the stairs? Her breath stopped as there came a soft knock.

"Julie, I want to speak to you."

With the negligee crumpled under one arm she flung open the door. Trafford's eyes as they met hers were the clear, direct eyes of the man who had teased her in the cabin. His voice had a smile in it as he commanded:

"Hold out your left hand. We came near wrecking our emergency measure by forgetting this." He slipped the narrow wedding ring she had so hastily discarded on her finger. "Good-night!" Without even a pressure of her hand he turned away. Julie listened at the partially opened door as he ran down the stairs singing softly:

" 'You remind me of my mother,
My mother was a lot like you,
So many little things you do
I find —' "

The girl closed the door and shut out the song. She seated herself before the mirror. Elbow on the dressing-table she moved her left hand back and forth and watched the flash of the diamonds in the narrow circlet. The eyes of her vis-à-vis widened in a laugh as she confided:

"My first ring. Captain Phin was right. 'Ye never can tell at sunup what you'll bump into before sundown.' "

Chapter XI

Julie stood in the shaft of sunlight which streamed in at the window recessed in the deep walls of the old kitchen at Brick House. She pictured the broad beams above her hung with corn and dried meats, the huge fireplace piled with once split logs, the spit at the back of the wrought-iron fire-dogs sizzling and dripping with cooking meats. Beside the fireplace a Rumford oven with its brass-handled door was set deep into the brick wall. On the other side of the hearth were copper boilers each with its own fire-box beneath. In a cupboard generations of brass and copper kettles glowed richly.

"What a wonderful kitchen! Do you ever use it?" the girl asked Sarah Beddle who was doing the honors of the old room. Marcella, the yellow coon-cat, brushed against the woman's skirts; a gray kitten caught playfully at her ground-gripper heels.

The housekeeper was in character with her background, Julie thought, just what she had imagined a New England spinster of the black-walnut age would be. She was tall and angular. The zebra effect of her gray streaked dark hair was complemented by her print gown of black and white stripe. Her third-degree eyes were in keeping with her thin lips. She had a tinge of that I-am-as-good-as-you manner which some flaunt as a badge of American citizenship. She punctuated her sentences with a sniff as she answered the girl's question.

"Use it? Certain, certain. We use it at Thanksgiving and Christmas. It makes the work hard but we Traffords ain't ones to let old customs die out because they mean work. Some day I'll show you the china. There's never been a piece broken nor a nick put in my time." Her sniff was redolent of suggestion as to what dire devastation had been wrought before.

"I should love to see it. I am off to the old mill now. I like to read my letters there." Julie slipped the note in her hand into the pocket of her white frock which already contained an envelope. It held her mother's answer to the announcement of her marriage. She was eager yet dreaded to open it.

"You've been in this house just a week and it seems to me you've spent most of your time on the brook or Glass Pond," Sarah Beddle commented disapprovingly. Julie slipped a friendly hand within the triangle formed by the woman's angular elbow as she agreed:

"I have, but I'll tell you a secret. Mr. Jaffrey has been teaching me to shoot the rapids. The boat went through like an eel yesterday and the day before with me at the wheel. I was to try it again to-day but the note that came was from him. He had to correct proofs and couldn't come."

Sarah jerked her arm free and regarded the girl with stern displeasure.

"Does Mr. Jim know you're doing that? — You shouldn't be doing nothing so reckless. You're a Trafford now and responsible for the next generation. You ain't got the right to take chances of leaving him a widderer."

Indignant color flew to the girl's temples. Anne Trafford had warned her that Sarah would take an undue interest in her activities. Martha Marshall would have sighed in sympathy with the housekeeper had she heard the tone in which Julie answered:

"I shall take any chance I like. In fact, I think I will shoot the rapids again to-day without Mr. Jaffrey. The tide will be right at twelve-thirty. If I am late for luncheon don't wait for me."

She ran into the garden with the housekeeper's voice shrilling after her:

"You know The Trafford has to have his lunch prompt! Don't shoot them —"

Space deleted the woman's warning, laughter diluted the anger in Julie's eyes and cooled the flush in her cheeks. She had not the slightest intention of shooting the rapids alone; she had threatened it as a defiance to Sarah, she thought, as she sped down the garden walk. The color along the enclosing brick wall had changed, she noticed. The pinks and blues of the week before were being supplanted rapidly by the crimson and gold of autumn flowers. Scarlet gladioli, red cockscomb, clumps of nasturtiums running the gamut of shades from claret to lemon, nuggets of golden-glow, the orange heads of calendulas, the yellow and bronze blossoms of marigolds nodded and swayed. The fragrant breeze which came straight from a thousand pines was snappy with a premonition of September. On the top of the wall the peacock had his jeweled tail spread to its gorgeous limit. He semaphored raucously as the girl passed between the open wooden doors, the iron trimmings of which had been wrought by some long-ago blacksmith on the Trafford estate.

Outside the wall Julie stopped and whistled. As the black spaniel raced from the direction of the garage she entered a wide path. Checkered with green sunlight, patterned with fantastic dancing shadows it led through the woods to Glass Pond. It was the bridle path along which the Trafford who had built Brick House had ridden to the mill; it was the path along which the present owner rode. Would it be used for generations to come, the girl wondered.

The word generations swept fancy from her mind and presented fact. Sarah Beddle had suggested family responsibilities. How little she suspected the truth of the emergency marriage. Julie visualized the housekeeper's expression of frozen incredulity when she knew. It would not be many days before Jim Trafford would be free to scramble out of the bramble-bush into which that miserable Cheever had flung him. That cabin experience ought to remain an enduring warning for Julie Lorraine to look before she leaped. It ought. Would it?

"You can't change a leopard's spots. I never think of consequences when I see a thing to be done, Sweetie-peach," she confided to the spaniel who had run back with a stick in his mouth. "But I am not regretting, at least not the cabin part," she assured him as she flung the stick. She waited till he proudly capered back with his trophy before she added, "But had I known what I was to bump into before sundown, I shouldn't have

158

jumped from the train to page you, no I shouldn't," she repeated to the dog who had laid his stick at her feet and was imploring an encore with snapping black eyes.

The path swerved when it came to a gate but Julie climbed the bars under the lowest of which the spaniel squeezed his plump self. She swung down into a fern-strewn, rock-blotched pasture. The sheep who were grazing daintily on its slope gave it a near Corot effect. They raised their heads at sound of her whistle, gazed at her curiously for a second before they kicked up their heels and scampered. One dingy drab animal stood its ground like a graven image. As the dog barked at it shrilly it moved toward the girl with a purposeful glint in its granite eyes. Julie's whistle trickled into silence. Her heart did a series of cartwheels as she smashed her own speed record toward the bars at the upper end of the field. She tumbled over them to safety.

The spaniel raced up to inquire in his best canine manner why his mistress was sitting on the ground leaning against silly bars when a woodsy trail, teeming with thrilling possibilities, stretched invitingly before her. She answered his eyes and his agitated tail.

"That sheep had a wicked eye, Sweetie-peach. Shall I ever be a well-balanced sport, I wonder? I've been shooting the rapids with

Billy without a qualm yet cows and sheep on the loose give me the merry-pranks. You saw what a spectacle I made of myself. Yes, I'm coming!" She responded to the dog's tug at her skirt, sprang to her feet and resumed her whistle.

Impatient as she was to know the contents of her mother's letter Julie waited until she reached the old mill before she drew it from her pocket. Even then she did not open it. Seated on the moss-covered ground under a tall pine, elbow on her knee, chin in hand, she gazed dreamily at the pond. It looked placid but when the tide turned in the bay outside there was a swift undercurrent. Something like her life at present, the girl thought. The low stone building near her was at the mouth of a stream which emptied into Glass Pond. It was connected with the opposite shore by a stout bridge. The great water-wheel which had revolved tirelessly in other days stood majestically silent. The wisps of gray moss which hung from it suggested haunting wraiths of bygone years. Dark shadows darted through the deep pool under it. Moored to a float on the shore was the slim launch, *Easy Money*, in which she and Billy had shot the rapids.

The smile which the remembrance of the exhilarating experience brought to Julie's lips dimmed as she thought of Sarah Beddle's horrified, "Does Mr. Jim know you're doing it?" He did not. She could not have explained to herself why she had carefully refrained from mentioning her latest accomplishment to him. Even now she edged away from the thought. But why should she feel guilty? Carfax had taken Pamela Parkman over the falls.

She would not have gone had she apprehended danger. Her sporting spirit was confined to her language and her habits. Billy had announced that his pupil was entitled to a diploma. It was a simple enough stunt. It was a matter of tide and a firm grip on the wheel. In spite of Julie's reasoning the irritation of mind occasioned by Sarah Beddle's objection persisted.

The housekeeper might be an angel as Mrs. Trafford asserted but she was a domineering angel. She ran the house with the beautiful precision of clockwork. The Trafford might fling sand into the machinery by being late to meals, by leaving a trail of burnt matches and pipe ashes, by bringing salesmen home to lunch unexpectedly and the fond Sarah smiled upon him adoringly, but let anyone else transgress and her temperature dropped out of sight.

Julie's lips widened in an irrepressible smile as she thought of the woman. In spite of her thorns and prickles she loved her. She loved everything about her life at Brick House, even to the mill whistle which seemed to regulate her day. Once unobserved she had watched the hands pour from the mill to take their noon meal out of doors. They looked to be a clean-hearted, self-respecting lot of men and women. She didn't wonder that Jim Trafford had gone white when he thought of their belief in him being shattered. And it might have been had she not consented to that marriage —

She gazed unwinkingly at the shore which lay warm and softly shining under the noon-day sun and thought of her first evening at Brick House. For a few days after it she had lost her breath for an instant whenever she faced Trafford at table or accompanied him to Shorehaven in the roadster. That reference of his mother's to the cave-man propensities of his ancestors had assumed heroic propor-tions in her imagination. She had held herself rigidly aloof but as day followed day and he continued to be the same sympathetically un-derstanding companion he had been the first time she met him, her apprehensions had dwindled to the anaemic substance of a hazy dream. She was almost as happy and friendly with him now as she was with Billy; were it not for the lurking shadow of that emer-gency marriage, she could dispense with that qualifying "almost."

Julie shook off her abstraction and opened her letter. A robin who had been bathing near shore with one bead-like eye fixed on the motionless figure against the tree-trunk abruptly cut short his morning ablution as the white sheets fluttered in her hand. He shook his wet plumage and flew to the top of a mammoth pine where he preened in the sunshine. The black spaniel who had been dozing, nose comfortably snuggled between silky paws, raised his head suddenly, sniffed experimentally and with a stealthy look at the absorbed girl beside him sneaked off on a private hunting expedition.

Julie was unconscious of his departure as she read the opening lines of her mother's letter.

"My DARLING GIRL:

"Why not devise a cabalistic sign to be used on the envelope of a letter, a sign which will denote *explosives!* I should then be prepared when I opened it to have my composure blown to smithereens. (Perhaps you know what a smithereen is. I don't, but you will agree with me that it suggests infinitesimal fragments.) If the suggestion sounds flippant, forgive it, Julie dear; it serves merely as a sort of inky cocktail to warm and stimulate my pen to express in some slight degree all that your father and I feel about your marriage. Our first impulse was to board the next train to you, then we thought it over and said, 'No, Julie will be better off without us.'

"I waited for your father before I opened the letter. When I began to read it did not occur to either of us to wonder that you had gone back to a description of your journey to Clearwater. We laughed at your pursuit of the runaway spaniel and your Dad chuckled, 'Wasn't that like Julie?' I could feel him stiffen as I read on to where you defied the man Cheever with the announcement that you were married. 'Dear God!' he groaned. 'Oh, dear God! My littlest girl!'

"I kept on as steadily as I could. Whether you had withheld it for dramatic effect, or whether it just happened, up to that you had not mentioned the name of the man who had adventured with you. Then it came. Your father dropped into the arms of his Morris with an abandon which shocked a groan of repletion from the rugged chair.

"For you see, dear, your father and I know of The Trafford and your aunt's hopes and plans. She has talked James Trafford, written James Trafford since he settled in Clearwater and took on the responsibilities of the mill. We have wondered how she could know so much of his ideas and his ideals. Probably she gleaned them from his mother for whom she seems to have a profound admiration. Martha was obsessed to bring you and Jim Trafford together. Discounting her nonsense about planets and horoscopes your father and I began to covet him for a son. Your sisters' husbands are hard-working, well-intentioned, successful men, but their conversation is as inelastic as a map. It is bounded on the north by business, on the south by stocks and bonds, on the east by golf and on the west by musical comedy and the bootleggers' price list. You are our youngest, the light of our eyes, dear, and for you we coveted a broader outlook. For you we wanted a man who was a champion for, but not a slave to, the great god Business; one who loved and believed in his country to the extent of sacrificing his own comfort to uphold its laws; a man who would inspire you to your best, who would keep alive in your heart and soul the appreciation of life's spiritual values.

"Has Martha told you that it was not coincidence that you and James Trafford were on the same train? She knew the date on which he was to return from a conference in Boston and planned that you should go to her the same day."

Julie's eyes blazed as she looked up from the letter. How maddening that events should have played into her aunt's hands. She would be more cocksure than ever that she was a divinely appointed deputy. She wouldn't be so cocksure the day after election, the girl gloated as she returned to the letter.

"Martha wrote that she knew the reason you gave for your delayed arrival was a smoke-screen, but that she had sufficient faith in you and James Trafford, plus the planets, to ask no questions. So you see, her apparent belief in your story was but pretense. In your letter I felt a tinge of contempt for her credulity. Don't discount your aunt's intelligence, dear. She may seem a bit mad on the subject of astrology but in other ways she is to be regarded with admiration slightly tinged with awe.

"Your father and I will faithfully keep the secret of that cabin adventure. To each of your sisters I have written the news of your marriage. Fortunately for the meagreness of my explanation those quarantinable first-cousins, measles and chickenpox are rampant among your nephews and nieces. The girls have their hands too full to give much thought to you. I have asked your brothers in-law as a favor to me, to bombard you with neither questions nor presents."

"Presents! Ye gods! I hadn't thought of that! Whatever would I do if anyone gave us anything?" Julie distractedly demanded of a squirrel who was regarding her curiously from under a scrub-oak. As the chipmunk chattered an unintelligible answer she returned to her letter.

"Why not put all thought of the annulment of your marriage out of your mind till after election, dearest? Live each day as it comes and trust to God and The Trafford to bring you safely out of the maze. You wrote that Jim was the dragon-slayer of your favorite fairy-tale come to life. Trust him to slay your dragons.

"Dear, if I have seemed to answer your letter lightly it is only because I feared to say too much. My heart goes out to you. My first waking thought in the morning, my last at night is this prayer:

" 'Dear God, keep my little girl fine and true and happy. Help her to stand for the best that she may steady weaker souls than hers. Let her count in the life of the nation.' It is the petition your father and I would offer had we been blessed with a son, that he might count in the life of the country his ancestors toiled and died to save. Help the last of the Traffords to make good, Julie.

"Devotedly,
"MOTHER."

Julie struggled with a lump in her throat and blinked furiously to clear her eyes of tears before she read the few words her father had added.

"Your mother has said it all better than I could, Julie. God bless and keep you, my littlest girl. May He help you remember that, swept into this marriage on a wave of impulse as you were, you must meet its obligations with a steady sea of determination. Stand stanchly back of Trafford in his fight for clean politics, work with him, for him. Don't be too severe in your condemnation of Cheever. Remember, that there must be at least a spark of the divine in everyone. If I could hold you in my arms a minute, dear — but I can't, so I'll start on my parish calls and try to bring heart-healing to some other father's daughter.

"Dad."

With a sob Julie pressed her lips to the letter. What dears they were. How they understood. She had known that they would. How characteristic of her father to make that plea for Cheever, but — What was that? It sounded like a cautious step on the dried pine-needles. It was a step! She crushed the letter into her pocket, sprang to her feet and turned. Against a tree her hands thrust into the pockets of her poppy-red sweater leaned Pamela Parkman. Julie's welcoming smile faded as the girl remarked with studied insolence:

"Married only a month and kissing a letter, Mrs. Trafford? Of course it is from a man. Hadn't he as much money as Jim?"

Chapter XII

The imputation effectually dried the tears which the letter had brought to Julie's lashes. She carefully brushed a pine-needle from the shoulder of her white frock before she met the hostile eyes pillorizing her and inquired in a faintly surprised voice:

"Were you speaking to me, Pamela?"

"I was and that isn't all I have to say. It is only fair to warn you that I intend to find out what black art you employed when you persuaded Jim Trafford to marry you."

The words loosed a yelping pack of memories in Julie's mind. Cheever's contemptuous comment, which had faded somewhat in the last two weeks, flashed back with cinema-like clearness:

"The girl has turned a clever trick, Jim. There are advantages in being the richest man in the county —" Had he insinuated that she had tricked Jim Trafford into marrying her? Was that what Pamela meant? Even her lips were white as she defied coolly:

170

"Why not ask him what magic I used?"

"I will. You can't deceive me with your lie about having met during the war. Why did you wait before you announced your marriage? There is something back of it, some absurd quixotism of Jim Trafford's. I mean to find out what it is at the same time that I help elect Ben Cheever."

"Will it help him for you to be disloyal to your guardian and her son?"

"That maddening guardianship is one more reason why I should like to hurt them both. I was eighteen, quite old enough to manage my own business, when my father, who admired Anne Trafford and her archaic ideas and ideals, died and left her the right to mix into my affairs. I don't belong to her era. I've waded out of the sluggish pool of restraint for good. I love Jim Trafford. If I can't have him I —"

Julie interrupted the passionate fury of the words imploringly:

"Oh, please — please — *don't!*"

"My advanced views would undoubtedly make a minister's daughter *pretend* to squirm, but after the way you noosed Jim Trafford you can't put that stuff across on me. You have always been poor, haven't you? No wonder you jumped at the first rich man who came your way. Have you thought how much more a wife with money could help him? I hope that you are not counting on your aunt's? Perhaps you don't know that her fortune goes back to her husband's people when she gets through with it?"

The quality of her tone as she went on showed her appreciation of the color which stole to Julie's hair:

"I know that Jim's absurd New England conscience plunged him into this mess. He belonged to me by right. I wouldn't marry a man who was practically engaged to another girl."

"Have you been asked to?" then as her question reduced Pamela to dumb fury, Julie added crisply:

"As a minister's daughter I have been brought up to consider a brawling woman about the lowest form of animal life, Pamela. At the present moment you come dangerously near being indexed in that class." Her eyes traveled from the poppy-red hat to the immaculate white shoes and back to the smoldering dark eyes before she added:

"I suggest that you investigate the record of your candidate before you devote much time to his campaign."

Pamela laughed.

"Piffle! Do you think that if Jim Trafford knew anything against Cheever he wouldn't use it? No one can make me believe him as quixotic as that even if he did marry —" her eyes wandering derisively over Julie to give point to the interrupted sentence rested on the corner of the envelope in her pocket. Her lids narrowed triumphantly.

"I wonder — I wonder if Jim had seen you kissing a man's letter if he wouldn't feel justified in demanding his freedom? I wonder —"

"Why waste precious time wondering? Why not ask him?" defied Julie flippantly.

"I will. I'll meet him as he comes from the mill. Thanks awfully for the suggestion."

With a triumphant laugh she turned away. With hands outstretched as though to clutch her Julie took a step forward. Then her arms dropped to her sides. It would be the height of folly to permit Pamela to think that she feared her insinuations. She watched the flashes of color as the red hat and sweater appeared and disappeared among the trees.

When it gleamed and vanished for the last time Julie looked up at the sky. What had happened to dim the glory of the day? Had the sun clouded? No, it still shone brazenly. The fault wasn't in the atmosphere, it was in herself. She felt as though leaden weights had been attached to her spirit. Of course it couldn't be the effect of what Pamela had implied about Jim and herself; hadn't Billy and Martha Marshall both suggested that there was an understanding between the mill-magnate and his mother's ward? And hadn't Jim Trafford that night in the cabin admitted that he was in love? Like a wet sponge across a slate swept the memory of her first evening at Brick House. It magically erased the man's first confession and left only his steady, "I love you," staring at her like the caption on a screen.

"Shall I never forget that?" Julie demanded of herself furiously. Would she never be free from that sense of intolerable burden?

"I know how poor old Hercules felt when Atlas dropped the Earth on to his shoulders. And it is all your fault, Sweetie-peach," she admonished the spaniel as he raced up to her with his erstwhile silky coat bristling with twigs and his nose brown with moist earth. Julie dropped to her knees and held him by his floppy ears while she vigorously removed the dirt with her handkerchief. The attack relieved her overcharged feelings to a degree. She released him and sprang to her feet as the whistle of the mill rent the hot air.

"Unless I intend to defy the divine Sarah and arrive late for luncheon, we had better start for home." The spaniel barked peremptorily. "What do you want now?"

The dog looked down at the stick at the girl's feet, poked it with his paw, shook his long ears over it, ran a few steps toward the water and looked back wagging his tail excitedly. He voiced an imperative yelp. Julie laughed and picked up the partially chewed portion of a branch.

"You are a spoiled child if ever there was one, Sweetie-peach. I'll throw this once more, just once. Go get it!"

She flung the stick into the pond as she had flung it dozens of times before. The spaniel waded for a few steps and then swam for the floating wood which had drifted in the current. He caught it in his mouth, went on for a few seconds and turned. Before he could get back to quieter water he had been carried a few inches down-stream.

Concern dashed the laughter from the girl's face. She ran to the water's edge and clapped her hands.

"Come! Come!" she called sharply. She could see the little black creature struggle to obey but the current was too much for him. It seemed to Julie that his dark eyes implored her across the water that separated them. A dry sob lodged immovably in her throat as she ran to the float to which the launch was tied. She unfastened the painter, jumped in, and pushed off the boat. She hastily adjusted grease-cups, tank-cock and needle-valve. She shifted the big oars which always seemed to her such useless cargo. She threw in the switch, rocked the wheel and started in pursuit.

"Julie's coming!" she called to the dog whose black head bobbed in the current. Her heart stopped as it disappeared for a moment. It rose again. The launch seemed to crawl. Far ahead she could see the low bridge and the white patches beneath it where the current boiled over rocks on its swift rush to the bay. If the dog went over those — but he wouldn't — she would reach him before that — she was almost alongside him now.

"I'm coming!" she called again. As though the girl's voice had inspired him with fresh courage the spaniel made a desperate effort to head toward shore.

"You're making it! You're making it!" Julie encouraged exultantly. "Keep trying! I'm coming!"

She steered as near the struggling dog as she dared. As the boat bore down on him she leaned far over and caught him. For an instant she lost her balance, then pulled herself up with the dripping little creature in her arms. She hugged him convulsively before she dropped him to the bottom of the boat and caught the wheel. She heard his panting breath as she looked about to get her bearings. She was only a half mile above the falls.

It would be a hard pull against the current to go back. Had she gas enough to make it? She dared not leave the wheel to investigate. She had much better keep on and go over the falls. The tide was right for the adventure and Billy had assured her that she was manoeuvre-perfect.

She rehearsed mentally his instructions.

"You can't do anything well until you know why you do it, Marble-heart," he had begun in his best pedagogic style the day he had introduced her to the motor-launch. "This pond is eight feet above the level of the bay. The average tide here is eleven feet. In consequence the rising tide starts filling the pond an hour before flood. The outflow starts an hour after flood and increases in volume as the fall from pond to bay becomes greater. Then boulders and ledges poke their heads through a rushing film of water. That is the psychical moment to shoot the rapids. Just below the bridge a ledge lies squarely across the channel. The outflow rushes over this to a lower level of granite covered by a foot or two of water. Below this, directly in mid-stream, is the Boiler, a granite boulder that breaks water after the hour limit and parts the flood into two narrow rock-strewn channels. One is impassable, the other skirts the Trafford shore. Do you get it, Marble-heart?"

Julie's mind had been a jumble of levels, tides, boulders and rapids, but she had tried to appear intelligent as she answered:

"Intermittently. I shall understand better when I have been through it. It sounds complicated."

"It isn't. It is as simple as navigating a frogpond — when you know how. You don't take even a gambler's chance if you keep your head."

"Remember that it is as simple as navigating a frog-pond," Julie reminded herself as she gripped the wheel. She knew that Billy had not intended her to attempt the stunt alone, but she had been practically forced into it. When it was over and she told him about it he would approve heartily.

"Barring your aversion to the dark and the lowing kine, you are one good little sport, Marble-heart."

She wouldn't be too toppy about it but it would be fun to mention casually to Jim and the others:

"I shot the rapids quite by my lonesome today." The thought of Trafford brought back the smart and sting of the unpleasant encounter with Pamela by the old mill. Had she broken Jim's slate and Pam's by her impulsiveness? She forced the thought from her mind. The adventure upon which she had embarked required her undivided attention. She appraised the glistening wet rim on the shore. The time to make the drop from pond to bay on the ebb-tide was right to the minute.

Splendidly unafraid Julie whistled softly as she kept her eyes straight ahead. A languid breeze stirred the soft hair at her temples. The late August sun blazed down on her uncovered head. Its heat grilled woodsy fragrance from the timber along the shore. Its light gilded the tide-pools in the marshes till the floating grass took on the semblance of writhing golden eels. Rocks poked sinister heads above water as though to breathe after their noon immersion. A sand-bar was alive with peep who looked as though their tiny bodies were mounted on tinier stilts. The sky was mottled with clouds. On the banks sumach waved like rivuleting fire. Pines nodded their stately tips in condescending encouragement. A cicada shrilled in the bushes. A gull screamed at the slim launch below him. The spaniel slept peacefully.

As *Easy Money* neared the falls a roadster swept to the bridge above and stopped. Julie's eyes flashed up for an instant. Had the driver slowed down to watch her? If he had he had a grandstand seat. He would get the full effect of her spectacular drop, she thought with a thrill of nervous excitement.

179

She forced her mind back to her wheel. She must watch her step, not think of an audience. She stole a look at the engine. Every cylinder hitting! She was through the first whirlpool! There were eight more before she reached the bridge. Billy had counted them. Her triumphant eyes challenged the rapids to do their worst.

With a loud snap her bubble of satisfaction burst. What had happened? She did not dare take her eyes from the boiling water ahead to look at the engine. She listened. Nothing wrong there. It was running perfectly, it was not missing a beat.

She flung the wheel over. The boat did not respond. The rudder-rope had broken!

The launch spun like the propeller of an airplane. It banged against a rock and catapulted into the next cauldron. For an instant Julie's heart stopped, then raced on pluckily.

" 'You don't take even a gambler's chance if you keep your head,' " she reminded herself as she seized the frayed ends of the rudder-rope and attempted to tie them together. They were jerked violently from her hands. She caught up the boat-hook and ineffectually tried to keep the launch clear of the rocks. The tool might have been a wooden toothpick. It snapped at the first impact.

The girl's lips whitened as she watched the

pieces swirl away in the current. The spaniel disturbed by the crash of the launch against a boulder sprang to the seat and began to bark. Julie dropped down beside him and caught him in one arm. With the other hand she clutched the gunwale. Her wide, strained eyes were on the foaming water ahead, but her voice was valiant as she encouraged:

"Don't be frightened, Sweetie-peach! 'Shooting the rapids is as simple as navigating a frog-pond — when you know how.' "

Chapter XIII

The creases between Jim Trafford's eyes were deep as he rode home from the mill. The bridle hung loose on the horse's neck. It was his custom when at the office to wait until the whistle blew and go out for lunch when his employees went. His grandfather and great-grandfather had followed the same program. It gave an opportunity to exchange friendly greetings with the workers. But today their descendant had found it impossible to remain indoors after Ben Cheever's call. It was the first time his political opponent had visited the mill since his accident and save for an ugly red scar on his cheek the representative to the legislature had seemed as sound as before that epoch-making night in the cabin.

He had been friendly. He had smoked and discussed the division of a consignment of wool that they two had ordered months before. He had been too darned friendly, Trafford thought with a darkening of his eyes as he stared ahead at the shady path filigreed with golden sunshine. His business statements and propositions had been of the fairest. He had not mentioned the campaign. He had referred once with a sigh to the two weeks he had lost out of his life, the weeks that he could not remember. Couldn't he? Had he forgotten or was he keeping up a superb bit of bluff? With his hand on the office door Cheever had turned back with a smiling apology:

"I sure acted like a goof the day I was presented to your wife, Jim. My only excuse is that I was still dazed from my accident. Before that time — I didn't admit it because I wanted her myself — I could have sworn that you and Pamela — Don't scowl. I won't say any more except that I'm obliged to you for leaving the field clear for me."

The lines between Trafford's eyes deepened. Cheever must know that until his appearance at the gate of Brick House there had been no announcement of the marriage. Pamela would inform him as to that fact. Was he playing possum? If he were it behooved him to get all the fun out of it he could now, for after election — Did Julie think that that insult to her would go unpunished? Trafford's hand clenched on the reins. A savage thrill twisted into a muttered:

"Good Lord, I'll choke him to his knees.

He —" Fury strangled the words in his throat. His face was white, the muscles of his jaw rigid as his thoughts doubled back to the interview in his office. Cheever had been almost convincingly sincere. Had he forgotten or was he making a virtue of necessity? He must realize that a word against Julie would cost him his election. He must know that the girl with her beauty, her sweetness and tact, which she had doubtless acquired from the demands of her life at home, had the village at her feet. If there was speculation about the sudden marriage — and of course the town must seethe with it or it wouldn't be a small town — no hint of it had seeped through to him. He leaned forward to stroke the satin of his horse's head. The remembrance of Julie's ultimatum at the cabin relaxed the tension of his jaws.

"While I am at Shorehaven I shall think only of myself."

Her initial venture on the all-for-self program had been her dash to succor the dog. Next she had made that mad declaration to help a man whom she had known but a few hours. She had been at Brick House but a day before she had hunted up his mother's old ladies to coddle them in true Anne Trafford fashion. She seemed blithely, unconcernedly happy. She pretended to have forgotten his avowal on the night of her arrival at Brick House but her involuntary start when he spoke to her betrayed her. Well, he could bide his time as long as he had her within arm's reach. He touched his heels lightly to the satin flanks under them. As he turned into the drive at Brick House he hummed:

" 'I find they bring to mind my mother,
I never thought there'd be another
Would have that sweet appeal
Or could make me feel
That the old fool world was real —' "

He broke off his song and pulled in his horse as he saw Pamela Parkman in her roadster evidently waiting. Her red hat and sweater drew the light as the sun draws water. Her dark eyes were triumphant, mocking, as they met his. Her tilted head was a challenge. He dismounted and threw the bridle over the horse's neck. The intelligent creature, after an inquiring look at his master, trotted off to the stable and his dinner. Trafford stuffed his soft hat into his pocket and held out his hand.

"Good-morning, Pam. Have you come to lunch with us? Julie will be delighted."

"Will she? Then she will have to hurry some to express her delight. I left her by the old mill kissing and weeping over a letter."

185

Trafford overtook and strangled the exclamation on its way to his lips. His eyes and voice were warm with concern as he substituted:

"Weeping! Poor little girl, I wonder what has happened. I will ride back and meet her. I may be able to help."

Pamela abandoned her air of smiling confidence. Her dark eyes contracted unbecomingly as she advised:

"Better not butt in, Jim. It was a man's letter."

Trafford's face whitened but his eyes smiled. "Was it? Then I won't go back. I won't be needed. Julie has a score or more boy confidants who pour their troubles into her sympathetic ears. If you are sure you won't stop for luncheon I will go in. You know that I am a slave to the divine Sarah's rules and regulations. We are dining at Shorehaven to-night so I'll see you later."

"I had not said that I was not staying for luncheon but as it is evident you don't want me, I'll go."

For an instant the angry eyes of the girl met Trafford's. Her roadster leaped forward as she jammed in the gears.

"You'll wreck your machine if you do that again," he cautioned unwisely but she drove on without answering.

186

Trafford looked after her. He had been unpardonably raw to dismiss Pam like that but she had infuriated him with her insinuations about Julie. Was she jealous? She had no right to be. Since she had been flung into the life at Brick House he had treated her with frank friendliness. Never had he been in the least attracted to her. In fact had it not been for complicating the already complicated situation for his mother, he would have avoided the girl.

Had Pamela seen Julie kiss a letter or was she trying to make trouble? For the last week she had been enthusiastically championing Cheever. He had been a frequent guest at Shorehaven. There was no apparent reason why he should not be. Few persons knew that Anne Trafford opposed his attentions to her ward; only she and Mrs. Marshall knew of the dastardly part he had played at the cabin. Managing Martha had been sworn to secrecy so why shouldn't she welcome so important a man as the state senator? Trafford's thoughts flashed to Julie. Had she kissed — of course not — it was too unlike her. Had she not confided frankly:

"Men and boys bore me stiff when they wax sentimental."

His lips widened in a laugh as he visualized the girl as she had made the crisp statement.

The remembrance of her aversion to sentiment had helped steady him when he was with her. She was his. She must love him. She would love him if he didn't lose his head and antagonize her, he warned himself for the hundredth time. As he entered the house he assured himself once more that he had not believed that infernal yarn of Pam's, not for an instant. At his study door Sarah Beddle charged upon him.

"Jim, did you see Julie?"

The informality of her address proclaimed her perturbation. Since he had become head of the house she had prefaced the boyhood "Jim."

"No. Why?"

The housekeeper's hands gave an excellent imitation of a wringer in operation.

"Because I hoped you'd see her and stop her."

"Stop her! Where has she gone?"

"Now don't get excited. Perhaps she said it only to tease me. She had a letter from that writer-man Jaffrey this morning. I guess 'twa'n't much of a letter. Just said that he couldn't take her shooting the rapids."

"Shooting the rapids!"

"Yes. That Mr. Jaffrey's been teaching her. She said she'd go alone. I tried to stop her but she ran out laughing and called back over her shoulder:

" 'The tide will be right at twelve-thirty! If I am late for luncheon don't wait.' " Sarah snapped her lips together and stared. The last of the Traffords had bolted for the garage.

Pamela had been right, Jim Trafford assured himself doggedly as he started the roadster and shot into the drive. She had seen Julie by the old mill, for the boat she would use to shoot the rapids was moored there. It didn't necessarily follow that the rest of Pam's yarn was true; the hectic bit about the letter might be an invention of her inflamed imagination. She was furiously angry because he and his mother opposed her friendship with Cheever. Had it been Jaffrey's letter which Julie had been reading? It might be. She had frankly confessed that she cared more for Billy than for any man beside her father. Caring wasn't loving. But she had spent hours of late with her old pal. There was magic in vacation air. Had constant outdoor companionship changed the quality of her regard for her friend from affection to love? He couldn't believe it. He wouldn't.

The roadster swung into the highway. Had Julie intended to shoot the rapids or had she threatened it to tease the housekeeper? Sarah could be maddening. Whether the girl had been in earnest or not he wouldn't take the chance of not being on the bridge when *Easy Money* shot under. Of course she could make the drop safely. It wasn't much of a stunt. It needed a level head and a steady hand, that was all. Why the dickens was he in such a fever about it? There was hardly a breath of air stirring, nothing to mix signals for her. Good Lord, but it was hot!

He wiped the slight beads of moisture from his forehead which were not occasioned by the sun overhead. Below the road a smooth sapphire sea thinned to lace-edged daintiness as it frilled the shore. Trafford dragged his eyes from the road long enough to appraise the wet kelp.

"The tide is on the ebb. She's right as to time," he approved and stepped on the accelerator. Gulls screamed raucously as they wheeled above him. Never before had he realized the distance from Brick House to the bridge. Shrubs and trees on the upper side of the road flashed by him like a panorama. On the water side the sea and foam were a blur of color. It was fortunate that the highway was deserted, he congratulated himself grimly. Jaffrey had no right to take Julie over the falls without consulting him. The autocratic spirit of the First Trafford rampaged through the mind of his descendant. If once he got her back to Brick House he would keep a watchful eye on further adventuring with the pal of her Dutch-cut days. Was she in love with him? The roadster slid on to the bridge. The thought was the motive power behind the hand which ground on the brake. As the car groaned to a sudden stop, Trafford looked up the pond.

A boat was coming smoothly down. It was his boat. He caught the glint of Julie's hair. She was safe! His tense muscles relaxed with a suddenness which left him limp. With his hand on the door of the car he leaned forward in his seat to watch her. The sun beat out the high lights in her hair. She stood erect, boyishly slender, her capable hands firmly on the wheel, her eyes straight ahead. Was she whistling? He thought the breeze brought a few soft notes which he heard above the roar of the water below. She had looked up as the car stopped. Had she recognized him? It had been but an instant before her eyes were back on the swift current. Thank the Lord she had made the first whirlpool. Only eight more. Good God, what had happened?

Trafford's face was livid as he sprang from the car and rushed to the rail of the bridge. The boat spun. It banged against a rock and catapulted into the next cauldron. Julie had abandoned the wheel! What was she doing in the boat? She had the boat-hook! Didn't she know it wouldn't hold? It had gone! She had picked up the spaniel. Good Lord, she wasn't planning to jump, was she? He made a megaphone of his hands and leaned far over the rail.

"Take the oar!"

He had thrown his voice against the wind. Could she hear? Would she understand? Yes! Without looking up she had seized the unwieldy thing. God! The boat almost turned turtle that time!

She was through the sixth pool. Five to go before the falls. The falls!

With his eyes on the valiant figure in the boat which seemed like a toy in the raging water he tore at the straps of his leather leggins. Why wouldn't the darned things unfasten! "Steady, Jim, steady!" he admonished himself and attacked them carefully.

Four to go! The last pool had given the boat a vicious twist. It had wrenched the oar from the girl's hand, had whirled it about and shot it downstream. Thank the Lord, his puttees were off! Eyes on the tossing boat he flung his shoes aside. He pulled off his coat and swung over the rail of the bridge. He clung by one hand and shouted:

"Head straight for me!"

Had she heard? The rush of water was deafening. Yes! She waved her hand. She seized the remaining oar. Trafford's eyes burned. His throat contracted. Two to go and then the falls. Could she keep the boat steady?

Chapter XIV

As *Easy Money* spun in the second whirlpool Julie instinctively closed her eyes. She could do nothing now but grip the spaniel and the side of the boat and pray that it might keep right side up as it went over the falls. If it did she would be quite safe, if it didn't — she shivered. It couldn't be her time to die. Die! She fought back the thought. One didn't pull through crises by folding one's hands in resignation, she reminded herself; one fought till one's last breath. Was that a shout? For the first time she remembered the roadster on the bridge.

"Take the oar!"

In an instant she had dropped the spaniel to the seat and obeyed the shouted command. Her spirits rose like a balloon which has cast off excess ballast. Her imagination had almost flung her overboard instead.

Against the breeze came another call. The bulky oar was wrenched from her hand, whirled about and shot down-stream. Her eyes flashed to the rail of the bridge. A man hung there. Jim Trafford! Julie laughed. She was safe. Nothing could harm her now. What was he shouting? She leaned forward.

"Head straight for me!"

The girl waved her hand. She seized the remaining oar. Hope steeled her arms as she attempted to keep *Easy Money* head on. Jim intended to drop into the boat. A sick faintness swept her at the possibility of his missing. She rallied sharply. It was up to her to make sure that he couldn't miss. As the launch shot out of the last whirlpool the man dropped from the rail. He landed in the middle of the boat. He grabbed the oar with a sharp command:

"Sit down! Hold tight!"

Julie swept the dog from the seat and held him between her knees as in a vise. She gripped the gunwale with both hands and shut her eyes. She had the sensation of hurtling down a bottomless pit. The boat smashed into a rock, careened crazily, shivered into steadiness and shot into smooth water. A hand, warm and compelling, loosened her clenched fingers. A voice sounded as from a long distance:

"Open your eyes, Goldilocks. You are quite safe."

Julie looked up into Trafford's livid face,

into his flaming eyes. She controlled her quivering lips with an effort as she smiled:

"The dragon-slayer to the rescue." Then as he continued to regard her with glowing intentness she asked unsteadily: "How did you know that I was shooting the rapids? The rope broke or I should have made it." Her defense was a last shuddering defiance of the disturbing eyes which held hers. He straightened.

"Sarah told me. The Inferno can hold no terrors for me now. I passed through hell before I reached you." He cleared his voice before he called to a boy near shore:

"Hi, Pete! Pete Sparks! I'll land on the rocks. Take this launch up pond on the flood to-morrow, will you?"

At his call a man beside the boy who had been watching the boat in a trance of fright turned and scuttled up over the rocks with crab-like gait. The spaniel rumbled and shook with a throaty growl as he spied the white bulldog at his heels.

Willy Small again! Had Jim seen him, Julie wondered. Apparently not, for his eyes were on the freckle-faced boy whom he had hailed; a boy whose skinny legs, bare, burned and prodigally nicked, dangled over the edge of an immense boulder as he fished for flounders. He had nodded a dumb acquiescence to Trafford's request. His eyes, of the sculpin type, threatened to pop from his head, his mouth to remain permanently open. He closed it with a fish-like gasp before he answered:

"Gee, but you had me knocked for a gool! Cracky, but you took a chance! I thought the old tub was gonna turn turtle. Whatcha let your wheel go for? An' with a girl aboard too! Sure, I'll take it back. I'll come get it now."

Julie felt herself labeled and pigeonholed by that scornful "Girl." The color burned in her cheeks as steadied by Trafford's grip on her arm she slipped and slid on the rocks which he climbed easily in his stockinged feet. In silence he helped her to the bridge, in ominous silence he pulled on his shoes, tossed his puttees into the car and slipped into his coat. The flash of his eyes as they met hers reminded the girl of heat-lightning; it indicated a storm brewing. She whistled for the spaniel who was barking at the boy. Her tone was elaborately casual as she announced:

"As I am late for luncheon I'll walk to the village and get —"

"Oh, no, you won't. You are coming with me. Were you to meet your pal, Billy, there is no knowing what crazy stunt you and he might pull off."

Julie's eyes blazed indignation but they might have been limpid pools of concession for all the impression they made on the man who faced them. He settled the collar of his coat with painstaking care, then before she realized his intention, he had picked her up, deposited her in the roadster and had dropped the dog at her feet. She was still struggling for adequate expression when he backed the car from the bridge and turned toward home.

He drove slowly. Was he preparing to indict her, Julie wondered. She hoped not, for she had a hundred things to say to him, and a hundred thoughts which were too deep for expression. She wanted to tell him what it had meant to her when she had seen him hanging from the bridge, her sense of security for herself, her terror for him. An appreciation of his help had been on her lips but his autocratic command had aroused the horrid little demon of opposition which was forever stalking her common sense. He and Managing Martha had much the same effect upon her. They must be cousins under the skin. The thought curved her lips. Trafford saw the smile. His face had not yet retrieved its normal color.

"I envy you your sense of humor. As yet I can see nothing funny in your last escapade," he commented gruffly. Julie was penitent. If she had been terrified at her own plight back there in the rapids what must a looker-on have felt?

"Neither can I, Jim. I wasn't laughing, really. It was my nerves unknotting. Nerves do curious things when they straighten out. They began to untangle when I looked up and saw you on the bridge. The sight poured the elixir of courage through my veins. I knew that nothing could happen to me."

"I wish that I could have been as sure!" The color rushed back to his face. "Why did you try to shoot the rapids alone?"

Eagerly, breathlessly Julie told him of the dog's plight and her rush to his rescue.

"But you told Sarah that you intended to try it."

"I said it merely to tease her. She is such an autocrat. I was half-way to the bridge when I pulled Sweetie-peach out of the water. It meant a long hard pull for *Easy Money* to go back, I wasn't sure of the gas, and I had shot the rapids almost every day with Billy. The last three times we went over I had the wheel. We had planned to try it again to-day but Billy sent word —"

"Did he telephone?"

"No, wires have ears, and we don't let Aunt Martha know all that we do. One of the Shorehaven chauffeurs brought a note —"

"A note!"

"Yes. One might think from your tone that I had said an automatic. I should have come through the rapids without the least trouble had the rudder-rope held. That break wouldn't happen once in a thousand years. I may shoot them twenty times more and —"

"You may — but you won't."

Julie's fate flooded with indignant color. She buckled on her armor of defiance. She was passionately grateful to him for his help but he must be made to understand that her gratitude did not carry with it a right-of-way across her independence. She asserted herself in a voice of amused patronage:

"From your tone one might think that you had a right to dictate to me."

"Haven't I?"

"No. I don't like to appear ungrateful after what you have just done but we had better come to an understanding. You are as domineering as Managing Martha; you are fast getting to be a — a *Sheik*."

Trafford threw back his head and laughed. His eyes were alight with dancing sparks as they met hers, fiery with indignation; his rich voice held a caressing note.

"A sheik! No such luck. If I were one you would at the present moment be smothered in my burnous — isn't that the name of those white flowing things the sheiks wear in the movies? — thrown across the saddle-bow of my trusty Arab-steed while we flashed across the desert."

His mounting spirits were more disturbing than his anger had been. The picture his words presented had a tingling realism which set Julie's pulses pounding.

"Go on, state your other objections to me. You have an aversion to the Arab streak, what else?"

His light tone fired the girl with a desire to hurt him.

"I think that a man who was engaged to a girl should be willing to acknowledge it — at least."

"If you are referring to me I can assure you that I have never been engaged. If Jaffrey or Carfax told you that I had they are liars."

"Jim!"

"If you don't care for the word we'll modify it. I'll call them psychopathic liars. That relieves them of all responsibility."

"They were not the only ones. If the story is true you can easily get engaged again after election."

"Julie, look at me!"

Involuntarily the girl's eyes met his. He laughed.

"I thought for an instant that you believed that statement, that you had forgotten what I told you the evening you came to Brick House, but I see that you haven't. By the way, your mother suggests that I bring you home to her after election."

"Mother! Suggested *that!* When?"

"When she answered my letter."

"Your letter?"

"Did you think that I would rob your parents of their littlest girl without giving them my side of the story, Julie?"

"That accounts for it."

"Accounts for what?"

"Something in the letter I read from Mother, this morning."

"Were you reading it out by the old mill?"

"Yes, why?" the surprise in her tone was submerged in indignation. "Did Pamela tell you that — that —"

"She did. Was it your mother's letter?"

"You can find that out from your informer."

"No. I shall wait for you to tell me."

His tone was as crisp as hers. She looked at him from under long lashes as the silence between them persisted. He was bending slightly forward, intent eyes on a shambling figure ahead. She recognized the hitching gait. She had not told Trafford that she had seen Small at Blue Heron Cove. Events had moved so quickly up to the announcement of the marriage that she had forgotten it. After that what harm could Willy do?

"Do you see that man ahead, Julie?"

The girl nodded.

"That is Small, the bleak-eyed witness Cheever relied upon to corroborate his story of finding us in the cabin. I had hoped that this time he had disappeared forever."

"Has he the disappearing habit?"

"Yes. In his youth he was the town's bad boy. If anyone wanted a shady transaction put through they would give Willy fishing tackle or money and he was their man. Then he'd go away for a while. He isn't vicious. He's just too darned lazy to work and if a man won't labor for a living he's rather sure to lie or do something worse for it. I wonder why he came back — just now?"

The lids narrowed over his gray eyes. Ought she to tell him that she had seen Small at the Cove? She opened her lips —

"If Willy Small tries to speak to you, don't answer him; do you understand, Julie?"

"Ye-es, but —"

"In this case there is to be no 'but.' You must do as I say."

He stopped the roadster at the door of Brick House. Julie disdained his extended hand and sprang from the car. Autocrat! The fact that he had listened to Pamela's tale still rankled unbearably. He talked with persons who had a slight regard for the truth and *believed* them; why shouldn't she have the same privilege? She wouldn't tell him now that she had seen Willy at the Cove. He could find that out for himself.

Trafford followed her into the hall like a relentless destiny. She ignored him as she smiled radiantly at Sarah Beddle and explained gaily:

"It took me rather longer than I thought it would to shoot the rapids. I am sorry to have kept luncheon waiting. Please do not scold us."

The housekeeper sniffed.

"So you did that fool thing, did you? I guess The Trafford can have his meals any time he likes without no one's thinking it necessary to apologize for him. Charity'll serve lunch as soon as you've both washed up," she announced and disappeared in the direction of the kitchen.

Julie started up the stairs. In the peaceful atmosphere of the old house her resentment, her latent fear of the owner misted into vapor. She stopped and looked back over her shoulder.

"I will be down as soon as I 'wash up.' By that time Sarah will be hovering over you and will have forgotten that I was the unworthy cause of the delay. Teacher's pet!" She made an adorable gamin face at him.

Trafford seized her by the shoulders. His eyes met and held hers. His voice was gruff:

"Julie, my self-control is mighty near the snapping-point. If ever you wrinkle your nose at me like that again — I shall kiss you, so watch your step!"

Chapter XV

"As you come through the village, if it ain't too much trouble, I wish you'd get some chloroform, M's. Jim. M's. Trafford told me before she left that if I didn't put the old cat, she's this one's mother, to sleep before she came back she'd have Phin Snow do it. I wouldn't trust that old woman-hater to drown even a female rat. I've fed and loved that animal for ten years and it seems as though 'twould break my heart to put her out of the way."

Julie slipped the proffered money into the pocket of her violet sweater. She smiled sympathetically at the angular woman who blocked the doorway of her room with tawny Marcella rubbing against her knees.

"I will do it for you, Sarah. I'm an expert. Dad's parishioners have turned to me for everything from making out mail-orders for their clothes to dispatching their age-battered pets." She stooped to stroke the yellow coon-cat who purred against her gown.

"I never see Marcella so took with anyone as she is with you, M's. Jim. If it wasn't for that black pest of a — my land! Here he comes now! Marcella! Marcella! Come here!" she implored as with a yelp of anticipation the spaniel dashed into the room. For an instant he stopped to regard grinningly his hereditary enemy who was arched like a recumbent interrogation point, and whose red jaws and topaz eyes snarled defiance. Julie crushed a soft hat over her fair hair.

"I'll take him out at once, Sarah. I haven't forgotten the havoc those two wrought the last time they had a tooth-to-tooth combat in these rooms. Sweetie-peach, you're a torment! Come along! Quick!"

She ran down the winding stairs but the spaniel escaped her and doubled back. The housekeeper swept him out of the room and slammed the door.

"There, you cantankerous critter," she sighed in relief as they reached the lower hall. "Just wait a minute, M's. Jim, till I get the bottle for the chloroform. No use paying that drug-clerk ten cents extra. Seems as though I was forgetting everything since Phin Snow told me this morning that it looked as though Ben Cheever might get elected."

"How can he —" but the housekeeper had disappeared. "How can he be elected, how can he?" Julie demanded of space resentfully. "A man like that —"

"A man like what?" her argumentative self demanded. Except for his dastardly behavior at the cabin — and his world did not know of that — what reason had she to think that Ben Cheever would not be a useful man in the legislature? He had been a model of courtesy and consideration since his accident. Jim Trafford evidently knew something to his discredit and as evidently was determined not to use the knowledge as a weapon in his campaign. Julie frowned down upon the dog who was gazing up at her expectantly.

"Suppose that I were to find out what it was? Would I use it, Sweetie-peach?" The spaniel shook back his long ears, barked imperiously, stood up on his hind legs, settled back on his haunches, tilted his head and whined ingratiatingly. Laughter sunned the shadow from the girl's eyes.

"You are a fascinator but you are not going with me. You have been a bad boy, do you understand?" She spoke to the housekeeper as she appeared with the bottle. "Please shut the dog into the garage after I drive out, Sarah. Don't expect me too soon. It is a glorious afternoon and I may do a little exploring. Don't let Sweetie-peach follow me, will you? He must be disciplined."

Julie made her purchases and drove slowly from the village. She had thought it unnecessary to tell Sarah that her objective point was the field above Blue Heron Cove. Since Billy had told her of the villagers' superstitious avoidance of the cliff and the copper-mine she had wondered if the bleak-eyed man whose head had popped above ground like a prairie-dog's might not be responsible for that c-curious, l-luminous mist Billy had described? He had been sent to prepare the cabin for Cheever; might he not be working for him at the mine? Jim distrusted Willy Small. Did he suspect that he was his opponent's tool?

It seemed unbelievable that in these twentieth century days a man of Cheever's importance would dare indulge in such clap-trap melodrama as spectral mists. Whatever Jim suspected he had given no hint of it in the campaign which had been waged with renewed but friendly vigor since Cheever's recovery. Julie had had no opportunity to ask Trafford how the fight was going. She had avoided him during the week which had elapsed since he had dropped from the bridge to her rescue.

Through Sarah and the boy Pete, undoubtedly, the news of her narrow escape had spread. Her aunt had been angry, Mrs. Trafford tenderly disapproving, Pamela Parkman contemptuous, Carfax amused. They had all ignored the fact that she had started out to rescue, not to do a dare-devil stunt. Billy had scolded her roundly.

"A nice position you have put me in, Marble-heart. I can see Jim grind his teeth when he looks at me and I don't wonder. Oh, I understand that you went to the rescue of that confounded dog, but he would have fought his way to shore. If you belonged to me and had tried that stunt alone I'd keep you on bread and water for a week. Trafford was jumpy enough before but now when I speak to you he looks as though he were holding a stopwatch on us."

Billy was right, Julie meditated. Although Jim appeared never to look at her she felt as though she were under observation whenever he and she were in the same room, which situation occurred as seldom as possible. She was expending most of her gray matter these days devising routes and methods to dodge him. Thank heaven, there was but one more whole day before election. After that he and she could begin to untangle the mesh in which Fate, ably abetted by the black spaniel and Cheever, had caught them.

"Stick your head in the sand, Julie, if you please, but you can't alter the fact that I love you."

The words shot to the surface of the girl's mind. She whistled a difficult aria to shut out the memory. It began to look as though the only way out of the mix-up would be to ingloriously cut short the golden vacation in which she was to think only of herself and go home. Home! *Impasse!* That road was blocked. Her mother had invited Trafford to come with her.

Her eyes strayed to the sea which scintillated like a many faceted emerald shot with blue. A purple haze veiled the horizon. Toward the west a few cloud-puffs had taken on a tint of rose. She loved the place. She didn't want to go home, she would feel shut in. She loved Brick House and — who was in the low red roadster speeding toward her?

It was Cheever. She straightened in her seat. Could she pass without being hailed by him? He had been at Shorehaven whenever she had been there this last week and had been insufferably attentive. He had reminded Julie of a big blue-bottle fly who persisted in buzzing about the person whom it annoyed the most.

When his car approached her sedan he shut off his engine, evidently preparatory to a heart-to-heart talk, the girl thought with a twitch of her vivid lips. She slowed down. He swept off his hat with his conqueror's air. His eyes — ooch, how she hated his eyes when he smiled —

"Good-afternoon, Mrs. Trafford. Out for an airing?"

Always he made Julie conscious of a note of amusement in his "Mrs. Trafford." The little veins at her temples throbbed with resentment as she answered:

"No, Mr. Senator, I am out for a vote. Good-afternoon."

She bent to the gears and the sedan shot ahead. She listened for the sound of Cheever's engine; apparently he had not started it. Was he watching her out of sight? Did he suspect that she hoped to locate Willy Small? Why should he? He might think that she was after Willy's vote for Jim. Wasn't she, in a way?

The breeze which blew from the water was salty and invigorating. Julie filled her lungs with it. The air was heady with vitality, rich with that "Open sesame!" quality which made one sure that one had but to knock imperatively at any obstinately closed door to swing it open.

Just ahead the road divided. The right fork forsook the primrose path of highway to zigzag into the green plateau which crowned the cliff above Blue Heron Cove. There it dwindled into a footpath. Julie turned the sedan into the field and shut off the engine. Now that she had embarked on the adventure her nerve-centres tingled a warning. She left the car slowly. The field in front of her stretched smoothly to the fringe of berry-bushes, she remembered. Beyond them the sea flashed on and on illimitably. The fragrant darkness of pines and spruces, lightened in spots by flaming maples and yellowing birches, stretched for miles behind her.

As she started across the field she smiled defiance at the NO TRESPASSING and DANGER signs she passed. The world seemed uncannily still. Only the monotonous lash of the sea against the cliff broke the silence. She looked up startled as far above her a hawk swooped and sailed and shrilled its strident battle-cry.

Julie walked slowly with her eyes on the turf. There must be something to indicate that opening in the sod, she assured herself. She would go to the fringe of berry-bushes, locate the spot from which she had seen Willy Small's head emerge, then work forward. Eyes downbent she advanced. A warning growl followed by a whine of pain drew her eyes to the left.

"Thank heaven I didn't bring Sweetie-peach," she thought as she saw a white bulldog biting furiously at his back. At her low exclamation of sympathy he turned with a menacing snarl. In spite of it the girl took a

213

quick step toward him. His small eyes set in pink rims were anguished, pleading, his nose and neck resembled nothing so much as a white cushion stuck full of pins. With an imploring whine the dog crawled to her feet and looked up beseechingly.

The tortured eyes twisted Julie's breath into a sob. She dropped to her knees. She didn't attempt to touch him but her voice seemed to comfort the sufferer.

"Poor dear! Will you let Julie look at your nose? You've had a fight with a porcupine, haven't you? Where is your master? Is anyone here?" she called.

The bushes stirred. A head rose above them. The girl looked up at the grotesque face upon which wind, sun and self-indulgence had lavishly dabbed their colors.

"Come here, Willy Small. Is this your dog?" she inquired, as the man hitched nearer with crab-like gait. His bleak eyes were blurred, his voice cracked with emotion as he answered:

"He is, ma'am. Hooch an' me have traveled together fer years. He never got stuck with one of them d— one of them hedgehogs before. This time a black an' white pointer comes an' barks an' Hooch here rubs noses with him an' the two run off together like kids as is up to some innercent mischief. When my dog come

214

back he was like this. Ye can't tell me that pointer hadn't framed up the hunt an' come fer Hooch ter help him."

He knelt beside the girl. The dog dragged himself closer and looked up imploringly. He whined continuously.

"You don't know nothin' to ease him, do you, ma'am? When he first come back he raced round and round tryin' to git at his neck. I thought he'd gone mad. Then I tried to pull out some of them spines. I must have hurt him terrible." He laid his dirty hand with its broken discolored nails tenderly on the white back. Julie swallowed hard.

"Poor old Hooch! I wish that I could help him. One of my dogs got into a mess like this and I had to chloro— wait a minute — wait a minute!" she interrupted herself breathlessly. "Lift his head from my lap, Willy Small. I had better not touch him. Keep him quiet till I come back. Nice Hooch! Be patient till Julie comes! She'll make you all comfy," she crooned tenderly before she sprang to her feet and started across the field.

She pulled gloves and a bunch of waste from the pocket of the sedan, rummaged in the tool box for the slenderest pliers, seized the phial of chloroform and a newspaper and raced back to the bushes. Hooch turned agonized, bloodshot eyes upon her.

215

"I'll try — to give — him some — chloro-form," she panted.

"Ye ain't plannin' to dope him an' put him out of his misery, are ye, ma'am, because I —"

"No, no, I am trying to help him. I'll be honest, Willy. One never can tell just what effect the stuff will have upon a dog, but it is his only chance. If we can make him inhale enough to paralyze his muscles I can pull out those spines. Shall I try?"

"Sure, ma'am. Go to it."

Julie pulled off her sweater and turned back her sleeves. Deftly she rolled the newspaper into a cone and stuffed it with waste. She drew on her gloves. She talked softly to the dog as she made her preparations. He whined a heart-wringing accompaniment. The girl was quite unconscious of the two big tears which ran down her cheeks as she directed:

"As soon as I pour the stuff on this waste roll Hooch over, Willy, and grip him so that he can't move. He'll struggle, so hold tight. Now! Quick!"

With amazing dexterity the man followed instructions. With teeth set hard in her lip Julie applied the cone. Tears followed tears down her face as the dog protested with dumb anguish. Then it seemed but an instant before he relaxed and lay terrifyingly still. Julie swiftly applied the clumsy pliers. She was subconsciously aware of Small's hard breathing; once a big drop splashed from his chin to her glove. After she had cleared nose and neck she had the man force open the dog's mouth while she extracted six big spines from the pink roof of it. As she drew out the last spiked, thorned quill she dropped the pliers and sank back on her heels.

"They're out! Do stop those bushes. They're whirl—" The world went black. Willy Small's distracted voice pursued her into the darkness.

"Fer God's sake don't faint, ma'am! Ben Cheever might come back. He'd think I tried to frighten yer, an' I ain't never frightened a woman, whatever else I done. I ain't never frightened no woman!"

Julie opened her eyes. She tried to smile.

"Of course you haven't, Willy. Don't worry. I sha'n't faint. I never fainted in my life but I was so anxious to help poor old Hooch, — I felt every one of those awful things I pulled out. If — if I could have some water —" She braced her elbows on her knees and dropped her head into her hands.

"Sure, ma'am. Just you keep quiet an' I'll get some. Don't you faint while I'm gone, will yer? I won't be a min—" His voice died away as he ran sideways down the field. Julie remained motionless till the sensation of faintness passed. She raised her head and looked at the dog. She stroked his rough coat. Poor old Hooch. He had seemed to know that she would help him. Poor Willy Small —

Willy Small! The thought dispersed the last wisp of dizziness. Where had he gone? He had feared Ben Cheever's return. Was she on the verge of a discovery which might help Jim Trafford? She took her bearings. Behind her a flaming sumach nodded and swayed in the afternoon breeze. It was the one bit of brilliant color among the bushes which fringed the field. At a sound she turned. In a straight line from the burning bush a piece of ground was suddenly thrown back. As a head popped from the opening Julie dropped her face into her hands.

"Here it is, ma'am. It ain't much of a cup but it's clean an' full of spring water."

Julie looked up and accepted the dripping can colorfully adorned with an impossible tomato. She drank thirstily. She returned it with a pale smile. Did the man remember her as the girl he had seen in the cabin, she wondered. She tried to hold his bleak eyes but they shifted like a dog's. If he remembered her evidently he had no intention of taking advantage of the fact. Jim need not have forbidden her to speak to him. She picked up the pliers and the phial and stood up. She looked down at the dog who lay with eyes half open.

"Hooch will be all right when he wakes, Willy. He will appear chastened for a day or two, after that he will look for revenge. You had better keep him close. He may not come out of the next porcupine fight so well. Do you live near here?"

"I don't live nowhere, ma'am, I'm a traveling man," Small corrected with a sudden flash of humor. "Hooch an' I, we pick up our livin' where we can find it. Jest now I'm actin' as caretaker fer a man, but I'm quittin' the job. I'm much obliged to yer fer helpin' Hooch. Seems as though I hadn't got no words to say it." He cleared his throat. "Was you here fer anything special?"

"Here in this field? I came to see the view. Glorious, isn't it? I have seen rather more than I expected. I must go. Pat Hooch for me, Willy. Good-afternoon."

"Good-bye, an' thank you again. Be careful you don't step down no holes," he cleared his throat once, twice before he added:

"Jest a minute, ma'am. Don't let Ben Cheever put anything acrosst on you. He ain't never lost his memory. Not for a minute."

Chapter XVI

For an instant the bleak eyes met Julie's. As they shifted she caught the man's arm.

"What is Ben Cheever trying to put across, Willy?"

"You'll have to spell thet out fer yourself; I can't say nothin' more."

The girl thrust her hands into her pockets and looked out to sea where the slanting sun was transforming a string of cabin-topped dories on their way to the fishing grounds into golden gondolas sailing an enchanted ocean. Jim Trafford's election might depend upon her reply to Small. Self-indulgence and sloth had clogged the man's normal impulses and intelligence with the ashes of failures but deep down under them a spark of conscience had flickered when she had helped his dog. Could she fan it into a flame? His heavy lips instinctively responded to her smile as she looked up.

"Ben Cheever was here before I came, was he not? Why didn't he take poor Hooch to the veterinary in the village?"

"I asked him, wouldn't he, an' he laughed an' called Hooch a mongrel cur an' when the dog growled he up an' kicked him."

"Kicked him! When he was suffering! Oh, no. Willy, no!"

"He did, the da— mean cuss. I tells him then an' there that he could git another party to do his work. I was through, ter-day."

"To-day! I'm sorry, Willy. I wanted to see Hooch again; he's my patient, you know. Wait until Monday. I'll bring him the nicest, juiciest bone I can find. When I come perhaps you will show me through the old copper-mine. I want to explore it and I suspect that you know it better than anyone else."

Small's eyes which had been on the unconscious dog met the girl's. Something stirred behind their bleakness. It was as though an imprisoned spirit were fighting its way to look through bars, Julie thought. "Help me to free it! Help me to free it!" she prayed fervently.

"Ain't you afraid to go down in the old copper-mine with me? Jim Trafford wouldn't let you if he knowed. He's had me watched like a lynx since the day you come through the rapids with him."

Julie's heart gave one thump and quieted.

"He doesn't know you as well as I do, Willy. He didn't hear you say a few moments ago that never had you frightened a woman."

The imprisoned spirit shook at the bars as the man reaffirmed doggedly:

"An' I ain't never, an' so help me God, I never will. Why can't you come ter-morrer?"

Julie struggled to keep the mounting excitement from her voice. "I couldn't get away on Sunday, Willy."

"Then come Monday at about four. It'll be election day — too late to do any good this year but you may see somethin' that'll help Jim Trafford next year; mind yer, I only say yer may. You'd better be goin' now, ma'am, an' goin' quick. Cheever might come back an' if he was to see us together — well, good-night to yer plan of comin' Monday. You won't ferget that bone?"

"No, Willy. I'll bring it. Good-bye."

He was back beside his dog before she had finished the sentence. Julie's thoughts rioted with melodramatic possibilities as she drove to the village to have the phial refilled. She did not dare face Sarah Beddle without it. What could Willy show her that would discredit Cheever? She must be cautious. Were Jim to suspect that she was in communication with Small he might do more than forbid her to speak to him. His mother had been right. There was a cave-man tinge in the Traffords. She stirred uneasily. There had been a smile

222

in the depths of the present mill-magnate's eyes but determination in his voice when he had warned her not to wrinkle her nose at him again.

As he was not there to see she indulged herself once adorably at his expense before she again caught up the thread of Small's disclosures. Whatever evidence she gained would be kept up her sleeve as a sort of hand-grenade. Willy had intimated that Cheever's loss of memory was a blind. What could the state senator hope to gain by it? Did he intend to blare his version of the cabin episode at the last minute? If he did, possibly — just possibly — by Monday night she would have a nice, fat bomb rammed to the fuse with TNT to fling at him in return.

Monday night! That was the evening of Martha Marshall's reception to the villagers. Every citizen in town had been invited to meet the new senator. A marquee was to be erected on the lawn for the employees of the two mills, there was to be a caterer and two orchestras from New York. Julie had protested:

"But think how unpleasant it will be for the defeated candidate," and her aunt had answered crisply:

"It will give him an opportunity to show that characteristic which you and Billy are

223

forever glorifying, his sporting spirit."

Was Cheever waiting for that occasion to recover his memory? Julie's heart tripped and stumbled on. Willy had warned her for some reason. Should she tell Jim? What good would it do? It she did he would find out that she had talked with Willy Small; he might cross-examine her till he discovered the plan for Monday. She would keep her own counsel.

It was dusk when she reached Brick House. The September twilight was cool and crisp and fragrant. In the living-room a cheery fire of cannel coal blazed and crackled in the Franklin grate. The silver water-kettle on the tea-table steamed industriously above the alcohol flame. The fat Canton teapot snuggled in its cosy, between its lemon and cream ladies-in-waiting The yellow cat in her accustomed place beneath the Duchess blinked wise eyes at the muffin-stand. Julie pulled off hat and sweater and hailed her:

"I could eat you, Marcella, I am so hungry! I — Heavens, how you frightened me, Dal," she exclaimed as a figure rose from the wing-chair. Carfax passed his hand hurriedly across his eyes. In the faint light he looked white and shaken.

"What has happened? Has Aunt Martha — Billy —"

"No, no, Julie, nothing like that. I heard —"

224

he broke off and caught her two hands in his. The lips he suddenly pressed upon them were white.

"Julie, I love —"

The girl, who at first had been too stupefied with amazement to move, snatched her hands from his. She clenched them behind her. Her tone was more incredulous than angry as she demanded:

"Dal, have you gone mad?"

"No. Will you marry me when this farce with Trafford is annulled?"

"Dal!"

With the horrified exclamation Julie shrank away from him. She backed into the tea-table with a force which set its appointments jangling just as the lights flashed on and a voice from the door inquired:

"Why try to serve tea in the dark, Julie?"

In the sudden glare the room was a blur, then the girl's vision cleared. She gripped her composure and smiled radiantly at Trafford.

"That is better, Jim, thank you. One lump or two, Dal?" she inquired as she poised silver tongs.

"I won't stop for tea, Julie. Billy asked me to drop in and tell you that the fishing-trip was on for Monday —"

"Monday! I can't — did he say morning or afternoon?"

"Morning, of course, with a picnic lunch at the old mill. He thought it would help you bear the suspense of waiting for election returns. How's the battle going, Jim?"

"It is almost over. I'm speaking to-night and then I'm through."

"To-night! But we are to dine at Shorehaven!"

"Sorry, Julie, but Cheever has staged a last rally. Take my regrets to Aunt Martha, Carfax."

"I will. Good-bye, Julie. I'll see you at dinner?"

The girl avoided the question in Carfax's eyes. She appeared absorbed in the cup she was filling.

"Ye-es. Don't forget to tell Aunt Martha that Jim is not coming."

When Trafford returned from accompanying his guest to the door he snapped off the lights and plunged the room into flame-tinted dusk. He leaned an arm on the mantel and steadily regarded the girl by the table.

"Was Carfax annoying you, Goldilocks?"

Cap to dynamite. Julie's self-control blew up. The surgical operation she had performed on the dog had insidiously undermined it.

"Annoy me! What has happened to you all? First you smash our friendship and now — now —" her voice broke; tears dimmed the blaze in her eyes. She made a precipitate dash for the door. Trafford caught her by the shoulders.

"I can't let you go like this, Julie. You are right, something has happened to our friendship. You haven't looked at me for a week. You have dodged me every chance you could get. We seem to be drifting farther and farther apart and I won't have it."

"It is your own fault. You glare every time I play with Billy and —"

"Then my glare must be an almost continuous performance. What other sins have I committed?"

Julie warmed to her grievance.

"You know how I hate sentiment — that I only came to Brick House to help — and you take advantage of that and spoil everything by telling me that —"

"That I love you? Forget it, if that is what is wrecking our friendship. Put it out of your mind."

"I can't! I think of it all the ti—" she held back the word but too late. Trafford caught her close with an exultant laugh.

"Do you, my Sleeping Beauty? Then put this memory with it!" he whispered huskily before he crushed her lips beneath his.

For a dazed instant the girl's eyes remained closed. Then she rallied and twisted herself free. Her face was white as she defied him.

"I won't speak to you again until you apologize for that."

Trafford's eyes and voice were recklessly triumphant.

"Must a man apologize when he kisses his wife? This one won't. I shall do it again at the first opportunity."

The color scorched to the girl's hair, then drained away. There was an incredulous gasp in the voice in which she warned:

"If you do I — I shall run away with Billy."

Chapter XVII

Arrayed in silk shirt, khaki knickers, and hip boots, with a rakish tilt to her soft felt hat and a basket slung over one shoulder, Julie cast her line into deep water in the dark depths of which she had seen a darting shadow. Beside a huge boulder and beneath an overhanging tree-root the trout pool lay still and mysterious, undisturbed by the rippling song, the never-ending murmur of the brook which leaped and plunged, splashed and eddied its way through the woods on its pilgrimage to merge into the pond. The sunlight flirted audaciously with spray and foam, now transforming it into miniature rainbows, now into a thousand sparkling gems. Crisply fragrant with balsam, pine and cedar, keen with September energy the breeze whipped a glorious color into the girl's cheeks. Her eyes watched the swoop of a hawk far, far up in the realm of wings. She followed the pirate as it circled and melted into the unfathomable blue of the sky. Her attention returned to the matter at hand. She cast tentatively for a while then reeled in her line and confided to the barnyard hackle which camouflaged her hook:

"This pool is a total loss. Why did Billy recommend it? Bille-e-e! Bille-e-e!" she called. She listened. From up-stream Jaffrey sent his robust and not unmusical voice ahead of him in the one song of his repertoire:

" 'To-re-a-dor! To-re-a-dor! For thee a fond heart waits. For the-e-e a fond hear-a-art waits!' "

Julie looked up the brook and laughed. Down the middle of it came Jaffrey slipping and sliding over rocks which invited by their mossy greenness and betrayed by their wetness. He puffed from leg and voice exertion as he joined her.

"Unlimber your rod, Marble-heart. Dal and Pam are to meet us at the old mill. They are to motor over with the lunch. Catch either of those two children of luxury tramping. We'll cut through the woods. Quit, you rascal!" he protested as the black spaniel in close proximity shook the water from his coat.

At the girl's whistle the dog dashed ahead of her into the trail. She drew deep breaths of piney fragrance as she and Jaffrey trod lightly in Indian file. They crossed a small clearing where the grass was waist high, where fireweed blazed and goldenrod swayed in the breeze. A cloud of brown butterflies winged upward at their approach and settled back upon the blossoms. They crossed a bit of corduroy road and came out upon the bank of the pond near the old mill. Jaffrey looked up and down the shore.

"Pam and Dal haven't come and I could eat raw dog, I'm so hungry."

"They may expect to meet us at the upper mill."

"They wouldn't have to walk a step if they stopped there. I'll bet a hat they are waiting for us to find them. We don't go. This is the best place on the shore for a fire."

"Go after them, Billy. Don't grumble, that's a dear. I'm starving. Take Sweetie-peach with you. I adore him but he frightens the wood-folk away and some may appear if I am alone."

"I'll go. Do you know what I think? That the man-eating Parkman on her way here detoured to district headquarters to entice Trafford out for lunch with her."

Julie paused in the process of tying up her rod.

"Billy, is Pamela really in love with Jim?"

Jaffrey grinned. "She may be but she means to marry the man who is successful to-day. Somewhere she has heard that classic 'As Maine goes so goes the country.' She figures that if she starts here, no matter how humbly, she's bound to land in Washington. She has the lady-of-the-cabinet bee in her bonnet."

"But Jim is married."

"Permanently? I wasn't born yesterday, Marble-heart. When Pamela told the story of the runaway dog I suspected in a flash that you and Trafford were the girl and man who had rushed to the rescue. The suspicion settled into conviction when I read of the sale of the prize-winning spaniel. Your expression of shocked surprise betrayed you. Haven't I known you all your life? Haven't you rushed to the aid of someone or something ever since you put up your hair? Did you think that I or anyone else believed that war-time-romance explanation? It was a pretty bit of fiction but not colorfast. Already there is a faint rumor that the marriage was a political move of Jim's"

"Then that miserable Cheever is behind it."

"Oh, ho, so Ben is the dusky gentleman in the wood-pile, is he —"

"Billy, I'll confide —"

"Don't! What I don't know I can't tell. I'm sorry to bring this up now but an understanding between you and me is a bit overdue. I put you wise to that rumor because I had a hunch you ought to be prepared to meet it, not have it jumped on you. You and Jim met some-where — love isn't a matter of time, it is a matter of ignition. Apparently you picked up a hang-over germ of that married-in-haste war epidemic. That is the stand I have taken against the flood of conjecture in the village. And I'll say right here, Julie, that whatever happened I'd trust The Trafford anywhere, in any situation, in spite of the fact that at present he is seeing me as through a glass, darkly. I don't mind. I'm flattered pink to have him jealous of my red head and super-waistline." He indulged in a gratified chuckle.

"As for you, I never know where your big heart will land you, you are a curious combi-nation of child and woman, but I do know that you are as straight and true as God makes a human. Whatever your experience was it has changed you. You try to be your old gay self, but I sense spiritual conflict, poor old Christian lined up against Apollyon."

"You are right, Billy. I am trying to down one of the spiritual verities Mother and Dad have bred into me and it won't down."

"And there are dumb-bells who claim that the influence of parents doesn't count. It's the gyroscope which steadies the world kept whirling by love."

"Billy, you are a dear! Never have you given an inkling that you suspected —"

"Why should I? For some reason you and Jim are putting up a stiff bluff. Why should I ball it up?"

"I'll tell you the whole story after election, Billy."

"Meanwhile remember that if ever you need help I'm standing by, Marble-heart. Now I will break the rule of a lifetime and warn one woman against another. Look out for Pam. You are the most straightforward girl I ever met. You play fair with men. You have as much idea of coquetry as Sarah Beddle and Pamela is past-mistress in the art."

"Thank you for rating my charms with the divine Sarah's."

"Don't be snippy! I've delivered my warning with the usual result. If we want lunch I suppose I shall have to round it up. Shall I take the dog?"

He whistled to the spaniel who after an inquiring look at the girl dashed on ahead. Jaffrey turned back.

"Just one word more, Marble-heart. Keep out of Dal's way until you can tell the truth about your marriage."

He did not wait for the girl to answer. Julie watched him out of sight before she dropped to the ground. Elbows dug into soft pine-needles, chin in hands she considered Jaffrey's warning. It had come about forty-eight hours too late. There had been something more than self behind Carfax's impassioned "Will you marry me?" His voice had suggested the clink of armor, had held the chivalrous timbre of a knight's tilting madly in defense of his lady. What could it mean? Did Dal think that she was not married? Was that what Billy had meant by that "Permanently"? How could they think that The Trafford would do anything so preposterous as to pretend that there had been a ceremony? She flushed hotly as she remembered that that had been her first flurried suggestion.

Billy had been a dear to warn her about that rumor; it had not been easy for him, she had known by his heightened color and the apology in his eyes. So the marriage was spoken of as a political move. She and Jim had called it an emergency measure. Jim —

The thought of Trafford brought a surge of smothering memory. He held her close. His lips crushed hers. She could see the flaming triumph of his eyes, hear his husky, "Do you, my Sleeping Beauty?"

Would she ever, ever feel cool again? The memory of his lips on hers turned her blood to fire — and it recurred with maddening persistency. What had he thought of her silly threat to run away with Billy? She had been so furiously angry that she had hurled the first words that came to her mind.

"Christian lined up against Apollyon," Billy had said. He was right. The Prince of the City of Destruction urged a break of that marriage contract while she repelled him with the thought, "Whom God hath joined together —"

"But it wasn't God, it was that miserable Cheever," the girl protested brokenly under her breath.

She gazed unseeingly into the woods. Great boulders of granite which broke the serried phalanxes of trees were luxuriantly green with rock ferns. An occasional partridge berry which had escaped the hungry birds made a ruby spot in the rich pattern of moss which carpeted the forest. The girl did not move when the noon whistle of the mill sounded, when from afar drifted the excited yelping of a dog who had treed his quarry. She lay so motionless that a portly hedgehog which had been watching her backed down from the fork of a tree and with quills rustling lumbered into the underbrush. A squirrel overhead scolded shrilly. A partridge drummed on a hollow log. The girl was unconscious of the sounds.

Jaffrey's warning, his blunt, "Look out for Pam!" was rotating in her mind. He had confirmed what Pamela herself had brazenly proclaimed. Billy need not have been so brutally frank about her own lack of charm. He was right, though, she had not the remotest idea how to open up a flirtation skirmish. She liked men as friends. When they abandoned that firm ground and — she sprang to her feet.

"You have too much leisure in which to think, Julie," she admonished as she collected wood for a fire. "Did you find them, Billy?" she called as Jaffrey appeared upon the bridge.

"Yes. It was as I suspected. Pamela and Dal picked up Jim and Cheever at their respective headquarters. She insisted that they would have to eat somewhere and promised to drive them back immediately after lunch. Jim was ready enough to come. He had protested against being at headquarters today, didn't believe in it, but his backers overruled him. Put on more wood. I'll clean the trout."

Why did Pamela have to drag Cheever into the party, Julie queried indignantly as she tended the fire. If he would only hover about the man-eating Parkman, but he didn't. He persisted in dangling about herself. Was it a stirring of his comatose memory which prompted him? But Willy Small had warned: "He ain't lost his memory, never for a minute."

Jaffrey from a flat rock near the water looked up from the fish he was cleaning.

"This would be a peach of a day to shoot the rapids but I suppose you are off that sport for the rest of your young life. The Trafford —"

"Jim here?" shouted a voice from the trail above them.

"It's Captain Phin! Do you suppose that he has news of the election?"

"It is too early. Get him down here and I'll stir him up to talk. Uneducated as the man is he represents Public Opinion in this neighborhood. I'm putting him in a story."

"Here we are, Captain Phin!" Julie called eagerly. "Have you heard who is ahead?"

Snow appeared at the top of the bank. His glassy eyes were clouded, his tone was worried as he answered:

"No, about half the district ain't voted. The tellers don't know just what to make of it down to our pollin' place. Not a hand from Cheever's mill's been in yet. It'll be evenin' now before we know —"

Jaffrey indulged in a prolonged whistle.

"Looks as though Cheever were preparing a coup, doesn't it?"

"Looks as though he was up to some devil-try. Where's Jim? I telephoned headquarters an' they said he'd gone to lunch. There's an express package at the office which they won't deliver to me without written order from him. I flivved to Brick House an' Sarah Beddle didn't know where he was. Said you was lunchin' here, so I jest rushed through the woods thinkin' I might locate Jim. I know he wants thet package to-day."

"He is coming here for lunch, Captain Phin. Sit down and cool off. Don't worry, The Trafford must win. Here he comes now," she added as Carfax and Cheever, Pamela and Trafford appeared on the bridge. The last two lagged behind, the girl looking up, the man bending toward her as though communicating something of tremendous import.

Julie caught her breath in an indignant gasp. Billy had been right. Pamela Parkman evidently had already opened her campaign. Jim seemed to like it. As she mixed the ingredients for the dish she was preparing her thoughts raced on. It was curious and altogether disturbing that not one of the four persons approaching could she greet with sincere cordiality. Pamela had been unforgivably insulting; Carfax seemed bent on ignoring the fact of her marriage; she distrusted Cheever; as for Jim — she banged the door of her mind against him. With unnecessary vigor she broke eggs into a frying-pan which already held bits of onion, potatoes and bacon done to an appetizing brown.

"May I ask the name of that wicked-looking stuff you are concocting?"

Of course it was Cheever, Cheever smiling ingratiatingly from the flat rock Billy had vacated. Julie controlled an unholy desire to make a face at him. The black spaniel barked at him aggressively. The dog obeyed Trafford's sharp whistle but a growl rumbled an accompaniment to his padding paws as he ran to his master who was signing a slip of paper as he listened to Snow's whispered communication. Did Sweetie-peach remember the man in the cabin, Julie wondered even as she answered his question:

"Slumgullion. Wait until you try it; you'll think it wickeder. Had you better indulge, though? It is hardly the diet for an invalid."

The girl's cheeks were a lovely pink from the glow of the sun and the fire. The breeze fluffed her hair about her vivid face. Her violet eyes were dark with concern as they met Cheever's which smoldered with disconcerting admiration.

"I am not an invalid. I am more fit than I was before the accident. The enforced quiet did me good."

"Has your restored health retrieved the two weeks your memory lost, Mr. Cheever?"

Were the man's eyes wriggling beneath their surface boldness or was it her imagination? A slight color tinted his yellow pallor.

"No. Curious, isn't it? The doctor tells me not to worry, that remembrance will return suddenly. Excitement is likely to send it surging back." He stopped to light a cigarette before he joined Carfax who sat where he could not see the girl by the fire.

Julie motioned to Jaffrey to serve the dish she had concocted and sank back on her heels. She felt limp. Had Cheever unconsciously shown his hand? Had she been right in her suspicion that he had timed his return of memory for to-night at Shorehaven? Through the laughter and badinage about her she felt the strain of suspense though no one mentioned the election. The contest which centred in the white-spired village below might have been raging for the choice of a ruler in a South Sea island for all indication either of the candidates present gave of being interested.

Julie became tinglingly conscious that Trafford had dropped to the bank above her. He had not spoken to her, apparently had not looked at her, but try as she would to ignore him she was irresistibly aware of his every move. Her mind shrugged as Pamela Parkman commanded:

"Take my hand, Jim; the moss is slippery. I'll have my lunch with you."

Steadied by Trafford's firm grip she seated herself beside him. She smiled an answer to something he said in a low tone. Her red hat and sweater took the color from everything near them. Her voice was lazily content as she observed:

"Isn't this a perfect day! What a wonderful night Mrs. Marshall will have for her festivity."

Julie roused from her furtively indignant contemplation of the two on the bank. Her mood was reflected in her voice.

"I wish that the planets had forbidden her old celebration."

"How sharper than a serpent's tooth it is to have a thankless niece," paraphrased Jaffrey. "Her blare of hospitality is more for you than for the successful candidate, Marble-heart. Aunt Martha's first idea-seedling has grown with the rapidity of Jack's beanstalk. The last lusty sprout was to order wedding-cake, tons of it, in little white boxes with silver initials lovingly intertwined."

His tone was light but his eyes met and held Julie's. Was he preparing her, the girl had just time to wonder before Trafford repeated sharply:

"Wedding-cake! Who is to be married?"

"Boy! You and Julie were, weren't you?"

Cheever bent to knock his cigarette against his shoe. His eyes were hidden as he contributed:

"Has the happy bridegroom so soon forgotten the ceremony?"

Julie's heart pounded in her throat. The sarcasm in the man's voice confirmed her suspicion that he was waiting to spring his trap. She stole a glance at Trafford. His face was white, his gray eyes flames as he answered:

"No, Cheever. He remembers every word of the service which gave him the girl he loved." There was an instant of charged silence before he inquired coolly:

"What do you think of the day, Captain Phin?"

Perched on an overhanging tree-root from which his long overalled legs swayed in unison with the moss on the mill-wheel, Snow looked up critically at the blue sky and sniffed the air. "It's a weather breeder. You'll hev to look out fer yer crimps, girls; we'll git a thick fog before night."

"A fog!"

Cheever flung away his cigarette with the exclamation. He made a movement to rise, then sank back at Snow's chuckle.

"What's the matter, Ben? 'Fraid you won't

get them votes of yours in before the sun is shut out, or are ye bound ter keep a date with the roamin' Duchess when the weather's thick?"

Chapter XVIII

Julie caught the look of warning which Trafford flashed at the old fisherman. Was she the only one who had seen it? Cheever was as usual lighting a cigarette, Billy and Carfax were talking with Pamela and had missed the chuckled question. Evidently Captain Phin was in Jim's confidence. Did they suspect that the present senator had an ungodly interest in the copper-mine? The girl's heart quick-stepped to the tune of excitement. It looked as though she might become a party to the secret this afternoon. This afternoon! Suppose there should be a fog? Would Willy expect her? She would go whatever the weather. Ought she to take Billy with her? She had sworn to herself that never again would she jump recklessly into a bramble-bush, and her appointment with Small might lead into a jungle of them. She would think that point out later; at present she must pay attention to what her companions were saying. If she appeared distrait Cheever might suspect —

Why worry! No one was conscious of her. All eyes were on Captain Phin who was discoursing. Was he garrulous to cover his malapropos question or had Billy succeeded in stirring him up? If he had he would get a trifle more than he expected, the girl thought with a smile. A little of the old fisherman's philosophy might open his eyes wider. Billy was a dear, but from her father's point of view and her own, he was not standing for what he might. They believed that a talent for expression like his brought grave responsibilities in its train. Captain Phin's gummy voice slid into her revery:

"Mark-my-words, Billy Jaffrey, what the world needs ain't a lot of consecrated missionaries; it needs rich fellers like you and Dal Carfax an' Pamela — I understand Julie's folks ain't got much so I don't count her in — should stand fer the best. Fer one thing, cut out yer encouragemnent of rum-runnin'. You people who are encouraging bootleggin' are rangin' yourselves with the greatest aggregation of crooks, hold-up men, thugs, gamblers, thiefs, double-crossers that's ever been got together. They're the scum and the dregs of the country. An' you're draggin' some that might be decent down with you, too. I know a feller —"

Snow broke off his sentence to cough. Had Jim raised his hand from design or accident?

With the thought Julie's eyes flew to Cheever. His face was undisturbed and serene. Evidently Captain Phin's peroration had not touched his conscience, and she had been quite sure of the sort of evidence she would find in the copper-mine this afternoon. Jim had said that he was a master of bluff. The present senator's voice was grave; he might have been addressing the legislative body as he agreed:

"Snow is right. Men like you had better show up at the primaries and the polls, work to repeal the laws which you don't like and substitute something better if you object to what you get."

Julie caught the smile in Trafford's eyes as they met the fisherman's. Carfax's face was a lively crimson, Jaffrey's flamed but he laughed as he acknowledged:

"I get you, Cheever. Captain Phin, I take it that 'God give us successful men with ideals' would be your slogan?"

"You've said it. Gorry-me, but it takes you writer-folks to boil a lot of thoughts into a few words, don't it?"

"It depends upon how much he gets per word how much he boils, doesn't it, Billy?" demanded Carfax and skillfully steered con-versation into less turbulent waters. Trafford sprang to his feet.

"Pam, I hold you to your promise to take

247

me back to headquarters. If you and Cheever are going with us, Dal, you'll have to come now." He held out his hand to Pamela who clutched it and lingeringly struggled to her feet. "I shall be at Brick House in time for tea this afternoon, Julie. Plan to be there. I want to talk to you." There was a "no appeal" glint in the eyes which met the girl's.

It was the first time since his arrival that he had directly addressed her. Before she could answer, with Pamela beside him he turned into the path which led to the old mill. Cheever and Carfax nodded *au revoir* and followed. Captain Phin ambled in the direction of Brick House. Julie's eyes followed Trafford as he crossed the bridge. He never came home for tea. Why should he make an exception to-day of all days when he was supposed to be immersed in politics? Did he suspect that she had a rendezvous with Willy Small? Why should he? She looked at Jaffrey. He was staring indignantly at the disappearing figures on the bridge.

"Well, of all the cool proceedings, Marbleheart. They have gone and left you and me to pack the basket. Do they expect us to carry it home?"

"We won't, Billy. I will send one of the men for it. Have you anything on for this afternoon?"

"No. Do you want me to hang round the village with you and watch developments?"

"No, I want you to go somewhere with me."

"But Jim wants you at Brick House."

"I have another engagement. Won't you help me without asking questions?"

"I will. Now and forever. Where will you pick me up?"

"I will call on Aunt Martha. You can be in the hall and I'll say, 'I'm going on an errand. Do you want to come, Billy?' And you will say, 'Sure, Marble-heart.' Will you?"

"Sure, Marble-heart."

At half after three, dressed in the heliotrope frock she had worn on her arrival in Clearwater, its frills at neck and wrists as crisp as fresh organdie and Martha Marshall's maid could make them, Julie tucked a slicker and sou'wester beneath the seat of the sedan. Captain Phin had prophesied a fog and she would not risk being obliged to abandon her expedition because of the weather. As an additional plank in her platform of preparedness she slipped a ball of stout twine and a flashlight into one of the pockets of the car. On the floor she deposited a bulky bundle which contained the reddest, rawest, juiciest bone the village had offered. As she manoeuvered the machine noiselessly from the garage, hoping to escape the observation of Sarah Beddle, the woman's voice, shrill with anxiety, hailed her.

"Got any returns from the election, M's. Jim?"

"Nothing definite yet."

"Better not go far. There's a fog rollin' in."

"It won't catch me before I get to Shore-haven."

"Perhaps you'll hear how things are going there. Take this fer M's. Trafford, will you? Someone from the mill left it. It's about the Girls' Club, I guess." Sarah ran down the steps and handed Julie a note. She looked toward the sea and shook her head. "It's comin' in thick. I don't think much of your going even that far."

"I'm not afraid of a fog. I almost forgot — The Trafford will be here for tea, Sarah. Set the table by the fire in his study and have —"

"Ain't you going to be here to pour it? Suppose, jest suppose Jim don't win and you ain't here when he comes? I never knew a Trafford wife yet who wasn't always to home —"

Julie stepped on the accelerator. As the roadster shot forward she turned and waved her hand. Disapproval shadowed the house-keeper's thin face. As she craned forward to watch the car her long neck seemed to lengthen like that of Alice in Wonderland. The girl increased speed. It would not be out of character for Sarah to try to stop her, so much and so heavily did the responsibility of the Trafford family rest on the shoulders of her New England conscience.

Julie lingered on the steps at Shorehaven to look off to sea where a slight haze hung. The breeze which blew from the water was damp and cold. There was the taste of salt on her lips. Fog or no fog she should keep her appointment with Small, she decided as she opened the door. She hoped that Billy would be ready. Every moment counted.

"Short stories here, Julie," she reminded herself as she entered the hall. Its warmth and color were a stimulating contrast to the gray world outside. The brass gates of the fireplace were thrown back to give an unobstructed view of the blazing logs. There were flowers everywhere. From behind the closed doors of the dining-room came the tinkle of silver and the click of china. Weird shapes in black shrouds filled the minstrel gallery. Everywhere was the bustle and evidence of preparation. The bottom seemed to drop from the girl's heart. Had Billy been right? Was this festivity of Managing Martha's primarily to celebrate her niece's mock-marriage? She crushed back the apprehensions which crowded in the train of the question. She must not think of that now.

Mrs. Trafford in a leaf-green frock was curled up in one corner of the mammoth couch. Mrs. Marshall, *grande dame* from her beautifully coiffed white hair to the jet buckles on her satin slippers, smiled at the girl from behind the tea-table. Anne Trafford sprang to her feet.

"You, honey-girl? Any news of the election?" Julie shook her head. "I suppose that it is too early for results. Is it possible that the divine Sarah allowed you to venture out this foggy after-noon when you had a party on for to-night?"

Julie smiled in sympathy with the laughing voice. "I had a suspicion that she contemplated locking me in my room so I bolted. No tea, thank you, Aunt Martha. I am on my way to do an errand." This was Billy's cue; where was he? "I stopped to leave this note which came from the mill for you, Mrs. Trafford."

"Thank you, Julie. Why not drop that Mrs., dear? You might call me Mother Anne — or —"

"No, oh no!" Julie attempted to wipe out her vehemence. "It — it sounds too old for you and —" Her inventive faculty was conserved by Martha Marshall's intervention.

"Don't get tired, Julie. I want you to look your best to-night. This reception is partly to introduce the Trafford bride to the county."

Julie had a sensation as of walls closing in upon her, as though she must smash her way out of this wildly impossible situation. Why — *why*, when both these women knew the truth did they persist in ignoring the facts of her marriage? Exasperation tinged the voice in which she inquired:

"Won't your party fall flat if the groom is defeated?"

"Why should it? Jim is a good loser, is he not? If the voters elect Cheever they will be given an opportunity to-night to congratulate him. They can't justly accuse me of showing favoritism. That note you gave Anne reminds me, Julie, that one was left here for you. It is extremely soiled and smells to heaven of cheap tobacco. It is doubtless from one of your fishy admirers who has had that flashy stationery stored with his savings since the dark ages. If you insist upon being democratic in your choice of friends please request your correspondents to sterilize their communications." In the tips of her patrician fingers she extended a brilliant pink envelope of the type and color which is perennially bunched on the bargain-counter. Julie studied the address.

"It must be from Captain Phin. He asked me to buy some records for him the next time I went to the village. My last classical purchase was 'Toot! Toot! Toots, good-bye'!"

She whistled a bar of the popular air.

Her eyes shone with laughter as she opened the envelope. The corners of her vivid lips curved in a smile. She felt them stiffen in consternation as she read:

"Fer the love of Mike, don't come to the mine ter-day."

There was no signature but through the paper beneath the scrawled message was thrust a barbed porcupine quill.

Chapter XIX

"Fer the love of Mike, don't come ter the mine ter-day."

It seemed to Julie that she had been staring down at the words for hours when her aunt picked up the thread of conversation where she had dropped it to present the note.

"Stay here and dress, Julie. I will send Carlotta for your clothes and we'll 'phone Jim —"

"No, oh *no!*"

That protest of hers was in danger of becoming chronic, Julie thought, even as she determined to ignore Small's message and keep on to the mine. Something exceptionally queer must be on the *tapis* or he wouldn't have tried to head her off. Was Cheever's concern about the fog tied up with Willy's warning? Her pulses raced. She wouldn't tell Billy of the note. He would refuse to go with her; he certainly would block her going if he knew of it. He was coming, singing his one song. The approaching sounds reminded her of Wagner's method of preceding the entrance of the characters in his operas by his or her own orchestral motif.

"To-re-a-dor! To-re-a-dor! For thee a fond heart waits, for th-e-e-e a f-fond ha-ha-heart —" Jaffrey ended with a trill which would have smashed any self-respecting disc which tried to record it. As he reached the foot of the stairs he raised his brows in an inquiring arch and at the girl's imperceptible nod approached the group near the fire.

"My usual luck! You are arriving just as I am departing, Marble-heart."

"I am going too, Billy. May I give you a lift?"

"Sure."

"Then get your oilskins and join me at the car." As Jaffrey hummed his way toward the coat-room she added: "I will report for duty early this evening, Aunt Martha. I'll see you all later. I must run along or Billy will scold."

Jaffrey was waiting when Julie reached the sedan. He took his seat beside her in silence. As she eased in the clutch and the car slid from the drive into the highway which led to Blue Heron Cove he leaned forward to clear the windshield of mist and suggested:

"Now that you have me snugly corralled perhaps you'll explain the reason of this mysterious expedition. Is it to work off steam

256

while you await returns?"

"No, but it is indirectly connected with the election. I am on the trail of evidence against Cheever. It will be too late to use it this year, but it will keep. If you can't concoct a best-seller from the facts I am about to relate, plus your hectic imagination, you had better be psycho-analyzed to find your *métier*. Last Saturday —"

The fog thickened as she related the story of her trip to Blue Heron Cove and the events which followed. The regular throb of the engine had an uncanny sound in the curious stillness of the atmosphere. The tinkle of a cow's bell came weirdly through blank, impenetrable gray walls behind them. Jaffrey sat motionless, his sharp-shooter green eyes contracted to steel points. He turned to her as she concluded.

"Can you find the spot where you helped the dog?"

"Yes. It was near a flaming sumach. The opening in the ground is in a straight line with that. I brought a ball of twine so that if Willy Small didn't materialize we could find the place ourselves."

"Clever kid. The gods be thanked that you thought of bringing me along. It would have been so like you to go it alone," Jaffrey observed dryly. "Of course Small will meet us. Why shouldn't he?"

Julie's conscience administered an admonishing pinch but she let his remark pass without comment. Even if Small did not expect her he might be in his dugout and they could find him. They might find someone with him. Her imagination reeled with excitement. She had left home craving adventure, anything different from her round of duties; it looked as though she would get it, good measure and running over. She had made a fairly brilliant start with the affair in the cabin. Her brows creased. If only Aunt Martha had not staged that ridiculous wedding reception for to-night. It was so like her to plan it without asking Jim or herself if they would like it.

"Darn!" she muttered between clenched teeth.

"You use that wicked expletive only under stress of great emotion, Marble-heart. What's wrong?"

"I was thinking of that silly party to-night."

"One thing at a time. You had much better concentrate on the crazy proposition upon which we've embarked. Holy smoke, isn't this fog thick!"

Julie closed her eyes for an instant to rest them from the strain of peering into the mist. When she opened them she could see the path which zigzagged across the field which

258

topped the cliff. She ran close to a mammoth pine and shut off the engine. She put on her slicker, stuffed her soft hat into the pocket and pulled a sou'wester low over her fair hair.

"I'm ready. Take the flash-light, Billy. I have the twine."

"Do you want the bone?"

"N-no, we'll leave it in the car till we meet Willy. He can come here for it."

Drip! Drip! Drip! Mist transformed into water dropped from the tree branches to the hood of the sedan and rolled off. Drop chased drop down the girl's slicker as she and Jaffrey crossed the field. The fog dripped from their sou'westers, it beaded their eyelashes, it playfully cavorted down their noses. Except for the oily lash of the waves against the cliff the world was intensely still. Suddenly out of the mist ahead two weird shapes shot into the air. Ghoulish wings flapping, long legs trailing, they vanished as though conjured out of sight by some sorcerer of the skies. Julie caught Jaffrey's arm.

"Only the blue herons. Why the dickens am I whispering?" he added with a joviality slightly overdone. "Shsh! Listen!"

The girl held her breath. Was it imagination or did she hear water slapping against the side of a boat? Whatever the explanation of the sound Billy had heard it too. He gripped her hand and together they proceeded cautiously.

"Go easy! Look out for holes! Are we near the sumach?"

Julie nodded. It was not difficult to locate the flaming bush. Its crimson leaves and blossoms were jeweled with a million tiny beads of moisture.

"Is this the place? Where's Small?" Jaffrey demanded in a sharp whisper. The girl shook her head. Why tell Billy now that she had not expected to find the man? Her heart leaped to her throat as from the shore a hollow voice floated through a gray wall of mist.

"I sha'n't wait for Campbell. Tell Jones to pick up Old Man Grindle and stand by till the others come!"

Jaffrey crushed the hand he held in a warning grip, and pulled the girl down behind the berry-bushes. There was the click of an oar in a row-lock, then only the sound of the sea. Julie wondered if her heart intended to park permanently in her throat. She could feel it pounding there. She and Jaffrey raised cautious heads and peered toward shore. What was that unearthly light? Did she really see it or had her unconscious mind flung to the surface that absurd story of the roaming Duchess who searched for her sapphires? She impatiently brushed the moisture from her lashes and looked again. Her imagination had not tricked her. The light was there. A pale flame-colored mist floated half-way up the cliff beneath which she and the others had lunched that never-to-be forgotten day when Jim Trafford had announced the marriage. She put her lips close to Jaffrey's ear.

"Do you see it too, Billy?"

He nodded.

"Pirates? Smugglers? B-bootleggers?"

The whispered words jostled one another for expression. Julie understood now why Small had sent the warning. He had said that he was acting as caretaker for a man. Evidently he had received word that the boats were coming. Cheever had known that they would come if the day turned foggy. How much did Jim Trafford suspect? She remembered the warning hand which had checked Captain Phin.

"They've gone! Give me that twine! Quick! I'll locate the trap-door," whispered Jaffrey hoarsely.

Hardly daring to breathe for fear some movement might betray them Julie produced the ball. Jaffrey knotted one end securely to the flaming sumach. The girl's slicker brushed against a bush. That mustn't happen again! She pulled it off and dropped it on the ground. Jaffrey discarded his and side by side they crouched forward, paying out the string as they went.

As though in league with the two investigators the fog closed in densely. Globules of moisture dripped from their sou'westers. The girl's erstwhile crisp frills were damp rags. From feet to knees she was wet to the skin but she was quite unconscious of physical discomfort. Her eyes were dark with eagerness, her vivid lips tense with determination as on hands and knees she felt her way along.

"It ought to be about —" Julie interrupted her strained whisper with an exclamation of pain as she clutched one knee. What had she struck? She groped in the grass, now a bilious yellow in the fog. She gripped an iron ring.

Jaffrey seized it. With an impatient hand he waved her away. She hitched back on her sound knee. She watched breathlessly as he tugged at the ring. The door flew up with an ease which tumbled him backward. It proved to be an iron grating overlaid with sod. Evidently it was one of the protections against a shaft opening which the present owner of the mine had had placed there. The thing must be on springs to open so easily.

Jaffrey laid his finger on his lips and beckoned. Julie crept toward him where he lay flat on the ground, peering down into the opening. She bent her head close to his. The air which came up to her was fresh and sweet with a tang of kelp. From the darkness came the monotonous drip of water.

"The tomb of Tutankhamen in the Valley of the Kings," chuckled Jaffrey. There was an infectious thrill in his whisper. Julie shivered from excitement She surreptitiously caught his arm as he flashed his light. She could discern a short flight of steps which descended into a rock-walled space perhaps ten feet square. The floor was covered with white sand. There was a pile of dry kelp in one corner. Jaffrey snapped off the light.

"I'm going down. I sense untold splendor."

"I'll go with you."

"Not on your life! You stay above ground. If you hear or see anything put your head down and whistle, whistle like the deuce."

"But you may get lost."

"I couldn't if I tried. Didn't you see Small vanish into the cliff and emerge here? This opening must connect with one of the tunnels in the copper-mine. Those all open out on the cliff. There is no danger. The boats have gone —"

"Then why are you whispering?" Julie laughed as her spirits suddenly ballooned.

"From abundance of precaution. Hold the light. Now I'll take it." She bent over the hole and watched his descent. "All right!"

The sepulchral whisper chilled her blood. She sat back on her heels with a shiver and looked about her. Rocks and shrubs and trees were shadows in the mist. The yawning hole drew her. She should have insisted upon going down with Billy. She would have been perfectly safe with him. It was her personally conducted expedition, why should she be denied any of the thrills of it simply because she was a girl? What was that? She tilted her head and listened. The sound of soft drumming, a far faint humming trickled through the mist above her.

An airplane! Had that hollow voice from the shore referred to this arrival when it had announced that it would not wait for Campbell?

" 'The Campbells are coming, heigho, heigho,' " the girl whistled softly under her breath. Her lips widened in a laugh as she threw back her head to look upward in the direction of the sound. She saw a shadowy biplane circling far above her as though looking for a place to land. It shot up and out of sight. Then, it seemed but an instant, before she saw a great gray mass hurtling down upon her.

Chapter XX

Jim Trafford looked down at the perfectly appointed table before the fire in the study at Brick House. The fat silver water kettle faithfully and shiningly reflected each tiniest spurt of flame. The Canton cups and saucers of his grandmother's day neutralized the modernity of the mushroom sandwiches which Sarah Beddle knew he particularly liked. The feast was set but where was Julie? The old clock caught its breath and boomed:

"One! Two! Three! Four! Five!"

Trafford crossed to the French window. Seen through the fog the gravel path which led straight to the shore was nothing more than a blurred outline. He returned to the hearth and pulled the old-fashioned tasseled bell-rope. Sarah Beddle answered. She gave the impression of having been waiting outside the door in anticipation of the summons. She was charged to the lips with indignation. Her small eyes flashed. Her prominent cheek-bones had the appearance of having been heavily dabbed with rouge. Trafford recognized the symptoms. He had seen them often enough in the era of his predatory attacks upon the cookie-jar, in those care-free days when he was the heir apparent and his grandfather was king.

"Do you want your tea, Mr. Jim?"

"Not until Julie comes."

The housekeeper pursed her lips into a mass of fine lines.

"I guess if you want it you'd better take it now. She drove off an hour 'n' a half ago. She told me you were comin' at five and when I asked wasn't she going to be here she just laughed and waved her hand and drove away. I don't know what the world's comin' to. Women didn't treat their husbands that way in your grandmother's and mother's time. But it's all of a new-fangled piece with you livin' in one side of the house and her in the other. I —"

"Sarah!" thundered Trafford. The woman flushed an unbecoming beet-color and busied herself among the tea-things. The voice in which she offered information was chastened:

"She said she was goin' to Shorehaven. I give her a note one of the mill girls left here for your mother. Do they know yet who's been elected senator? They don't? Now do sit down and rest while you drink your tea. It's

266

just as you like it and here are some of those mushroom sandwiches you're so set on."

He took the cup she offered. "Thank you, Sarah. I won't sit down. I want to find Julie. Did she say —" he absent-mindedly punctuated the sentence with a swallow of tea. It left the impression that his mouth had been thoroughly and painfully skinned. "Good Lord, why didn't you tell me this was hot?"

"Did you ever know tea to be cold in this house unless 'twas iced tea? That's one thing I'll say fer M's. Jim Trafford. She knows more how things had ought to be done than any girl I ever saw. That comes from bein' a poor minister's daughter, I suppose, though most girls with an aunt as rich as hers would have set back an' let her pay fer a hired girl. Julie's been doing all our buyin' — That reminds me, a boy came just after she left this afternoon with a note for her. 'T'was Pete Sparks, one of those shiftless Sparks kids, who when he ain't delivering goods from the store is forever fishin' with Willy Small an' that white dog of his —"

"Where is the note?"

The housekeeper snapped her eyes in her endeavor to pick up the thread of monologue Trafford had broken with his abrupt question.

"The note — the note — certain, certain,

here it is." She produced a bright pink envelope from behind a bowl of cosmos on the table. "Kinder pretty paper, isn't it? I love bright colors."

Trafford studied the illiterately scribbled name which had the appearance of being about to head hurriedly for the right-hand upper corner of the gay envelope.

MRS. JIM TRAFFORD
Important

The creases between his eyes deepened as he considered the triple underscoring.

"Did Pete suggest that he wait for an answer?"

"No. He just left it and run. You wouldn't expect one of those shiftless Sparks —"

"I am going to Shorehaven. I'll take the note. I have arranged with Captain Phin to take you to the party to-night, Sarah."

"Thank you. I hope he'll come early so I'll get there in time to see the folks come in. I guess all the village is turning out."

"I'll bet it is," Trafford supplemented to himself as he entered the garage. What marplot from the region of misfits had prompted Mrs. Marshall to plan the reception? If only it had occurred to her to consult his or Julie's wishes. Julie! Where was she? His mother's sedan which the girl had driven since she came to Brick House was not in its place. Of course she had gone to Shorehaven, he assured himself as he turned his roadster into the highway.

He drove slowly, his eyes strained to see through the mist, his ears strained to hear. If Julie were at Shorehaven — if — of course she was there. He beat back the threat which persisted in singsonging through his mind. "If you do I shall run away with Billy!" The words had tormented him since Saturday. He had not seen Julie until the luncheon on the shore and then he, like an idiot, had tried to make her jealous by devoting himself to Pamela.

His attempt had been a dismal failure. The delicate art of flirtation was as much out of his line as it was out of Julie's. He doubted if she had known he was talking with Pamela. Cheever had absorbed her attention when Jaffrey hadn't. Lately when the two had been together Ben had neglected Pamela to devote himself to Julie. What did he mean by it? Would he dare — There was a guttural sound in Trafford's throat. Two sparks like indicators which warn that the electric current is on glowed suddenly in his eyes. His thoughts flashed back to Julie. She had ignored his request that she be at Brick House for tea. He had left headquarters, first, because he had something to give her, second because he refused to longer stand about like a watch-dog. If the voters wanted him they would elect him. Was Cheever trailing him? His opponent had slipped away in his red car when he had left the village.

He had intended this afternoon to demand the truth about Billy Jaffrey from Julie. Did she love him? He had not decided what he would say to her if he found that she did — but he intended to know the truth.

He tried to relax his tense muscles. Of course he would find Julie at Shorehaven. There were nine fat chances to one lean one that Mrs. Marshall would not permit her to return in the fog to Brick House to dress for the reception.

Permit. Trafford's stern lips softened. Julie appeared not to know the meaning of the word in connection with her aunt. Curious that the woman should arouse such opposition in the girl. Was it? She had much the same effect upon him. He admired her keen grasp of business detail, she was generous, perhaps a little mad on the subject of astrology but most persons had a pet obsession these days, many Coued or crystal-gazed where she horoscoped, but she irritated him. He had thought that she disliked him. He had been more amazed than Julie when he had discovered that her attitude had been a part of her plan to bring her niece and him together. In spite of his aversion he realized that she was a loyal friend. His mother loved her.

His mother. He had forgotten for the moment that she was at Shorehaven. She would protest against the girl driving in the fog. She never antagonized. She was a wonder and he adored her. Julie had attracted him first because in a subtle way she had reminded him of his mother. It was her expression. A girl might or might not be born with beauty of feature but beauty of expression was acquired. They had both lived for others. Was it that which gave the sense of resemblance? Even the boys in the village had begun to be shyly friendly with Julie.

The thought circuited to the pink note in his pocket. A boy had brought that, a boy who was "forever fishin' with Willy Small." Was Small trying to frighten Julie with the fact that he had seen her in the cabin? He had feared it and had instructed the men on the Brick House estate not to allow Willy on the grounds. He was powerless to protect the girl outside except by forbidding her to allow the man to speak to her.

Julie was not in the hall at Shorehaven when he entered, neither was Jaffrey. Anne Trafford, her hostess and Pamela Parkman were sitting indolently about the fire as though conserving energy to expend on the evening festivity. Dal Carfax who was reading near a lamp waved a long cigarette holder in greeting. As Trafford entered the women sprang to their feet and chorused:

"Have you heard?"

He laughed as he put his arm about his mother's shoulders.

"Not yet. Cheever is holding back his votes. Preparing for a grand slam, I suspect. Where is Julie? Sarah said that she came here."

"She left before four o'clock."

"Did she go alone, Mother?"

"Billy went with her. Someone sent a note here for her and —"

"What kind of a note?"

"A brilliant pink."

"Did she open it?"

"Yes. I thought she seemed a bit startled at its contents."

"Has Jaffrey come back?"

"No. He may have stayed for tea at Brick House to be on hand to congratulate you if—"

Trafford's white teeth flashed in a laugh as he echoed:

"If! Say 'when'."

Pamela linked a shapely bare arm in his. Her eyes implored from between heavy lashes. Her flame-color frock absorbed the light from the fire.

"Stay here and we'll play Mah Jong to quiet our nerves for the evening festivities. I'm worn to a frazzle with the stir and bustle of preparation. Why do people have parties! You can send home for your clothes. You can't plead that old mill as an excuse at this time of day."

Trafford made a pretense of searching for his pipe. It freed his arm. There was a quizzical smile in his gray eyes as they met hers.

"Sorry, Pam, but I must go. In spite of your efforts for Cheever I have a hunch that the next time I see you I shall be senator elect from this district."

Carfax laid down his book and approached the group by the fire. "Ben has a hunch that he will. Each time he has won before it has been by finding a weak joint in his opponent's character." The words were totally underscored. "If he wins you had better try his tactics next year."

Trafford ignored the implication. "If he wins I'll try again, still without mud-slinging. I know at least five men like you, Dal, with plenty of brains, plenty of money, who could help enormously by going into politics. They won't do it. They won't subject themselves to the vilification which goes with a campaign. Perhaps if I demonstrate that it can be done without degrading personalities I may drum up recruits."

Even as he talked his mother's words, "She seemed a little startled at its contents," revolved in his mind. The note left at Shorehaven for Julie had been a brilliant pink. The note in his pocket must be a duplicate. If Willy Small had written both he must be desperately eager to reach the girl. Had he sent for her? The pressure on his heart lightened. At least she had not run away with Billy. He would open that note outside. If she had gone to meet Willy Small it would be wise to take someone with him when he followed her. He decided on the instant. He met Carfax's eyes and held them.

"I want to talk with you, Dal. Come out to the car."

"I'll get my coat." As Carfax started for the door Trafford called peremptorily:

"Hustle!"

His voice was strained. His mother's hand tightened on his arm. As her son's eyes met hers she gave it a tender pat and turned away. Martha Marshall left the throne-like chair which she affected. There was apprehension in her voice as she commanded:

"Find Julie before you do anything else, Jim. Under the affliction of Mercury by Luna and Neptune this day, she may be subject to subtle attacks and fraud. Of course with her alert and ready mind —"

Her prophetic tone clanged an alarm. Trafford interrupted with an inarticulate protest and bolted. He was furious that her words had power to frighten him. When he reached the roadster Carfax was waiting. His eyes were wary, his lips set obstinately. Without explanation Trafford tore open the pink envelope. His brows contracted, his face whitened as he read the contents.

"Fer the love of Mike, don't come to the mine ter-day." There was no signature but through the paper was thrust a barbed porcupine quill.

Julie had had an appointment to meet Small at the mine. He had warned her not to come. Had the note she received at Shorehaven contained the same message? What could it mean? Was the man attempting blackmail? Could she find her way there in this fog? Fog! Good Lord, this was the sort of day — with a sharp exclamation he thrust the pink envelope into his pocket and jumped into the roadster.

"Get in, Dal, quick!" He started the car before Carfax had dragged in his long legs.

"What's the rush, Jim?"

"I am anxious about Julie. I suspect that she has gone to Blue Heron Cove."

"My word, is that all? Why worry! Billy is with her. I'll bet a dozen golf balls that they have gone to the village for first-hand news of the election. Julie will go anywhere with him." His tone was deliberately casual as he added, "I have a hint from rather good authority that after today she will be free to go her own way all the time."

Trafford's jaw set like steel as he allowed Carfax's deliberate statement to pass unanswered. His motor-horn sounded hollowly in the still air as he bent forward to peer through the mist. His thoughts were in a turmoil. What had Dal meant? Had Julie told him that after the election the marriage was to be annulled? She would not do that, he was sure that she would not. Had Cheever begun to talk? Had his memory conveniently returned? Well, his enemy's conniving couldn't alter the fact that Julie was his, that he knew how to keep and protect his own. The thought lightened his voice as he replied to his companion's implication:

"It is dangerous to believe all you hear, Carfax. Did you ever see a thicker fog?"

"I suppose you know where you are going?" There was a biding-my-time tinge to Carfax's voice which twisted the corners of Trafford's lips.

"I do. I'm going to the copper-mine."

"To the copper-mine? You said that Julie had gone to the Cove. What the dickens would she be doing at the mine in this fog?"

"That is what I intend to find out. The thought frightens you too, I see. I don't know why she came but I suspect that Cheever —"

"Cheever!"

"What's that?" Trafford cut out his engine and listened. The two men sat like basilisks. Through the mist ahead of them drifted back the throb of a motor. Carfax unconsciously lowered his voice:

"It is a car. It can't be Julie. It isn't coming this way. It's running ahead of us. My word, you could chop hunks from this fog, it's so thick. What are you going to do now?" he demanded as Trafford drove into a field, shut off his engine and pulled two flash-lights from the pocket of the roadster.

"Take one of these, Dal. Fortunately I carry them to illumine sign-posts at night. We'll cover this field till we find some trace of Julie or are satisfied that she has not been here. That note you saw me read warned her not to come to the mine this afternoon. You know Julie. Had she a reason for coming she would come in the face of ten warnings."

"She would. But Billy is with her."

"I hope that he is but — it would be so like her to go it alone. I can't see more than three feet beyond my nose. Follow the line of shrubs on the left. I'll go to the right. If you find any trace of her or the sedan, shout. If you don't, we are bound to meet near the middle of the cliff. Keep close to the bushes. I have had the shaft openings in the field covered but I don't know what has been going on here of late. Move quietly. Let's go!"

Trafford cautiously skirted the field. He knew when he approached the promontory by the sound of water lapping the beach and the seaward swish of pebbles. He strained his ears for Carfax's call but no human sound broke the uncanny stillness. He must have reached the middle of the cliff, he decided. Should he wait for Dal to join him or keep on till they met? His foot struck something soft. He dropped to his knees. It was a slicker. Under it lay another oilskin with a soft violet hat crushed into the pocket.

Julie's! The other coat must be Jaffrey's. He was with her. Thank God! What had happened to them? Had they fallen over the cliff in the fog? Had they been pushed over?

"What have you found, Jim?"

Carfax dropped to the ground beside Trafford.

"Julie's slicker. This must be Billy's. They — Good Lord, what is this?"

He picked up the twine. Running with Carfax at his heels he followed its lead down the field. Twenty yards from the sumach bush they halted abruptly. They stared ahead at the mass which resembled nothing so much as a great prehistoric bird. Its bill had dug into the earth, its wings were crumpled, its ruptured belly had sprayed everything within radius with gasoline. Trafford's face was ghastly as he looked from the twine in his hand to the spot where it disappeared under the biplane.

"Good God, Dal! Can she — can Julie be under *that?*"

With one accord the two men furiously attacked the wreckage.

Chapter XXI

For one stunned instant as she looked up at the unwieldy shape crashing down upon her Julie was too frightened to move. Then she gripped the ring on the inside of the trap-door and drew it down as she swung to the steps which led underground. She slammed it shut and slid down the iron ladder. She clung to it and waited. Had she been dreaming or had she really seen that monstrous thing shooting straight for her? A crash above answered her question. She was awake. The force of the impact sent a portion of the dirt and rock wall crumbling to the sanded floor.

The girl felt as though her breath had been permanently suspended. Was she trapped in this hole? If she were she was not alone. Billy must be about somewhere. Had the pilot of the wrecked plane been killed? She listened. Except for the drip of water and the trip-hammer of her heart she could hear nothing. Billy had told her to whistle if anyone came but how could she whistle when she couldn't steady her lips?

She gripped the iron ladder. What should she do next? That was the identical question she had asked Jim Trafford after Cheever had left them in the cabin, she remembered. If only he were with her, if only his steadying arm were about her shoulders as it had been that night in the storm! She blinked her lashes furiously as she assured herself that she was not in the least frightened; it was merely what Billy had always ridiculed as her "congenital distrust" of the dark, plus the blackness of the hole into which she had plunged, plus that weird trickle of water. Plus — what *was* it?

The sound came from somewhere behind her. It was fainter than the drip-drip-drip, less measured, more human. Human, that was it. It was like a person breathing.

"Steady, Goldiocks, steady," she admonished herself in a mental intonation as much like Trafford's as she could manage. "You'll pull out of this mess if you keep your head. You know that you will. Didn't you get through those rapids safely?" After all, perhaps it was only Billy waiting for her to speak. The thought quieted her heart. She leaned a little forward as she whispered softly:

"Billy! *Billy!*"

There was no answer save her own voice

ricochetted back to her in elfin fragments.

She pressed her hand over her heart to still its thumping. It couldn't be Billy or he would have answered. Was the person behind her? Something had moved in the opposite corner. The place seemed full of eerie sounds, seemed peopled with furtive shapes. She might as well know first as last what she had to face. She bit her lips to steady them before she demanded in a tense whisper:

"Who are you?"

The walls batted her question back and forth like a shuttlecock, sent it weirdly through space to the accompaniment of dripping water.

"Who are you? Who are y-o-u—u-u?"

Fright gave way to indignation. Julie's mind cooled. Whoever was there might have had the decency to answer her question, she thought. If the person had been honest he would have done so. It behooved her to be prepared for a villain. She groped on the ground for a piece of the rock she had heard fall, for anything she could use as a missile. Instead of the rough granite she had expected she gripped a smooth, flat piece of lead. The feel of the stocky thing inspired courage. She gave it an experimental swing. It was not as heavy as she would have liked but properly administered it would crack what it struck, she was willing to wager. Her voice was steady, was grim with determination as she repeated:

"Who are you?" Her movie-unconscious or her adventure-unconscious prompted her to add theatrically:

"Answer or I'll shoot!"

The threat evoked a startled oath and the sharp scratch of a match. As the light flamed blue then orange Julie found herself gazing straight into the bleak eyes of Willy Small. His usually ruddy face had a purplish tinge as he demanded hoarsely:

"Fer the love of Mike! Whatcha doing here? Didn't yer git my warnin'?"

At the sound of his voice Julie's knees doubled like soda-straws when applied to hot chocolate. She clutched at the iron ladder. The billion or two icy prickles which had attacked her spinal column in solid formation at the scratching of the match melted into warm rills of pleasurable excitement. She had no fear of Small. He would help her assemble the fragments of mystery that she and Billy — Billy! Where was he? She clutched the man's frayed sleeve:

"Where is Mr. Jaffrey?"

"The writer feller? I don't know."

"But he came down here."

"When?"

The explosive quality of the question was a cross between a pistol shot and a blow-out.

"Just before I came. We found the trap-door and decided to investigate. When you did not meet me at the sumach bush —"

"Fer the love of Mike, I wrote yer not to come! I sent a line ter the Trafford place an' one to the big house on the chance that yer might not be to home."

"I must have left Brick House before your note came," Julie evaded. "But now that I am here won't you show me what you promised?"

The match had long before flickered out. The girl could taste and feel and smell the sea air. In spite of the fact that she could see nothing she had not the slightest fear of Small. She disliked the dark but —

"I don't know, ma'am, as I oughter. There's a chance thet the boss might come back, but if you want to risk it —"

"I do. But first we must find Mr. Jaffrey."

"Don't you worry about him, ma'am. The old mine has three tunnels an' they all open out in the side of the cliff. The worst thet could happen to him would be to step out sudden an' roll to the beach. Did he hev a light?"

"Yes."

"Then don't worry. He's all right unless —"

"Unless what?"

"Don't be scared. I was goin' ter say unless some of the gang come back, but that ain't probable; it ain't worth worryin' about." Breathing through his mouth as was his custom, Small lighted a miner's lamp of a bygone age. It reminded Julie of the shabby old lamp of Aladdin which his Princess sold to the wicked African magician.

"Now you foller close behind me an' —"

The girl's throat suddenly went dry. Her tongue felt several sizes too large for her parched mouth.

"Wait a minute, Willy. May I have a drink before we start?"

In answer Small moved toward the dripping spring. He knelt and set his lamp on the white sand. Its yellow light illumined the water which trickled down the rock wall into a shallow pool in a hollowed block of granite. From that it flowed in a thin stream across the sanded floor and disappeared into a mousehole-like opening in a rock.

The man dipped a tin and offered it brimming and dripping to Julie. She shifted her weapon of defense from her right hand to her left and took the cup. She drank thirstily. The water was ice-cold, crystal-clear, slightly brackish. She felt as though she had imbibed a magic potion. She was refreshed, she tingled with the flair for adventure, she was unafraid. She felt Small's bleak eyes regarding her. His voice creaked as he warned:

"Don't make a sound, ma'am. I'm takin' a chance, showin' you things here. My boss acted kinder queer ter-day, kinder as though he suspected me of double-crossin' him. Listen, if you see or hear anyone when we git to the big dugout, run into one of the openin's there an' keep a-goin' till you git to daylight."

"I understand, Willy. If you get out first you'll find the bone for Hooch in my car."

"Thank you, ma'am, I'm glad you didn't fergit it. When I heard — well, I took the dog down to Snow's place an' tied him so he wouldn't be in the way ter-day. Don't speak after we start. These old tunnels is reg'lar megyphones. Ready?"

Julie's voice balked in her throat. She nodded. Her wet frock twisted about her knees as she followed Small. The piece of lead she still carried in her left hand was heavy but she liked the sense of preparedness the feel of it radiated through her nerves. Should she have told Willy that they could not get out the way she had come in, she wondered. The biplane must be wrecked on the ground above the trap-door.

The billion or more icy prickles mobilized again as the girl followed the man's crab-like advance down two steps into a tunnel. Its sides were shored with great timbers. The fresh air suggested kelp and the sea. It seemed as though she groped on for miles before they entered a lighter, more airy space which had been broadened to the dimensions of a good-sized room.

Small stopped so suddenly that Julie collided with him. He flashed his light slowly about the walls. It illuminated a few decrepit wheelbarrows, rusty picks, portions of cable, sections of lead pipe and wooden benches piled waist high with bulky bundles covered with black enamel cloth.

What could the packages be, Julie puzzled. She had been prepared to find the place lined with casks and bottles but there were none, nothing but those funereal but harmless appearing black things. She looked at Willy and raised her brows in inquiry. He laid his finger on his lips and set the lamp on a wheelbarrow. His ragged sneakers made no sound as he crept toward the wall. With a huge pocket-knife of the old-trusty type he cut the cords which bound the black bundles. He slit perhaps a dozen before he threw back the enamel covers and with dexterous flourishes, of the drama of which he was quite unconscious, ruffled the contents of each into a miniature mountain.

Julie brushed her hand across her eyes. Was she dreaming a fairy story? Silks, bolts and bolts of glistening silks were heaped before her. The green of emeralds, the pink of tourmalines, the red of rubies, the blue of turquoise, of sapphires and aquamarines, the yellow of topaz, the violet of amethysts made the dull place glow like the jewel heaped cave of Aladdin. The color blazed and shimmered in the dim light. Small tiptoed back to her with his lantern.

"Seen enough?"

"Where did they come from?" Julie's question was a mere breath. She bent her head near the man's to hear his whispered answer.

"From the big cities. It's stole, most of it. All kinds and colors. It's sold across the line fer less than the stores can import it."

"Silk-smugglers!"

"Huh, you've said it. The men who come few this don't take no chance on anything else."

"Who is the brains of this enterprise, Willy?" Small raised his voice the merest trifle.

"I've shown yer the stuff, that evens up what yer did fer Hooch. I ain't sayin' nothin' about nothin' else. The rest is up to you."

Conjecture, doubt of the soundness of her conjecture, suspicion, conviction jostled each other out of line in the girl's mind. Her eyes questioned the eyes which weren't so bleak now before they feasted at the banquet of gorgeous color so lavishly spread against the dark walls. Did Jim know of this traffic going on in his mine? Did Captain Phin? Was that why Snow had discoursed on the evils of bootlegging till The Trafford had signaled, "Stop!"? Had they been testing Cheever? Silk-smuggling! No wonder the suspected one had been calm. What had he to do with so sordid an occupation as the one being flayed by the old fisherman? Who would — What was that sound? Julie gripped Small's sleeve. Her heart tripped up her voice as she whispered:

"Lis— listen, Willy!"

"Cr-runch! Cr-unch! Cr-runch!"

The man and girl stood tense, motionless. Was it the sound of gravel under a cautious foot? The light from the old lamp faintly illumined shadowy niches in the walls. The black bundles assumed gruesome significance. Small turned the light so that it shone on the mouth of a tunnel, on another, on still another. Julie met the man's curious eyes. She bent her head to his in answer to their speechless summons. She could barely hear his jerky warning:

"It's the boss! I thought he was trailin' me. Don't git frightened. Beat it soon's yer find which way he's comin'."

Julie nodded. She motioned toward the right-hand opening. The sound seemed to have come from the passage on the left. There it was again!

"Cr-runch! Cr-runch! Cr-runch!"

The sound reminded Julie of a play in which the tramp, tramp, tramp of an avenging god was heard at intervals off stage. The implacable Nemesis never appeared but the sinister sound of his footsteps worked the audience into a state of suspense bordering on hysteria. She wished now, as she had wished then, that the baleful influence would pounce and end it. She was not frightened, she assured herself, but she had a sense of the quick closing in of captivity.

Her eyes flashed to Small's. He nodded. She measured the distance to the right-hand opening and as he dropped the lamp to the ground she made a dash for the tunnel. Before she could reach it she crashed into something big and bulky and human, something which caught her and clapped a hand over her mouth.

"Unless some of the gang come back!" Willy's words racketed through her mind. The gang! They shouldn't stop her from broadcasting the news of their enterprise. With all her force Julie brought the leaden missile she had clung to like a life-preserver down on the head bent above hers. She shivered at the impact but the arm about her loosened and whoever had gripped her slid to the ground. Her heart contracted. What had she done! Had she broken open a head? No matter what happened now she wouldn't leave a human being helpless in the dark.

"Willy! Willy! Bring the lamp!" she called frantically.

"Allow me," the words came from somewhere behind her and the place blazed with light. For an instant the glare blinded Julie, then as her vision cleared she looked toward the voice. Cheever stood smiling indulgently at her. "The Boss," of course. She had expected that. She stared at him wide-eyed. Had he come back to meet his gang or had he suspected — who — who had she struck? For an instant she closed her eyes then with teeth set hard in her lower lip she looked down. She caught at her throat to choke back her cry of horror.

Billy Jaffrey lay at her feet.

Chapter XXII

"Billy! Billy!"

With the sobbed appeal Julie dropped to her knees beside the still figure. She lifted Jaffrey's head to her lap and examined it with tender, skilful fingers. One side of it seemed to have mushroomed but the skin was not broken. She breathed a fervent thanksgiving. For an impulsive instant she pressed her cheek against her pal's red hair. If anything had happened to Billy — the thought contracted her heart unbearably. She must get him out to the air, quickly! How? She looked about. The light came from two rusty old lanterns set in dark corners. Electricity! The c-curious l-luminous mist at the mouth of the cave! Who would have suspected it? Her glance came back to the man standing near. It lingered on his feet and as though magnetically drawn crept up and up until it met his eyes. Where she had expected triumph she saw only maddening commiseration. What did it mean? Was he posing?

Julie flamed with anger. How dared he assume that patronizing expression, how dared he? He must know that now she had information which would wreck his career. Of course he was the brains of this infamous smuggling business. Hadn't Small said that the "boss" was coming? Where was Willy? He must have made his escape thinking that she was safely on her way through the right-hand tunnel.

Julie laid Jaffrey's head gently on the ground and sprang to her feet. The light behind her transmuted her tumbled hair into a sort of halo, her not blue, not violet eyes were black with earnestness, her cheeks were pink with excitement. Her musical voice was like a tree-harp roughly shaken by an angry breeze as she derided:

"What a habit you have of making dramatic entrances, Mr. Cheever!" Then as he lifted his brows in questioning surprise she added, "I forgot that you had lost your memory. Well, shall we come to terms about this —" She shrugged and looked suggestively at the colorful heaps of silks which gleamed in the light. The man's eyes followed hers. Instead of the anger she was prepared to combat with damning facts they darkened with sympathy; his voice dripped regret as he exclaimed:

"*Terms!* My dear girl, my *dear* girl, you can't

293

bluff me. I shall be sorry to drag your name into it but it is my duty as a public servant to make this enterprise of Jim's —"

"*Jim's!*"

"The horror in your tone is extremely well done. I'm sorry but it doesn't get by. I've suspected that something phony was going on here. Now I know it. This afternoon I saw the dories steal in and steal out laden. I saw you and Jaffrey on the cliff."

Julie felt as though she were in the grip of a nightmare. The grieved conviction of the man's voice and manner clutched at her heart. Did he believe his preposterous suggestion? He couldn't. What sane person would for an instant accuse Jim Trafford of anything so despicable? She didn't give a thought to his accusation of Jaffrey and herself. She rallied her courage. Hadn't Jim said that Cheever was a consummate bluffer? Her light laugh was a triumph of will over words.

"You are a more finished actor even than I thought you, Mr. Cheever, but you can't put that stuff across. I know that yours is the brain behind this smuggling enterprise."

The man shrugged, drew a cigarette from his pocket, slowly tapped it against his thumb-nail, slowly drew a match against the sole of his shoe. His deliberation maddened the girl. How long did he think he could impose upon her, how long, she demanded of herself feverishly. The flare reflected in his eyes seemed like leaping imps of flame. His tone was indulgent as he inquired:

"If it were do you think I would use another man's mine? Ask the owner of this property how this stuff came here if — if you do not know, but you do, don't you?"

At his question a bit of catch-phrase advertising giggled hysterically through the girl's mind.

"This boy knows the answer. Do you?"

Julie fought back an hysterical desire to laugh till she cried. Heavens, she hoped that her nerves weren't giving way! The thought steadied her. She looked straight up into the eyes above her. Hers smoldered but her voice was under control as she accused:

"Cheat! Liar! *Smuggler!*"

There was the lightest pressure against her foot. She looked down. Had Billy stirred? No, his eyes were half-open as they had been when she had laid him down. She had forgotten him in the surprise of Cheever's accusation. Had she been wise she would have propitiated the man and prettily begged his help to get Billy up into the air. Was it too late now? Her flicker of hope went out like a snuffed candle as she met Cheever's eyes. They were all flame but his voice was suave.

"You'll take that back when the news of this smuggling business of Jim's gets round. However, every man has his price and I don't claim to be better than the average. If you don't want the story broadcasted at Mrs. Marshall's reception tonight —"

"To-night!" Julie interrupted incredulously. Was it still to-day, she marveled. She felt as though she had been underground for centuries. Would Cheever accuse Jim at Managing Martha's reception? Who would believe his story if he did? As many as would believe her counter-charge against their present senator, her common sense scoffed. She fenced for time.

"What story?"

Cheever considered her from beneath frowning brows.

"The story that he has been backing a nice fat smuggling proposition. Those silks are not the only proofs I can present. The men whom you and Jaffrey directed this afternoon in their loading were caught with the goods out by Old Man Grindle."

Jaffrey and she! The girl's eyes widened in horrified incredulity. The man's tone was so convincing that almost he made her believe that in some psychic aberration she had superintended the loading of those boats. Where had they been caught? Like a caption on a screen the girl's mind flashed the muffled command from the beach:

"Tell Jones to pick up Old Man Grindle and stand by!"

Evidently Old Man Grindle had double-crossed his boss. Who was his boss? Cheever's impersonal coolness had shaken her belief that he was. If he were not, why should he be so determined to fix the guilt on Trafford? Mud-slinging, of course. In spite of Small's warning, for the first time since Cheever had appeared at the garden gate of Brick House she believed that he had forgotten that episode in the cabin. She had tried to lull herself into a feeling of security but all the time there had been a doubt pricking. If he really had remembered that he would not abandon that bit of yellow-press news if he wanted to stunt Jim's political growth.

Julie set the teeth of her determination. The Dragon-slayer who was fighting to liberate the imprisoned princess Clean Politics shouldn't be vanquished if she could help. Her mind feverishly suggested and rejected compromises as she asked scornfully:

"Would you fight your opponent with this contemptible weapon?"

Cheever's more-in-sorrow-than-in-anger tone was a perfect thing of its kind.

"Contemptible weapon! Isn't it my duty to

the voters to let them know the character of their nominee? Suppose I kept quiet and a newspaper came out with the glaring headlines, 'Apostle of Clean Politics Turns Out to Be a Smuggler!' Do you get the comedy of that? However, as I suggested before every man has his price and I don't claim to be above the average. If you will promise to throw The Trafford over and give me a —"

"She won't, Cheever," contradicted a cool voice from the shadow.

"Jim! Oh, *Jim!*"

The exultant cry broke in a sob of excitement, as Trafford flung a steadying arm about her shoulders the girl hid her face against his sleeve.

"Steady, Goldilocks, steady!" He cleared his voice of huskiness before he faced Cheever who had his head clutched in both hands as he stared at him. The senator's voice was a hoarse whisper as he derided:

"Well, I'll be damned! Now I remember! I remember the cabin! I remember the girl's saying you were married! And you married her! Lord, but she was clever. She got the richest man —"

"Cheever, if you finish that sentence I'll break every bone in your body."

It seemed to Julie that the arm against which she leaned turned to iron; that Cheever

298

shifted personalities before her eyes. It was as though he had ordered the self speaking to "Right about face! March!" before his other self apologized in a voice which patted Trafford on the shoulder:

"I should deserve the punishment. Good old quixotic Jim! Forgive me; that was the before-the-accident Ben speaking." Trafford ignored his explanation.

"What are you doing in my mine, Cheever? Can't you read those no-trespassing signs?"

"Yes, I can read. I can also deduct. Now you've touched upon a subject upon which my duty as a citizen forbids my being lenient. I was just telling *Mrs.* Trafford that I shall have a thrilling bit of entertainment to contribute to Mrs. Marshall's reception to-night."

"Why spoil the party, Ben? Before evening we shall know who has won. If you have, be magnanimous."

Julie clutched Jim Trafford's arm. Was he placating the man in that smooth voice, with a smile in the depths of his eyes? The nightmare theory revived in the girl's mind. But she wasn't dreaming. It was all incredibly true, as true as those gleaming silks against the wall. Cheever seemed as astounded as she. The sanctimonious droop of his mouth inspired by the thought of his civic duty had been succeeded by a slightly dropped chin. He recovered his poise quickly:

"Magnanimous! I should be unworthy to hold office if I kept my constituents in the dark as to this blot on the town. It hurts me to do it, Jim, but I am warning you so that you can stay away from the party. Julie had —"

"Cut that out, Cheever!"

Trafford's voice was hoarse with fury as he chopped into the man's sentence. Two steady flames had supplanted the smile in his eyes as he stepped in front of the girl. She had no fault to find with his manner now. It breathed fire.

"Broadcast your story to-night if you think it advisable, Cheever, but if you do, I'll come back with this."

Trafford pulled a roll from his pocket and displayed a map thumbed and frayed about the edges. The flicker of an eyelash could have been heard in the silence as Cheever stared at the red and black lines which crisscrossed its surface. He met Trafford's steady eyes. With an inarticulate oath he grabbed for the betraying map. Someone caught him by the knees and threw him flat. It was Jaffrey. Jaffrey who dropped heavily back on the waist-line of his victim. His beatific grin was slightly denatured with pain as he observed jauntily:

"So this is Maine!"

300

Chapter XXIII

Jaffrey's voice roused Julie from the comatose state into which his sudden activity had plunged her. Regardless of the treachery of the heaving seat on which he perched she flung her arms about his neck and whispered brokenly:

"Billy dear! I never knew until I thought I'd killed you how much I cared!"

"Holy smoke! Have I been reincarnated in a dog? I never have I seen you grieved over a male human before, Marble-heart." Jaffrey's chuckle could not quite disguise the honest emotion in his voice.

"Let him up, Billy!"

Trafford's command was a growl. Jaffrey made a futile attempt to rise and dropped back with an abandon which jounced a howl of anguish from his victim and brought a furious protest from Trafford. As he got to his feet Cheever rolled in a most unstatesmanlike manner from under and sprang to his. He glared at the three standing against a parti-colored background of silks. The purple anger of his face, the fury of his eyes were burlesqued by the fragment of dry kelp which dangled in the middle of his forehead with the engaging juvenility of a Kewpie curl. It brought a sparkle to Julie's eyes which was struck out as he started for a tunnel exit. Would Jim let him go without making him deny his lies?

Trafford rolled up the map and thrust it into his coat pocket. Cheever smiled compassionately.

"That's right, Jim. Take care of it. Its possession will prove just one more nail in your professional coffin, my friend."

The black maw of the tunnel gulped him. The three left behind stood motionless as the "Cr-runch! Cr-runch! Cr-runch!" of footsteps grew fainter and fainter and diminished to a mere sign of sound, then silence. Jaffrey gripped Trafford's arm and protested hotly:

"Jim, are you going to stand for that accusation of smuggling? There is such a thing as being principle-logged. Boy! I had you sized up as a fire-eater and you let him get away with a bluff like that."

"Billy, if I can keep this disgraceful affair from publicity I'm willing for a time to let Cheever think I'm scared. The proper authorities will be informed but why blazon from coast to coast the fact that a man climbing the political ladder is a blackguard? Cheever won't dare accuse me but if he does try to bluff this situation on to me, and there is bound to be a sensation anyway, I'll come back with this map. Indicated on it as a distributing station for silks is this mine and Cheever's cabin as a place where the pilot of the plane was to drop information. That last fact will fix the responsibility. Come on, we must get Julie home. We'll go out the cliff opening."

"Shall I cover these gorgeous silks, Jim?"

"Don't touch them, Julie. Give me your hand. The way out is rough."

When the three emerged from the tunnel halfway up the cliff it was dusk. The fog was crouching back before the glow of the setting sun, the sea was opaque gray glass. High overhead a flock of geese in wedge formation honked their way south. The western sky was crimson. The reflection delicately tinted the girl's face, gilded her hair as she strained her eyes oceanward.

"Can you see boats? Cheever said that Old Man Grindle was holding them as evidence against you, Jim."

"Said *who* was?"

"Old Man Grindle."

Jaffrey's shout of laughter sent his hand to his head.

"Boy, that hurts. You swing a wicked right, Marble-heart. Cheever said that the boats had been caught out by Old Man Grindle. Old Man Grindle is a buoy on the ledges."

"Did you see the boats, Jaffrey?"

"I heard them, Jim. After they pulled out I bored into the mine to investigate. Just before Julie caromed into me I had heard stealthy footsteps. I thought that the boatman had come back. I clapped my hand over her mouth to prevent her making a sound when behold, I saw a great company of stars a-shooting. I dropped to prevent another attack of staritis."

"I thought that you were one of the gang, Billy."

"The light flashed before I had a chance to speak. As you seemed to be handling the situation plus Cheever with your usual efficiency I reclined and humored my thumping head till I should be needed. I flatter myself that my neat bit of interference reflects credit on my half-back days."

When they reached level ground the three made their way cautiously across the field in the moist dimness. Everywhere cobwebs like spun glass glittered pinkly in the sunset reflection. When they reached Carfax and the roadster Julie looked about her.

"Where is the sedan?"

"I have a suspicion that the pilot of the bi-plane is speeding toward Canada and safety in it."

"Is it possible that he wasn't hurt?"

"Apparently not so seriously that he couldn't make his get-away. If you plan to attend that reception to-night you'll all have to hustle. Sit next to Julie, Billy. Carfax, you adorn the running-board till we drop you at Shorehaven. All set?"

Trafford eased in the clutch. Julie stole a glance at him as with creases deep between his eyes he turned into the highway. He had asked no questions as to her presence in the mine. Why, she wondered. She wondered more after they had dropped the two men at the gates of Shorehaven. Her companion preserved a stern silence till they entered the hall at Brick House.

"Wait in the study till I come back, Julie. I have something to say to you."

"But, Jim, it is late. I told Aunt Martha that I would be with her early and I must dress. Look at me!"

Like a modiste's model she pivoted for inspection. Her once dainty frills were damaged beyond redemption, her heliotrope frock was crumpled and stained, a smooch accentuated the dimple in her chin, the pupils of her eyes were like dark pools, her face was flushed a delicate pink. Trafford's eyes lingered on her but for an instant.

"I won't keep you long. I want the curtains put on the roadster before we start for Shorehaven."

The girl hesitated then entered the study. Through the long windows she could see the bank of fog which hung on the horizon line of the bay. The stillness of the house dramatized the ticking of the old clock. She lighted the lamp on the desk, and looked about the room which she rarely entered. Always she thought of it as the dragon-slayer's stronghold in which unruly captives might be disciplined. The one bit of wall space not covered by books was the panel over the mantel in which was set the portrait of a white-haired Trafford in high stock and blue coat with brass buttons. The eyes under shaggy brows regarded the girl with the same relentlessness which had characterized his descendant a few moments before.

What could Jim have to say to her which was of such importance, Julie wondered uneasily. Would he — would he attempt — She pressed her hand against her eyes as she felt again the pressure of his lips on hers.

"Oh-h," her passionate protest was transmuted into a soft whistle as Trafford entered. The gay little air evaporated into silence. His face was white. Instinctively the girl edged behind a large chair. A wraith of a smile flitted across the man's stern lips.

"You won't need that bulwark to-night, Julie. Sit down. I want to talk to you."

"I prefer to hear what you have to say standing. You intend to scold about this afternoon, I suppose. How did you know where I was?" Her tone was ablaze with righteous indignation. If one could put one's inquisitor in the wrong one had the strategic advantage, she remembered.

"I opened a note in which you were warned not to go to the mine to-day. I suspected that Small was attempting blackmail."

"No, *no!* Willy is my friend."

"*Your* friend? He is Cheever's right-hand man. Didn't Ben appear soon after your arrival?"

"Yes, but Willy had nothing to do with that. Do you believe that Cheever's memory suddenly returned in the mine while he was talking to us?"

"Don't worry about that, Julie. His lies can't hurt us now. I didn't ask you to wait that I might 'scold' about this afternoon, I am too thankful that you are safe. I asked you to meet me here for tea because I wanted to give you these."

From a drawer in the desk he produced a

velvet case, opened it and held it toward the girl. With a low cry of incredulity Julie caught his wrist. From their white satin bed innumerable blue sparks blinked up at her.

"The sapphires of the Duchess!"

"A reproduction. You remember I told you that I was having them copied."

"How perfect and how beautiful."

"Take them. They are for you. I thought you might like to wear them to-night."

Julie shrank as though the blue flames from the Kashmir sapphires had scorched her.

"No, oh no. I couldn't."

"As you like." Trafford's face was a degree whiter as he snapped the case shut and dropped it to the desk. "Now, Julie, I want the truth —"

"You don't intend to leave the sapphires there, do you? The doors and windows of this house are almost never locked."

"There is no need of locking them in this village. Stop fencing for time, Julie; we'll have this out now. When you threw your arms about Jaffrey in the mine I knew that you loved him. You do, don't you?"

He hurled the question. Surprise sent a wavering pink to the girl's hair. She gazed dumbly at her interlaced fingers. Her confusion seemed confession. Trafford's voice was rough with repression.

"Your silence is answer enough. As you have repeatedly reminded me, our marriage was but an emergency measure. The only course for me is to arrange for its annulment that you may marry Jaffrey."

Marry Jaffrey! For an instant Julie saw green shot through with wriggly red flashes. She shut her teeth over a surge of protest. Jim was humiliatingly eager to hand her over to Billy. Had Cheever been right in his hateful insinuation? Had Trafford married her out of sheer quixotism? Pamela had intimated that too. Did they really believe that money had tempted her? Well, he shouldn't think that she cared.

For the first time in her life Julie employed one of those uncopyrighted methods girls have invented to make a man furiously conscious that he counts but as a super in her life, a creature to be endured but not enjoyed. Her eyes were the blue of the Duchess' sapphires, her cheeks were as pink as the heart of a Russell rose, her voice was honey-sweet as she murmured:

"Billy will be pleased, of course." Again for the first time in her life she experimented with coquetry. She glanced up at Trafford with alluring provocative eyes as she dared:

"Perhaps had I met you first —" The sentence dangled for him to finish as he liked.

She dropped her eyelashes as she had seen her sisters drop theirs. She had just time to assure herself that for a first attempt she had done exceedingly well when Nemesis descended. Trafford caught her in his arms.

"What do you mean by looking at me like that, Julie?"

Frightened at the tempest she had roused the girl wrenched herself free. Panic and resentment fought for supremacy in her voice as she backed away from him and reminded:

"Have you forgotten so soon that I am in love with Billy?"

With a furious ejaculation Trafford turned and left the room. Bewildering emotion flooded Julie's heart as she looked after him.

"Why did you answer him like that?" she arraigned herself fiercely. Why had she allowed Jim Trafford to go thinking that she was in love with Billy? Billy was a dear, but she would no more marry him than she would marry Dal Carfax. Dal! He seemed to have lost his common sense too. Why, oh why, couldn't men remain friends with a girl? Love spoiled everything. It opened Pandora's box and loosed a multitude of worries and heartaches and disappointments. She could have been perfectly happy at Brick House with Jim had he remained the friend he knew so well how to be. Now she would have to go away at once and she had begun to hope —

Go away! The thought which she had hugged to her heart through the first days at Brick House now tore it to shreds. A sense of unreasoning panic shocked the color from her face. She stood motionless, her violet eyes gazing unseeingly out into the dusk.

"Silly!" she flouted herself softly. "Silly, not to know that you were in love with Jim Trafford after seeing five sisters through hectic affairs."

Realization set her pulses hammering. Ought she to play fair and tell Jim? No — no, not yet. Perhaps in a year — in six months — when she was tired of thinking only of herself she might — she refused to think the situation out to its conclusion.

An excited voice in the hall startled her back to the present. Was it news of the election? Jim's passionate accusation, the emotional tide of her own discovery had submerged all else. She ran through the living-room. She collided with Phineas Snow who caught her by the shoulders and exulted:

"Here comes the sun! Julie, Jim's elected!"

"Really, Captain Phin! Does he know?"

The fire died down in Snow's eyes and voice.

"I told him, jest a minute ago. But he didn't seem to care a hang."

A guilty color reddened the girl's cheeks.

"Oh, but he does. He will. Did Cheever get many votes?"

"He did, mark-my-words, it was a close call. He held his voters back till the last minute, and Jim's friends jest sweatin' blood to know what was comin'. That was what made the returns so late. Ben thought he'd swamp Jim, but he didn't. Won't there be great doin' at Mrs. Marshall's party tonight?" For the first time he sensed the girl's appearance. His jaw dropped, his glassy eyes bulged like marbles. "Gorry-me, you ain't goin' in thet rig, are you?"

"Of course not, Captain Phin."

"Then put on the prettiest dress you got, Julie. Remember you're a senator's wife now. Why don't you wear them sapphires Jim signed up fer me to bring? I guess if the townspeople once saw them on you — they think you're all right, Julie — the roamin' Duchess would be set back hard in her frame fer keeps."

Julie cast a startled glance at the royal lady above the mantel. Her breath came in a sudden gasp of excitement, her eyes gleamed with laughter as she whispered:

"I'll wear them, Captain Phin. Don't tell anyone. Take Sarah to Shorehaven and come back for me —"

Snow swelled slightly:

"But I've got to dress myself, Julie. I've got some new —"

"Then come after you're dressed, that's a dear. And tell Jim that I am going with you — that I *prefer* to go with you."

"But, Julie —"

"Don't argue. Hurry!"

She waited until he grumbled his way into the hall before she flashed into the study. She caught up the case of jewels. Back in the living-room she opened it. The blue stones caught the light as like a votive offering she held them beneath the cynical eyes of the Duchess. Her low voice thrilled as she whispered:

"Here are your sapphires. The prophecy has come true. Those shining knights, Love and Fame, and Wealth, attend The Trafford."

Chapter XXIV

As Jim Trafford entered the hall at Shorehaven the musicians in the minstrel gallery
were playing for the benefit of the dancers in
the living-room. A baritone voice caught up
the air and sang the refrain:

> "You remind me of my mother
> When Mother was a girl like you;
> You look a lot alike you two.
> Her hair was just as fair, her eyes, too,
> Twinkled just the same as your eyes do.
> You remind me of my mother
> That's why I — love — you."

The wistful sweetness of the man's voice
crumbled the barrier Trafford had set against
his thoughts since he had fled the study, furious with heartache and anger. They swarmed
back. Memories of his admiration of the un-
known girl on the train, the evening in the
cabin, the days in his house when Julie had
been boyishly friendly except when she had

met his eyes, then she had colored adorably and he had hoped —

Why think of that now? Had he not heard her remorseful cry: "Billy dear, I never knew until I thought I had killed you how much I cared!"

She had sacrificed herself for him, for his ideals, and now that he had won, the least he could do was to set her free at the first opportunity. Won! How little his victory meant to him. How could he let her go? It would be like tearing his heart out by the roots. She was so sweet, so true, so altogether lovable.

He made a desperate effort to free his senses from the girl's pervasive charm and personality and looked about him. The house was alive with guests even to the second balcony off which opened the radio-room and the glassed-in apartment from which Martha Marshall observed the stars. Many were dancing, more were chatting in the great hall, couples were twosing on the enclosed verandas which were lighted by silk lanterns that glowed like precious stones. Groups hovered near the dining-room sniffing the aroma of coffee and casting furtive glances at the cakes and rolls in appetizing profusion which could be glimpsed through the open doors.

Trafford's heart warmed. These were his people and what a fine type they were. To-day they had shown their confidence in him. He must make good for them. He would. He would not allow his love for a girl who did not love him to bankrupt his life.

A smile flashed in his eyes as he observed the recently deposed postmaster who looked like a prize-fighter and talked like a professor glaring across the hall at his successor who looked like a professor and talked like a prize-fighter. The selectmen stood in an aloof group. A realization of their importance gave a pouter-pigeon puff to their waistcoats, their run-to-weed eyebrows frowned above eyes which scanned the beautiful hall with an appraising, we-must-raise-her-taxes glint in their depths.

In spite of the intolerable ache in his heart Trafford laughed as his glance fell on Phineas Snow. The Captain was attired in a belted suit of juvenile style and checker-board design. His glittering patent leathers might have been responsible for his heron-like posture as at half-minute intervals he drew one leg up under him and balanced precariously on the other foot. The outstanding feature of his festal array was his teeth, of startling whiteness, of standardized regularity. That they were a trifle unsettled in their strange quarters was evidenced by the restlessness of their owner's jaws. Apparently Snow had run up a flag of truce for the occasion for he was listening to Sarah Beddle. The housekeeper's stand-alone black taffeta clashed with jet at every movement, her cheeks were beacons of color.

Directly across the hall from the great stairway, on the steps which led to the cloister, which in turn led to the garden, stood Martha Marshall receiving her guests. The closed casement door behind her made an artistic background for her stately figure. Against the silver of her gown her priceless pearls gleamed softly. Near her stood Pamela Parkman in a cerise frock which accentuated the whiteness of her skin, the lacquered blackness of her hair and brows. She was listening to Carfax but her glance wandered restlessly about the hall.

What consideration would she mete out to the defeated candidate, Trafford wondered. He turned as his mother touched him lightly on the arm.

"Jim, come into the morning-room with me. I have been lying in wait to seize you, before you were surrounded. Everyone in the village is here from the town fathers to freckled Pete Sparks who is enthusiastically acting as self-appointed guide to the observatory and radio-room."

As they entered a small room, small only in

a relative sense, Anne Trafford caught his hands in hers:

"Jim dear, I am so happy that you have won. We lived through hours of maddening suspense this afternoon while waiting for returns. The situation was not eased by Martha Marshall's half-hourly reminder that under the affliction of Mercury by Luna and some other old planet this day, you, as well as Julie, were subject to subtle attacks and fraud."

Her eyes laughed up at him but Trafford saw the quick rush of tears before she pressed her lips to his sleeve and said softly:

"I am so proud of you, Jim."

Her son rested his cheek against her satin hair. He struggled to keep his voice light as he reminded:

"Mother, one might think from your jubilation and Captain Phin's that I had been elected to the presidency. I feel bound to remind you that I am but an humble state senator."

Anne Trafford blinked her lashes and laughed with him.

"I know, dear, but it isn't the distance you have run already that counts, it is the force and principle which you have within you that will keep you going up. Have you seen Julie? She is a picture in her pearl-beaded white

318

frock. Was there ever a lovelier bride, I wonder?"

"Don't, Mother."

Trafford's voice was hoarse as he turned to
examine a water-color on the wall. Anne
Trafford slipped her hand under his arm.

"What has happened, dear?"

"Julie loves Jaffrey."

"Of course she loves him, but as she would
love a brother. Why should you imagine anything more serious?"

"She acknowledged it. She would not drive
over with me to-night. She sent a message by
Snow that she preferred to go with him."

"I know that. She 'phoned me that she was
coming with the Captain."

"Telephoned you! Why?"

"Oh, a little detail of dress. You know we
women consult one another oc-ca-sionally."

The last word was mischievously drawled.
There was suppressed excitement in the tone.
The laughter in Anne Trafford's eyes was
dangerously akin to tears, her tender lips were
unsteady. What had happened, her son wondered. Something more than his election or
Julie's perfection was responsible for her
emotion. He caught her by the shoulders.

"Mother —"

"Have you told him, Anne?"

Major Thomas Buell effectually blocked

the door with his broad shoulders as he asked the question in a whisper which could have been heard in the rear rank of a battalion. The expression of his eyes gave Trafford the sensation of having glanced inadvertently into a holy of holies. He encircled his mother with his arms.

"You needn't tell me. I know. You have promised to marry the Major!"

"Who told you?"

"He, just now. Not in words, with his eyes. A man looks like that only when he attains his heart's desire."

"I should not have said 'Yes' had you not had Julie, Jim."

Trafford flinched as though his heart had suddenly been run through a wringer.

"Even if I hadn't Julie, Mother, I shouldn't allow you to sacrifice the rest of your life to me."

Jaffrey ducked under the Major's barricading arm and burst into the room. His face was almost as white as his shirt-front, his green eyes snapped, his red hair reared, his voice rumbled with excitement as he commanded:

"Jim, come out of here, quick! Cheever has asked Aunt Martha if he may say a few words of greeting to her guests! His defeat has made him flaming mad and Pam has fed the fire by snubbing him." He gulped and wiped his hot forehead.

"Where is Julie?"

"Up-stairs dressing."

"Dressing! I thought —"

"Don't stop to think, Jim! Come out!" rushed Jaffrey. "You won't let Cheever speak, will you?"

"Why not? Mother, go to Julie. Keep her upstairs until I send for her. Come on, Billy. Let's hear what the silver-tongued orator has to say." He put his hand into his breast pocket to make sure that the rolled map was secure before he led the way from the room.

The hall was full of expectant guests. Trafford and Jaffrey stopped outside the morning-room door. On their right the great staircase curved to the balcony; on their left Cheever leaned against the casement door at the top of the steps which Mrs. Marshall had graciously ceded to him. Trafford was reminded of the night his political opponent had backed against the door of a cabin. Then his expression had been malevolent; to-night it was one of condescending indulgence.

As Cheever began to speak Trafford watched the effect of his words on the faces about him. The defeated candidate expressed the usual appreciation of the support of his constituency, handed a few bouquets of artificial compliments to his successor, then with a quick change to confidential appeal he leaned forward:

"But before you congratulate yourselves on acquiring a new representative in the state senate, I suggest that you ask the gentleman if there are no — well — say — shadowy corners in his life. Ask him —" the speaker paused for dramatic effect.

"He's after you, Jim. Come back at him with that map," exploded Jaffrey in an excited whisper. Trafford clutched his arm to silence him as Cheever continued:

"Ask him to entertain you with an account of his melodramatic plunge into matrimony. Ask him —"

"Good *God!*"

Cheever hesitated at the hoarse interruption. He had flung his words at his listeners with such rapidity that Trafford had been caught in a maze of incredulity. He had expected an accusation of smuggling instead — "Good God!" he repeated as he wrenched himself loose from Jaffrey's clutch. Billy caught and held him with a choked:

"Wait a *minute,* Jim! Just a *minute!* Look! *Look!*"

The effect of his excited whisper spread in widening circles like the ripples from a pebble dropped into a still pool. Faces which had

322

been turned toward Cheever in amazed attention whitened or reddened in startled unbelief as they followed Jaffrey's eyes. The hall settled into the stillness of the palace of the Sleeping Beauty upon which an evil fairy had cast her spell as a woman ran half-way down the great stairway.

It was the Duchess of the portrait! The Duchess in blue satin and gold brocade, with a black spaniel under one arm and a sapphire bow against the braids of fair hair wound about her head, sapphires at her ears, sapphire buttons on her pointed bodice and the diamond setting of a great sapphire flashing on her finger.

Trafford brushed his hand across his eyes. Was he dreaming? Had excitement turned his brain? Could that be the Duchess? Of course not! It was Julie! Julie wearing the costume his mother had had made for the fancy-dress ball and the sapphires he had given her. The girl on the stairs held up her hand. A golden thread of camaraderie ran through the velvet of her voice as she pleaded:

"Don't be frightened, please. It is only I, Julie. Jim had the sapphires copied from those in the portrait. When they came to-day it occurred to me that if I were to appear in the gown and jewels of the Duchess we could all laugh together over the absurd story of her quest. Now I'll answer Mr. Cheever."

"You won't."

With the furious protest Trafford surged for the stairway. Jaffrey dragged at his arm. He shook with excitement. His voice was half chuckle, half sob as he pleaded:

"Jim, wait! Wait! Let Julie do it. Listen! Lis—" He stopped as the girl spoke. She smiled down upon the startled faces looking up at her:

"Oh, you can't know how I have wanted to tell you how, where and when Jim and I were married! You have been so kind to me and all the time you must have wondered. I feel as Christian felt when the load slipped from his shoulders. On my way to visit my aunt I jumped from the Pullman to chase this dog who ran away when the train stopped. Jim saw me and followed. The train left us. The storm caught us. We took refuge in a cabin. The thunder and lightning were terrific. There came a blinding flash, a crash, another flash that struck the pine outside. That last sent me straight to Jim. The next I knew from the shelter of his arms I was staring at Cheever inside the door."

She freed the wriggling spaniel and as he ran down the stairs she caught the carved rail beside her and leaned forward, her eyes starry with excitement.

"The man threatened to use the situation to defeat his opponent unless he withdrew from the contest. Jim had told me of his ideals for clean politics. Could I let him sacrifice his career to shield me? I declared that we were married. What could Jim do? If he denied it, he branded me a liar. Cheever rushed off to spread the news which he knew was not true and Jim and I took the midnight train to Portland and were married. When we reached Clearwater and heard that Cheever was unconscious and would not live I begged that the whole affair might be kept secret. But he didn't die and we acknowledged the marriage."

She flashed a defiant glance at Cheever who still stood by the casement door. He was smiling with cynical bravado. He shrugged as his eyes rested for an instant on the white shoulders in a cerise setting which were turned squarely against him. He bent his head as though listening for a distant sound as Julie concluded:

"That is the whole story. Jim has won the election without stooping to muddy methods, and I shall help him make good all his life if — if he wants my help."

Her voice trailed away in an embarrassed whisper as though for the first time she were conscious of the tearful eyes looking up at her.

There was an instant of silence, followed by happy laughter, tumultuous applause, a surge toward the stairs. As Jim Trafford reached the step beside the girl a deafening explosion shook the air. Across the sea of frightened white faces his eyes met Cheever's triumphant glance. Over the rail of the second balcony leaned a face white under its freckles as a boy's voice shrilled:

"Gee, folks! There's a big fire at the Cove! I'll bet the roamin' Duchess has blowed up the copper-mine!"

Chapter XXV

There was a second of stunned silence before Trafford caught the girl's hands. The flaming ardor of his eyes seemed to touch her hair, her lips, her throat. There was a newly possessive note in his voice as he commanded:

"When you are ready Captain Phin will take you to Brick House, Julie. I must go to the mine. Wait in the living-room until I come. Promise."

"I promise."

He spread her slender fingers on his palm, looked down at them, then up at her. His expression set the pulses in her throat to beating furiously.

"No, Jim. *No!*"

His low laugh was as disturbing as his eyes.

"I won't, Julie — now. The sudden ascent from despair has gone to my head — that's all." He crushed the hand he held and turned away.

When two hours later, with the cumbersome satins of the Duchess replaced by the soft whiteness of the pearl-beaded frock, Julie curled up in the wing-chair in the living-room at Brick House, his words came back to her with a distinctness which set her heart to beating suffocatingly. She had had the sense of being crushed in his arm though he had held only her hand. She had rescued that just in time.

The room was lighted only by the glow from the fire. She shut her eyes and leaned her head against the back of the chair. What a day! It seemed years long. She visualized the river and the old mill; she could hear the purl of water, smell the pines and crisping bacon. Her heart thumped reminiscently as she lived again the tense moment by the iron ladder when she had waited for a voice, she knew not whose, to answer her. She saw Cheever across the great hall, saw him lean forward as though listening, waiting. Then Jim had come and gone with that light in his eyes; Billy had administered a pat and a gruff, "You're one good little sport, Marble-heart!" before he had rushed off in Trafford's wake. She brushed her hand across her wet lashes as she remembered the white misery of Carfax's face and his broken apology:

"I was given to understand that your marriage was for political reasons only, Julie. Forgive me. I did not know that you loved Jim."

The girl's cheeks burned. Had she made the fact so apparent? It was so like her to bare her heart to the world, just as she had decided that she would wait months before she told Jim, she derided herself scornfully. Of course Cheever was responsible for Dal's information, Cheever who had blown up the mine to destroy all evidence of his smuggling activities. Captain Phin had monologued all the way to Brick House.

"Gorry-me, Jim kept what he thought Cheever was up to quiet till after election, didn't he? Folks are more hurt than mad about Ben's doin's. They won't take action against him. They've just advised him to leave town fer a spell, an' he's goin'. The Trafford didn't need to sling mud to win out. He didn't have to use thet map, either. He give it to me to put in his desk. You take care of it, Julie. I don't want to stop a minute after I set you an' Sarah down. I'm goin' to the mine. It's lucky we had thet heavy fog or this county might hev been wiped out by fire. Besides bein' planted with dynamite the log shorin' had been saturated with gas. Willy Small saw Cheever workin' there after you folks had gone. There ain't no doubt in anybody's mind who did the trick."

Julie had taken the map, she remembered. But when she had entered the house Sarah

Beddle, who followed her, had startled all thought of it from her mind by exclaiming with a fervor which set every individual jet to clashing:

"M's. Jim Trafford, I'm proud you belong to us!"

Julie forced open heavy lashes. The quiet of the room, the purr of the fire, her day of excitement seemed drugging her mind. What had she done with the map? Had she laid it on Jim's desk with the sapphires? She loved that wonderful ring — of course the jewels were safe until Jim came — she snuggled her head more comfortably against the cushions — perhaps if she closed her eyes for a moment and rested them —

It seemed barely a second before they opened wide in startled attention. She sat erect. Had she heard a door close softly? She had felt a breath of cool air. The sound had come from the study. The sapphires were on Jim's desk! Her heart thumped heavily. Cautiously she leaned forward. Through the French windows in the room beyond she could see the stars blinking drowsily as though making a superhuman attempt to prop up heavy lids which persisted in drooping and hiding their glimmer.

Julie tiptoed to the threshold of the study. In contrast with the dusk of the room a spark on the gravel path outside glowed like a beacon for an instant and winked out. The girl brought her white teeth down on her lip to force back a startled "Cheever!" Cheever and his inseparable cigarette. Her thoughts swirled and steadied. A disc of light scouted about the desk top for an instant. He was in the room. He had come for that incriminating map. She must get him out of the house before Jim returned. This would be the last straw to break the back of The Trafford's self-control.

She touched the button in the wall. The lamp on the broad-topped desk glowed into soft brilliance. Its light shot blue flames into the depths of the sapphires in the open case beneath it, shot red flames into the eyes of the man who stared back at her, threw into relief the network of fine lines at their corners, accentuated the thinness of the lips which twisted slowly into a smile.

The atmosphere of the room seemed electrified. Cheever straightened and casually picked up the map he had been examining.

"This is an unexpected pleasure, Mrs. Trafford. I drop in to congratulate our new senator and I find his charming wife. Doubtless you have come on the same errand. For fear I shall be *de trop* I'll go at once and leave you to present my good wishes."

He thrust the map into his pocket and took a step toward the long window. Julie reached it first. She turned the key and with the bit of metal clutched in her hand backed against the glass.

"You can't go until you have dropped that map." Her heart skipped a beat as she heard automobile wheels outside. "Be quick! Jim is coming. Do you want him to find you here like this? Do you want 'breaking and entering' added to your already smooched record?"

Cheever's eyes were alight with mocking admiration as he approached her.

"Just to look at you as you are now is worth any risk. Lord, but you're lovely! Don't glare at me. I've no quarrel with you. I hate Trafford. He turned against me. When he was a boy he took my word for anything. I didn't care what I did to smash his reputation."

"Or mine?"

"I'm sorry that I had to drag you in. I've been waiting for a chance to tell you that I knew Jim was on the level that night in the cabin. When I recovered from the accident I heard no mention of The Trafford's marriage. I knew then that you and he had counted on my snuffing out. When that day in the garden he presented you as his wife, I was staggered. Then I third-degreed the information out of

Willy Small that he had seen you board the Portland train. It didn't take me long to find the record of the marriage."

"What did it profit you to pretend you had forgotten?"

"It kept Jim on the anxious seat." He shrugged cynically. "All's fair in love and politics. All his life The Trafford has had things handed to him on a silver platter and then I, seizing a chance to smash him — fool that I was — handed him *you*. He has all the luck. Why couldn't I have been on hand to help you chase that dog? Then you would have married me."

For one horrible moment Julie feared that fury had paralyzed her. Even the strain of earnestness through the mocking voice did not palliate. She could neither speak nor move. Then the shackles burst. But even in her anger she remembered Jim's possible proximity. Her low voice shook as she demanded:

"How dare you imply that I would have married you? Not you nor any other man in the world but Jim Trafford."

Cheever's face reddened darkly.

"You needn't take what I said as an insult. I've been crazy about you since the night in the cabin when you brazened the situation out."

"Do you expect me to believe that after

your hateful question at Shorehaven to-night?"

"I was wild with fury. The people who had patted me on the back for years had set Jim up to worship. It was a false move. I know it now. I've lost whatever I had. But it was almost worth it to see you on the stairs. I love a fighter —"

"Then you'll have an opportunity at once to take one on," announced a furious voice from the threshold. Trafford's face was livid as he stepped forward. "There has been a thrashing due you since the night of the storm."

With an inarticulate protest Julie flung herself upon him. Trafford held her close.

"No, Jim, no. He has already apologized to me for that. There is to be no quarrel on my account." Her breath caught in a sob of relief as she felt the arm about her tighten. A one-handed man couldn't do much harm to his opponent. "Mr. Cheever came here for the map. I objected to his taking it without your consent, that is all."

"All! I heard him say —"

"That I love your wife. What of it? Isn't she everything that is lovable? Because I'm not an incorruptible like you, do you think I don't know a thoroughbred when I see one? That I want to marry a girl like Pamela Parkman if the other kind will have me?"

Cheever's face was only a degree less white than Trafford's as he lighted a cigarette. The glow of the match cast sardonic shadows on his face. Julie watched him in incredulous silence. Intrigant, smuggler, wildly improbable as it seemed, the man had ideals, the divine spark her father found in every human. With his faith and tenderness the domine would have fanned it into a steady flame. The thought softened her voice as she threw the key to the desk and implored:

"Leave the map and go, *please.*"

Cheever looked from her lips which quivered ever so slightly to the tense face, the blazing eyes of the man who held her in a possessive, white-knuckled grip. He shrugged:

"Why should I hurry? I —"

"Cheever, get out! Do you want to be thrown out? Take the map. I don't want it. I didn't need it in the campaign. I shall never need it."

Trafford's lips were colorless. Julie felt the muscles in the arm about her twitch. Cheever's mask of insolent indifference seemed riddled with surprise. His black eyes lost their malevolence. Awkwardly, as though incredulous, he picked up the key and the map. His expression twisted Julie's heart. Then it seemed as though she felt the tender touch of her father's hand upon her shoulder. She smiled through a mist as she said softly:

"Good-bye and good luck to you — in finding a girl to love."

For an instant the man stared at her. His face was dark with color as he inserted the key. On the threshold he turned:

"Good luck, Jim, and — and thank you for this." He thrust the map into his pocket and went out.

Julie stood motionless until the sound of footsteps on the gravel walk ceased. Then she freed herself. She locked the French window and after an instant's hesitation began to arrange the desk fittings in military precision. Her heart tripped as she looked up and met Trafford's intent eyes. He smiled.

"Exit Ben Cheever."

"But a different Ben, Jim?"

"For the moment," then in answer to her inarticulate protest, "We'll hope for the best. At least he has the discernment to appreciate you, you glorious girl." He steadied his voice. "Stop putting that desk in order or I shall never find anything. Come into the other room. I want to talk to you."

As Julie slipped by him into the living-room the yellow cat abandoned her post beneath the portrait of the Duchess and sprang to the broad windowsill. She doubled velvet paws neatly under her tawny breast and with wary topaz eyes peered from between the net curtains.

The girl seated herself on the broad arm of the couch. The firelight turned her white frock to rosy hyacinth. With his arm resting on the mantel Trafford smiled at her as he confirmed jubilantly:

"We've won."

The steadiness of his voice, the laughter in his eyes banished her self-consciousness.

"Congratulations, Mr. Senator. Now you will go on and on and —"

"Not so fast as that. Remember that I am elected only. I haven't made good yet. However, I know that I can or I shouldn't have entered the campaign. You effectually laid the ghost of the roaming Duchess to-night, Julie. What prompted you to appear in character?"

His friendly voice rescued her from the quick-sands of emotion and placed her on firm ground. Her eyes shone with laughter.

"Wasn't my entrance dramatic? After you had shown me the sapphires the idea sprang full grown in my mind. I was sure if the townspeople could see the jewels they would realize how silly they had been. I 'phoned your mother for permission to use the gown — and that's all."

"That question having been answered to my satisfaction I'll ask another. From whom was the letter you kissed, Julie?"

The sudden deepening of his eyes and voice set the girl's pulses racing, but her laughing glance met his audaciously:

"Don't you wish you knew?" Then as he took a purposeful step forward she parleyed breathlessly: "Please — please, I'll tell you. It was a letter from Mother and Dad."

Trafford caught her hands in one of his and drew her inexorably toward him. His face was white as he lifted her chin and tried to see the eyes hidden beneath long lashes.

"Why did you let me think that you loved Jaffrey?"

"Don't you think so now?"

Her tone of surprise was so well done that he dropped her hands and thrust his hard into his coat pockets. His voice was stern as he answered:

"No. Did you mean it when you said that you would help me all my life, Julie?"

"I said — if you wanted me."

"Wanted you!" Trafford cleared his voice. "Did you say that merely because you believe in the sacredness of a marriage contract or because —" he stopped as the violet eyes flashed to his. A smile curved the girl's lips. With tantalizing deliberation she counted on the tips of her pink fingers:

"That was reason one; two, was those 'tons

338

of wedding-cake in little white boxes'; think of the embarrassment for Managing Martha if we separated after that cake-shower — third, she has already added our pearl to her string — and fourth —"

Trafford had her in his arms. His voice was hoarse as he prompted:

"And fourth?"

"I discovered that I loved —"

He smothered the word upon her lips. He kissed her thoroughly, compellingly before he held her away from him the fraction of an inch. His eyes were turbulent, his rich voice unsteady as he demanded:

"Must I apologize for kissing you this time, Julie?"

Color stole into her face which had been white, laughter flashed into the eyes which avoided his.

"I should have insisted upon an apology if — if you hadn't," she answered with a breathless attempt at bravado.

Trafford released her only to crush her hands in his. The smile she loved was in the depths of his eyes as he announced:

"I am going away to-morrow, Goldilocks."

"Away? Where?"

He raised her left hand and pressed his lips to the glistening circlet on her third finger before he answered huskily:

"I shall take my wife to see her mother and her Dad."

A lovely light shone softly in the eyes which met his unfalteringly. A faint color stole to the girl's hair as she breathed a rapturous:

"Really?" Then added with an adorable imitation of Sarah Beddle: "M's. Jim Trafford will love that."

"Julie — you — you dear!"

The old clock ticked ponderously:

"You *dear!* You *dear!* You *dear!*" A red coal dropped in the grate. The firelight softened the eyes of the Duchess as she looked down upon the man's black head bent above the fair hair against his shoulder. The topaz eyes of the yellow cat peered out from between the laces. Suddenly they narrowed to black slits. Their owner soundlessly backed behind the hangings. The black spaniel dashed into the room. He stopped. He barked. Head tilted, long ears flopping, red tongue dangling, black eyes snapping, he grinned broadly and sat back on his haunches to observe the tableau before him. He barked again imperatively, ingratiatingly. Ignored, he flopped to the floor, dropped his head upon his outstretched paws and with a long-drawn sigh of resignation, tactfully closed his eyes.

More bright the East became, the ocean
    turned
Dark and more dark against the
    brightening sky —
Sharper against the sky the long sea line.
The hollows of the breakers on the
    shore
Were green like leaves whereon no sun
    doth shine,
Though sunlight make the outer
    branches hoar.
From rose to red the level heaven
    burned;
Then sudden, as if a sword fell from on
    high,
A blade of gold flashed on the ocean's
    rim.

— Richard Watson Gilder.

The employees of Thorndike Press hope you have enjoyed this Large Print book. All our Large Print titles are designed for easy reading, and all our books are made to last. Other Thorndike Press Large Print books are available at your library, through selected bookstores, or directly from the publishers.

For more information about titles, please call:

(800) 223-1244
 or
(800) 223-6121

To share your comments, please write:

Publisher
Thorndike Press
P.O. Box 159
Thorndike, Maine 04986